Looking Backward, From the Year 2000

Looking Backward, From the Year 2000

by

MACK REYNOLDS

THE ELMFIELD PRESS

LOOKING BACKWARD,
FROM THE YEAR 2000

Copyright ©, 1973 by Mack Reynolds

All rights reserved

ISBN 0 7057 0066 6

This edition is reproduced from the Ace books edition
published in U.S.A. in 1973

Published in the United Kingdom in 1976 by
The Elmfield Press, Elmfield Road, Morley,
West Yorkshire, LS27 0NN

Printed by John Bentley (Printers) Ltd.,
Todmorden, Lancs, England.

INTRODUCTION

For some years the present writer has been doing social science fiction, extrapolating in the field of socio-economics. During that period I have attempted to explore various future possibilities. This is the culmination. Old reader friends will recognize that I have pirated some of my own ideas in *Looking Backward, From the Year 2000* from early work. They will please forgive me but the story would be impossible otherwise.

The student of political economy will also note that I have called upon the ideas of such authors of the past as Proudhon for the medium of exchange of the future, upon Daniel DeLeon for the structure of industry, upon Edward Bellamy for much of the basic idea and upon many contemporary writers such as Vance Packard, Ferdinand Lundberg, Herman Kahn and Anthony J. Wiener, Michael Young, Robert L. Heilbroner, Arthur C. Clarke, John Kenneth Galbraith and the late Frank Tannenbaum. I have also drawn extensively on the many participants in the work being done by many contributors to the American Academy's Commission on the Year 2000 which appears in *Daedalus,* the Journal of the American Academy of Arts and Sciences.

I should also like to thank Raymond A. E. Klein, Director of the *Eidos* Theoretical Research group for his comments upon some of my pioneering ideas. A fiction writer is seldom blessed with a think tank to fall back upon.

"Man may be skeptical about following the flight of the dodo bird into extinction, but the evidence points increasingly to just such a pursuit.

"The planet and mankind are in grave danger of irreversible catastrophe if the political structure that now prevails is not drastically changed during the next few decades.

"We live in a high-risk environment, and the trends that create the present level of risk continue to increase the danger and reduce the possibilities of creatively control-

5

ling it. . . . There are four interconnected threats to the planet—wars of mass destruction, overpopulation, pollution and the depletion of resources. They have a cumulative effect. A problem in one area renders it more difficult to solve the problems in any other area. . . . The basis of all four problems is the inadequacy of the sovereign States to manage the affairs of mankind in the 20th Century."

Professor Richard A. Falk, *Princeton*

". . . those societies which cannot combine reverence for their symbols with freedom for their revision must ultimately decay, either from anarchy or the slow atrophy by useless shadows."

Alfred North Whitehead

"Is America's romance with practicality and efficiency enough to sustain it? Men serving a system with no other goal than its further advance have no transcendent aims."

David Riesman

"Why should men struggle to maximize income when the price is many dull and dark hours of labor? Why especially should they do so as goods become more plentiful and less urgent? Why should they not seek instead to maximise the rewards of all the hours of their days? And since this is the plan and obvious aspiration of a great and growing number of the most perceptive people, why should it not be the central goal of the society?"

John Kenneth Galbraith
The Affluent Society

"The present, for men who have no utopia, is inevitably constricting; and, similarly, cultures which have no utopia remain imprisoned in the present and quickly fall back into the past, for the present can be fully alive only in tension between past and future. This is the fruitfulness of utopia—its ability to open up possibilities."
Paul Tillich

Critique and Justification of Utopia

". . . through a strange alchemy of the Gods, there are a disproportionate number of kids coming along these days with IQ's that are soaring toward a level too high to measure. These kids have very cold eyes. They are the ones who, one day, will stop playing with transistors, diodes and microcircuitry and look at Barrentown and start asking the rude questions. Or build a machine that will ask."

John D. MacDonald
The Quick Brown Fox

". . . if we have learned one thing from the history of invention and discovery, it is that in the long run—and often in the short one—the most daring prophecies turn out to be laughably conservative."

Arthur C. Clarke
The Promise of Space

". . . one must either anticipate change or be its victim."

John K. Galbraith

"All human beings are equal in rights and dignity, and only such a system of wealth distribution can therefore be defensible as respects and secures those qualities."

Edward Bellamy
Equality

"I know of no safe depository of the ultimate powers of the society but the people themselves, and if we think them not enlightened enough to exercise their control with a wholesome discretion, the remedy is not to take it from them, but to inform their discretion."

Thomas Jefferson

"The major advances in civilization are processes which all but wreck the societies in which they occur."

Alfred North Whitehead

I

The transformation we're now seeing will make the Industrial Revolution of the 18th Century look like a pink tea.
Louis Levine
Chief Analyst in Employment Security
U.S. Department of Labor

Now

"Thirty years," Julian West said. "You mean all this has taken place in a third of a century?"

Leete nodded. "Don't underestimate thirty odd years in terms of history when times are ripe for change." He thought about it for a moment, pursing his lips as he attempted to put his finger on the illustration he wanted to use. "The Egyptians managed to go through thirty dynasties without any substantial changes in their culture, their socio-economic system, their science. It was during their early fourth dynasty that the great pyramid, that of Khufu, or Cheops as we usually call him, was built. Two thousand years later at the time of the Persian and then the Macedonian conquests, the Egyptians were substantially the same, their society fundamentally unchanged. They aren't the sole example. The Mayans of Guatemala and Yucatan came on the scene with a surprisingly advanced culture—we're not sure, perhaps inherited from the Olmecs. They maintained this culture for a millennium, for all practical purposes unchanged."

"That's what I mean," Julian West said. "It would take . . . why, a thousand years to—"

The other was shaking his head. "No. I was giving you the reverse of the coin. But take the United States in, say, 1840. She was a small, new country and, although the Louisiana Purchase had given her large portions of the West, had hardly penetrated beyond the Mississippi. Her economy was largely agricultural and based on slavery in the South. In world affairs she was a third-rate power, at best. Thirty-three years later she had spread from coast

9

to coast, engulfing such areas as Texas, New Mexico, Arizona and California and had become the most powerful country in the world, though it took Europe a time to realize the fact. The economy had become industrial, railroads spanned the continent, development had become a geometric progression.

"But perhaps that isn't the best example of what a third of a century can do in history. Consider Europe in June of 1914. All had been peace and progress since Napoleon's era. William Hohenzollern was Kaiser of Germany; Franz Josef, Emperor of the Austro-Hungarian Empire; Czar Nicholas the Second, Czar of Russia; all seemingly secure on their thrones. The airplane was a flimsy affair, not considered a serious military weapon. The submarine was in its infancy and when submerged most of the crew would sit on the floor, unmoving, to preserve trim. Weapons? The most dangerous were probably heavy cannon and the recently evolved Maxim machine gun. Lenin, unknown to the world as a whole, was a shabby refugee in Switzerland. Hitler was a paperhanger in Vienna, Mussolini the editor of a small so-called socialist newspaper. Thirty years later? Consider for a moment. The Nazi armies were reeling back from the interior of Communist Russia. The V-2 rockets, the first spaceships, were bombing England. The first atomic bomb was about to be tested in Alamagordo. In China, Mao's guerrillas were already making their plans to take over the most populous country in the world. Tito was largely in control of Yugoslavia, and shortly the Eastern half of Europe was to be under communist control. Fascism, a word unknown in 1914, was already a dead duck and within a year Hitler was to be a suicide and Mussolini hanging by his heels."

Julian West said, "You make your point. A lot of history can happen in thirty years. But all this—"

The other waggled a finger at him. "But there are new elements at work now. Back in your time, someone mentioned that ninety percent—or was it ninety-five?—of all scientists who had ever lived were presently alive and working. What would you say the percentage was today?"

10

:"Why, I don't know. I haven't the vaguest idea."

"Approximately the same. Ninety percent of all the scientists who have ever lived are at present alive and working. You see, during the past thirty years our universities have doubled, tripled and quadrupled the outturn of scientists, engineers, technicians. We have become a nation of such. I would estimate that at least half of our adults of the working years are scientists, engineers or technicians.

"But there is still another factor in which we differ from the past. About the year 1950 Dr. Robert Oppenheimer pointed out that human knowledge was doubling every eight years. Since that time, in some fields, at least, progress has accelerated. Of course, I don't mean that this is a progress that is steady and easily measurable. It comes in fits and starts. One science will forge ahead dramatically under the influence of several new breakthroughs, another will plod along. Archeology, for instance, is usually a plodder, although from time to time such discoveries as carbon dating will revolutionize the field. But medicine, physics, astronomy, biology, chemistry? Each discovery made leads for two or more others. Were it not for the International Computer Data Banks, no man could begin to keep up. Even with them, it is all but impossible, no matter how narrow your subspecialization."

He leaned forward in emphasis. "Consider the ramifications, Julian. Let us assume that when you took on your experiment the sum of human knowledge was expressed by the number one. In eight years, it had doubled to two. In sixteen years, it was four, in twenty-four years, eight. Today we have more than sixteen times as much information at our disposal as was available in your period, and in a few years it will be thirty-two times."

Julian West made a gesture of despair. "Even then, I was far from being up on most of the sciences."

II

Most Americans—citizens of the wealthiest, most powerful and most ideal-swathed country in the world—by a very wide margin own nothing more than their household goods, a few glittering gadgets such as automobiles and television sets (usually purchased on the installment plan, many at second hand) and the clothes on their backs. A horde if not the majority of Americans live in shacks, cabins, hovels, shanties, hand-me-down Victorian eyesores, rickety tenements and flaky apartment buildings. . . . At the same time, a relative handful of Americans are extravagantly endowed, like princes in the Arabian Nights tales. Their agents deafen a baffled world with a never-ceasing chant about the occult merits of private-property ownership . . . and the vaulting puissance of the American owners . . . It would be difficult in the 1960s for a large majority of Americans to show fewer significant possessions if the country had long labored under a grasping dictatorship.

Ferdinand Lundberg
The Rich and the Super-Rich

Then

Julian West said, "All right. How much time do I have?" There was a slight tic at the side of his mouth.

"If you take care, every care, you might have as much as a year, or even two."

"And if I don't?"

The doctor said slowly, "You might go next week, next month—or even tomorrow."

"I see. And what do you mean by taking care?"

"You must give up smoking and alcohol. And all other stimulants for that matter. Coffee, tea, cocoa. Even such beverages as Cocoa Cola or Pepsi Cola, both of which have a rather high caffeine content."

12

"So, I can't even drink a coke, eh?"

"Above all, you must avoid physical exertion. Never allow yourself to grow tired. Avoid ascending stairs. When you walk, walk slowly. And you must avoid as well, emotional upset. Don't get into arguments. Don't participate in sex."

Absently, Julian West fished his pipe from his jacket pocket. It was a gold-bound Barling shell briar, a gift from his fiancée, Edith Bartlett. The doctor looked at it expressionlessly. His patient ignored him, brought a tobacco pouch from his other pocket and began to load up.

He said, "I've been reading quite a bit about heart transplants recently. Down in South Africa and so forth."

The doctor nodded. "The field of organ transplant is in its infancy. I, myself, have performed three heart transplants. The most successful patient lived for six months. One died on the operating table, the other lived eight days."

"However, there wouldn't seem to be much choice in my case." Julian West brought a gold lighter from his pants pocket, fired his pipe, and sucked aromatic British tobacco smoke into his mouth. He exhaled through his nostrils.

In his mid-thirties, Julian West's hair was thick and dark, but there were touches of premature gray at the temples and a small amount in his mustache. However, these signs of age were an attractive counterbalance to his otherwise youthfully fresh complexion, to his flat stomach, square shoulders and strong arms and legs. He had never known it but the women who had loved him in his time had usually been attracted to the certain vulnerable quality about his eyes and mouth.

The doctor was shaking his head. "Were you otherwise in good shape, I might consider it. However, neither your kidneys nor your liver are up to the strain involved. Even though the heart operation was a success—" He let the sentence dribble away.

"In short, you offer me no hope whatsoever."

The doctor shifted in his chair, unhappily. "Mr. West, there is always hope. As I said, the field of organ transplant is in its infancy. However, amazing progress is already being made. Perhaps within six months or so major discoveries will be hit upon which would make an operation on you worth the risk."

"But you don't really expect such developments so soon?"

"No."

"How soon? One year? Two years? The absolute limit you give me?"

"No. You wanted the whole truth, Mr. West. Perhaps in five years, more likely ten, medical science will have arrived at the point where organ transplant is a standard operation with as great a chance of success as an appendectomy."

"But you could be wrong?"

"Yes."

"It might come as soon as six months?"

"Mr. West, I don't wish to arouse false hopes. As you told me when you first solicited my services, I am thought one of the outstanding specialists in my field. I do not expect organ transplanting to be a developed branch of our medical science in less than five to ten years."

Edith Bartlett, as ever, was late. When she came hurrying up, as ever, there was a whimsical, apologetic air.

Julian West came to his feet from the table tucked away in an alcove of the cocktail lounge. He put his pipe into a side pocket and held her chair for her.

Before she could say anything, he said, "Par for the course, sweetie. You're only fifteen minutes late."

"I got to shopping, Jule, and lost track of the time. I found the most darling—" She broke it off. "But that's not important, is it?" She put her bag on the table and looked at him.

He realized, all over again, that for him she was the most beautiful woman he had ever known. Perhaps not for the judges of the Miss America or Miss Universe contests. Perhaps not for those of Hollywood who had the job of selecting the sex symbols for films and television. But for Julian West. His taste ran to brunettes, to greenish eyes, to peaches-and-cream complexions in the English tradition, to figures less than lush and breasts smaller than currently in demand, to fine ankles and narrow feet, to full mouths and perky noses, to well-shaped ears and . . . in short, to Edith Bartlett.

"Martini?" he said, as the waiter came up.

"I suppose so."

"Doubles," he said. "A twist of lemon in one, two onions in the other. Be sure the glasses are preliminarily chilled."

"Yes, Mr. West." The waiter retreated.

She looked at him. "What did Doctor Almenroder say?"

"Do you want the good news or the bad news first?"

"Why . . . why the good news, I guess."

He took a breath and said, "Within five or ten years techniques will probably be developed that would make an operation a possible success."

She stared at him, uncomprehending. "Well, but . . . the bad news."

He said wryly, "I'm not going to last five years, not to speak of ten."

Her eyes rounded in disbelief. "But, Jule, you're no more than thirty-five."

The drinks had come. He took up the one with the lemon peel and made a mock gesture in the way of a toast. "That's the trouble with belonging to the jet set, I suppose. Evidently I not only burned my candle at both ends, but had it lit in the middle. Of course, the stint in the Asian War didn't help any. Evidently that liver and kidney infection never really completely cleared up."

"What . . . what did he say?"

"If I take it easy as it is possible to take it, I just might last as much as two years."

"Two years!"

"No alcohol, no tobacco, no nothing. I walk, I don't run. I don't climb stairs. I don't argue with anybody, not even Democrats, Civil Righters, or hippies. In short, I don't do anything except sit, real quietly, and wait."

"Darling." Her voice was urgent and she put her perfectly manicured fingers on his arm. "Let's get married immediately."

He twisted his face. "Among other things I avoid is sex."

"That's not important."

He was even able to laugh. "Don't go overboard, sweetie. The engagement is obviously off."

"You're being ridiculous."

"Almenroder told me never to argue." He flicked a finger for the waiter.

He took in Edith's glass, which had hardly been touched, and said to the man, "Another double."

When the other had gone, Edith said, "Jule, be sensible. That isn't the way."

"What is the way?"

Her mouth was tense and distress was in the greenness of her eyes. She shook her head. "He said no alcohol."

"And no tobacco and no excitement and no sex and no everything." Julian West fished his pipe from out of his jacket pocket, knocking the ash and unburned tobacco out against the palm of his hand and hence to the ashtray. He reached for his tobacco pouch.

"What did you think of Hemingway," he said.

She was surprised at the sudden switch. "Papa? Oh, he was great fun. A monster."

"When did you see him last?"

"Why, I suppose there during the *mano a mano* thing in Spain. In Torremolinos at a party. But, darling—"

Julian West said, "He was already going by then. And he knew it. He could have hung on, possibly, for a few more years. Possibly five or ten. But not as Papa Hemingway. No booze, watching himself, continual trips to the Mayo Clinic for everything from surgery on his kidneys, to treatment of his high blood pressure, to shock treatments for his chronic mental depression. But it wouldn't have been Papa. He called it quits instead. A lot of fools called him a coward."

The martini came and he took down almost half of it in one long swallow. The waiter looked at him nervously before taking off again.

Edith looked down into her own glass. "You're not thinking of suicide? That's silly."

He considered it. "No. Not really. But I don't expect to sit around like a cabbage, waiting for the end. I've got an idea."

"Jim," Julian West said, "I've got a problem for you."

"Fire away," his stockbroker said, crossing his hands over his well-larded belly.

"We've got a man who is going to disappear for ten years. During that period there will be no possible way for him to handle his financial affairs. He wants to put his fortune into something that will be absolutely safe, so that when he returns it won't have been stolen from him, eroded away by inflation or devaluation or by a collapse in securities values. So the problem is, what does he put it into?"

James Dempsey Lynch thought about it, only slightly intrigued. "How about one or more of the bluest of blue chips? Say, American Telephone and Telegraph."

Julian West said, "That was my first reaction. But the trouble is he wouldn't be around to supervise, in case something came up. For instance, every year that goes by the government gets further into business. AT&T is all but a monopoly and now with the coming of the communications satellites it's in the cards that the government might take over. The petroleum corporations? In ten years there might be some breakthroughs in nuclear power. If there are, what happens to oil? IBM? There you go again, almost a monopoly in the computer field. Computers are getting more important by the day. Might the government decide that their development is too important to remain in private hands?"

Lynch grimaced. "You've got a point."

Julian West said, "How about government bonds?"

His broker laughed. He was becoming more interested in the question. "Inflation is developing at the rate of more than six percent a year and each year that goes by the rate ups. Put your friend's fortune into bonds and in ten years he'd have a good chance of being broke. When I was a boy, back during the Depression, a pack of cigarettes cost ten cents, now you pay fifty. A glass of beer, when Roosevelt called prohibition quits, cost ten cents. Now it will be thirty-five or even fifty. Fords and Chevrolets cost less than six hundred dollars then. In a restaurant you paid a dollar for a meal that would cost five now. No, you couldn't put your fortune in any form of money, bonds, savings account or such. It might halve in value, if not worse, in ten years."

"Gold? Silver?"

Lynch considered that for a moment, but shook his head negatively. "Perhaps, but world money is going through a crisis. What the eventual development will be we don't know, but gold is no longer the ideal medium of exchange it once was. There's not enough of it, for one thing, to back all the international exchange necessary in the modern scene. They're going to have to come up with some alternative. What, I couldn't say. But when and if they do, there could well be a precipitate drop in the price of gold. It doesn't have a good deal of use, you know, other than as a backing of currency."

Julian West brought a pipe from his pocket, frowned at it and returned it. He said, "All right. What then?"

"Perhaps art objects. Old masters. As the world grows more affluent their value rises, and rises again. There is always a market for an old master."

Julian West said, "Paintings, eh? Say, the Impressionists?"

"No. Too recent. No contemporaries, either. The popularity of the more recent schools can ebb. Old masters, Rembrandt, Brueghel, Frans Hal."

"I think you're probably right," Julian West said. "Okay, old masters it is, but I think as a hedge some gold stashed away in Switzerland and also some blue-chip stocks, very conservative ones."

"What's all this about, Jule?"

Julian West said, switching the subject. "Jim, I want you to liquidate my holdings. All of them."

"What!"

"I want all my securities sold."

"Are you mad? With the market in the shape it is now? With money on the verge of being devaluated? And do you realize the chunk of capital gains Uncle Sam would gouge out of you?"

"Nevertheless, I want everything I possess in the form of cash, Jim."

"Have you considered this? Where is that going to leave me and the rest of our group, Jule? We'll lose vot-

18

ing control of Diversified, among other things. Your shares alone—"

Julian West said, "That's your problem, Jim, not mine. So far as I'm concerned, you fellows can pick up my shares—assuming you can raise the amount required. As I understand it, most of you are already overextended."

James Dempsey Lynch said desperately, "Julian, you can't do this."

"All right, but I am doing it. By the way, can you recommend any good art dealers, preferably some who have connections in London, Paris, Rome?"

Doctor Pillsbury said, "It would be murder."

Julian West made a negative gesture. "No. At the very most, suicide, perhaps, You see, doctor, I've checked you out very thoroughly. Without doubt, you're the leading authority in the field."

"Believe me, one needn't be very advanced in the subject to be its leading authority. Practically nothing is known. The science—if science it be, and most of the medical profession denies that—is in its absolute infancy."

Julian West nodded. "However, I understand that you and your associates already have some dozen or so persons in deep freeze."

"But they're *dead*. You evidently don't understand. It is one chance in a thousand, even less. These persons have died of cancer or some other now incurable disease. Immediately upon death, without even draining the blood from their veins, they are put into deep freeze. The idea is that some day in the future a cure will be found for their disease and also that medical science will have advanced to the point where it will be possible to revive them. But they are dead before we put them into deep freeze."

"As you say, as you say. I have read up on all available about your experiments, Doctor Pillsbury. However, this placing of cadavers in deep freeze is but one phase of your work. You have also experimented extensively in animal hibernation and the lowering of basal metabolism."

"But with *animals*."

19

"I'm an animal, Doctor Pillsbury. And my heart specialist tells me that I have possibly a year to live. It is his opinion that within five to ten years medicine will have advanced to the point where I could expect a cure."

"See here, Mr. West. It is quite true that I have induced hibernation in animals who do not practice it in nature. In rats, in monkeys. I reduce the basal metabolism far beyond the point where it would seem possible and have maintained life in stasis for as long as a year. I have successfully reduced the heartbeat to as little as one or two a minute."

"A year," Julian West said interestedly. "Without any food whatsoever?"

"I fed some intravenously. Those that were not so fed died in six months or less."

"What happened eventually to the one that lived for a year?"

The other was staring at Julian West, as though frustrated. "Nothing. A rat. He is still in stasis."

"And seemingly in good health?"

"Yes. It will be necessary to revive him to find if there has been brain damage or damage to other tissue. But we are speaking of a *rat*, Mr. West."

"An animal which has a great deal in common with man, so I understand. The reason the rat is so often used in laboratory experiments."

"But if I attempted to perform such an experimentation on a living person, I could be charged with homicide. At the very least, I would lose my license. I could—"

But Julian West was shaking his head. "No. You underestimate the power of wealth, doctor. I shall immediately begin to spread some of mine about. We shall present the whole matter as a breakthrough in science. We shall swath it all in a great aura of scientific experiment. You will be hailed as a pioneer. I will be held up as a volunteer, at the most a martyr, to science. There have been volunteers before in medical science. Convicts, for instance, who allowed themselves to be given supposedly incurable diseases so that the research boys could work on them. Believe me, doctor, I can handle this. I have an outfit on Madison Avenue that will put you on the lips of everyone in the country. You'll be famous overnight."

The doctor sank back into his chair.

Julian West pressed him. "You have been short of funds in your experimentations. All right. My offer is that I set up a foundation to subsidize you. You'll be most generously provided for. You'll be able to build your laboratories, the hospital of which you've dreamed. My only requirement is that my . . . body be taken care of until the day arrives that I can be cured. I will then be revived. However, the foundation will continue. You, or your scientific heirs if you have passed away by then, will continue to be subsidized by it."

"I am not ready for such an experiment. Perhaps . . . perhaps in another year or two."

"I do not have another year or two. We must proceed all but immediately."

At earliest dawn, he drove the Bentley up to Woodstock from Kingston where he had spent the night at a hotel. It was apple blossom time, save for the fall the most beautiful month of the year in the Catskills.

It had been a considerable time since he had been in these parts, but during his youth his parents had spent several seasons in the art colony. They had called it "for drying out" but as Julian recalled there hadn't seemed to have been much diminution in their drinking. He had liked the town much better than he had Antibes, Torremolinos, Paris, Rio, or even St. Moritz or Acapulco. Possibly because of the absence, comparatively, of other members of the set to which the Wild Wests belonged.

The Wild Wests, Barry and Betty, had long mixed gasoline and alcohol, an explosive amalgamation which had orphaned young Julian at the age of fourteen. In a sports car rally which had started in Paris and was to end in Cannes, they had made it only as far as Lyon before rendezvousing with a truck. The wrench hadn't been as great as all that. He hadn't really known them too very well. Their sole heir had been a drag on their pursuit of pleasure and their tendency was to leave him at this school, that resort, or staying with this schoolmate or friend, at any opportunity. Now, in his thirties, he was

21

hard put to remember either, without the aid of photographs or home films. Even then, his father in skindiving gear, or goggled behind the wheel of a Lancia or Porsche, or grinning from the cockpit of a soaring glider, didn't come home to him as a parent. Even less did his mother, bikini-clad perhaps, and looking like a madcap blonde teenager to the very end.

The Wild Wests had made their mark in the periodicals of their time, in the gossip columns, in the society pages. He wondered if there were anyone in the world now who really remembered them.

At the village square in Woodstock he turned right at the drug store and sped up the Rock City Road in the direction of Byrdcliffe and Overlook Mountain beyond. To his satisfaction, there was nobody on the streets at this hour. Art colonies aren't inclined to early rising. Not that it made very much difference, but he preferred not to be recognized—if there had been anyone who might have recognized the boy in the present man.

He tooled on past the Brass Rail, a former hangout favorite of Barry and Betty West, and noted that it was now called The Village Jug. The road began to ascend rather steeply and he slowed the heavy British car to accommodate the curves.

To his further satisfaction, Mead's Meadow, the furthest point to which it was practical to take a vehicle as low-slung as his, was also deserted. He parked near the rock-strewn road, little more than a path, that led to the unfinished hotel atop Overlook, took up his aluminum container and left the car there without bothering to lock it.

The doctor had said no strenuous exericse. All right, this would be the last and he would try to watch it. The road was steep. He would do it slowly. It would be too much of a cosmic joke on him to have his fatal attack at this stage.

The container, which looked like nothing so much as an overgrown briefcase of metal, had a handle grip on it and wasn't as heavy as all that. From time to time he shifted it from right hand to left and back again.

He had been up this way a score of times and more as

a lad. But he had never known just how far the summit was from Mead's Meadow. Two miles, perhaps three? He and the others had been able to all but run it in the old days. Not now. He was already puffing.

He had no difficulty in finding the place to turn off. It was at a point where the road turned and there was a gigantic boulder to the left. The vegetation was somewhat different. The trees seemed larger, the shrubbery more dense, but he had no difficulty in finding the small cave.

It came back to him . . . that first time. He had been alone and had scared up a rabbit which seemed to be crippled, possibly the victim of a hunter who had wounded without killing. It had darted into some tangled bushes at a point where seemingly it would be impossible to exit without passing Julian, or to find safe retreat. He pressed in after it and found the cave that should have been just about unfindable.

It was a natural for a boy of twelve, particularly when he had just finished reading *Tom Sawyer* and was intrigued with the idea of a cave in the way of a hideout. He hadn't told anyone about it, anyone at all, not even his closest friend. It was *his* cave and he was careful to approach it in such a way that he never left a path that might lead another to follow out of curiosity. In fact, he went to the bother of so arranging leaves and shrubbery that the secret spot was even more unlikely to be discovered than it had been when he hit upon it.

It was smaller than he had remembered, but then he was considerably larger than he had been at the age of— what had it been when he had last visited the place?— thirteen.

He pushed aside twigs, leaves and shrubs and managed to squirm inside.

The slingshot was still there. He remembered it now. The rubbers and leather pouch had almost completely rotted away but the prongs were still strong. He picked up the boy's catapult and thought back over the years. He snorted deprecation. He had never been a particularly good shot with it but at that particular time you couldn't be without a slingshot. His age group had been going through a slingshot phase.

He took up the vacuum-sealed container he had lugged with him and found a place for it in the furthest recesses of the cave. He placed it flat on its side and then covered it first with dirt and gravel and then with twigs and leaves. He stared down at the spot where it was hidden. It was slightly damp in the cave but the container was strong and completely airtight. In fact, its fabricator had assured him that it would remain a vacuum inside for a century or more. Eventually, it was going to be quite a project to reopen it.

He muttered, before turning to leave, "All right, Van Dyke, Rembrandt, Brueghel, Holbein—wait for me. I'll be back. The saying is, you can't take it with you. We'll see."

From the hotel in Kingston he phoned Edith Bartlett. It was early enough so that she was obviously still in bed, her voice sleepy. It was a warm sleepiness that he had always loved in her waking.

She murmured, "Darling . . . what . . . what time is it?"

Julian West said, "Sweetie, this is it. Today is it."

Edith Bartlett was suddenly completely awake. "You're not going to go through with that ridiculous experiment?"

"Oh, but I am. Edith—"

"Jule—"

"Edith, the engagement is, obviously, off. I might be gone as long as ten years."

"Darling, I'll wait for you."

"I was hoping you'd say that, It's a long time, Edith . . . sweetie—"

He hung up.

He took a deep breath and dialed again.

Pillsbury's voice said, "Yes?"

Julian West said, "All my affairs have been tied up as well as I can tie them. I'll be at the hospital within two hours."

There was a resigned quality in the doctor's voice. "Very well, Mr. West."

III

It is sobering that no sociologist predicted the magnitude of the Negro Revolt, that no prewar urbanist anticipated the postwar development patterns in American cities, and that, most troubling of all, no one has yet written systematic alternative futures seeking to chart the possible course of events in these fields.

Melvin M. Webber
The Post-City Age

Now

There was nothing but a flow, no place, no time. Only a flowing.

There was a salty taste of mouth and there was a feeling of prismatic vision though actually he knew there was no vision. There was pressure in his head; the air crackled silently.

He had the feeling of colored, multicolored musical notes floating about and now he realized that not all of the colors were of his world. His mental vision had penetrated the spectrum beyond the point his physical eyes had been able to.

There was unknown music somewhere, far, far in the background, from instruments unknown. He felt a compelling desire to laugh and laugh. Everything he could think of was uproariously amusing. The world, so insanely and pitifully amusing. The universe. All the pitiful, poor, sweet people. The laughter was transcendent, a sustained though gentle electric shock, an incomplete and continuing sexual climax. The laughter fell off into tears. The joke was on him, the cosmic joke was on him. He felt an edge of terror welling up. He wept, within himself, he wept at the tragedy of it all.

This is terrible. Let me out. Let me out, let me surface. I want to get back.

From a long distance, from ultimately long distances, a

voice said urgently, "Flow with it. Go with it. Let your-self be carried along. Don't fight."

But had there really been a voice? He was alone. He was cosmically alone. There was no way back. But per-haps the distant voice was right. Perhaps he should go along with it. Refrain from the fight.

But then, at long last, he felt he was emerging. He was flowing upward and out. Emerging.

"He's going to open his eyes. He had better see only one of us at first."

"Promise me, then, that you won't tell him. Not yet. I have the feeling that this is going to be a tremendous psychic shock."

The first voice was a man's, the second a woman's and both spoke in whispers.

"I'll see how he seems," the man said.

"No, promise me. I have a feeling about this."

"Let her have her way," a third voice whispered, an-other woman's.

"If I can. Quick, leave. He's coming out of it."

In the background, somewhere, there was a rustling of clothing.

Julian West opened his eyes. A man of about fifty-five was bending over him, curiosity on his face.

He was an utter stranger. Julian raised himself on an elbow and looked around. The effort brought on a feeling of nausea, all but overpowering. The room was an un-known. He had certainly never been in it before, or one furnished anything like it. He looked at the stranger.

The other smiled at him quizzically. "How do you feel?" he said.

Julian West attempted to override the desire to vomit. "Where the hell am I?"

"In my apartment."

"How'd I get here?"

"We'll talk about it when you're stronger. Meanwhile there's no call for anxiety. You're among friends and in good hands. How do you feel?"

"Queer. But I suppose I'm all right. What am I doing in your home? What's happened? How'd I get here? I was put under in a hospital. The theory was, I was to remain there under continual observation. It was all part of the agreement. The foundation."

"There'll be time enough for explanations later," the stranger told him. The smile was obviously meant to be reassuring. "It will be better to, ah, play it cool—wasn't that the term?—until you're a little more yourself." He took up a glass from a small table at the bedside. "Here, will you oblige me by taking a couple of swallows of this mixture? It'll do you good. I'm a physician."

"I should hope so. What in the hell's happened?" Julian West eyed the glass unhappily. "My stomach is churning. Where's Pillsbury?"

"Who? Oh, Herbert Pillsbury, of course. I am afraid he is not with us. Don't agitate yourself, Mr. West. I'd rather you didn't insist upon explanations so soon, but if you do insist I'll try to satisfy you, provided you'll take this down first. It should settle that stomach and strengthen you somewhat."

Julian West took the glass ungraciously and swallowed half of the contents. It tasted something like a Greek *retsina* wine, but the nausea immediately fell off.

He said, "All right. I insist on knowing where I am and what I'm doing here. Did the experiment go wrong? The theory was, I wasn't to be revived until an operation was possible. A heart transplant. I expected to surface in a well-equipped hospital and be hurried more or less immediately to an operating table. Under this kind of strain, my ticker might go any minute. Christ knows, I've ponied up enough money to you people."

The other leaned back in his chair. His mouth was straight but there was a crinkle at the side of his eyes. "Don't worry about your, ah, ticker. It's all right."

"What do you mean, it's all right? Are you completely around the corner? Doctor Almenroder gave me two years, ultimate. He actually expected me to go any day. The theory of this whole experiment was—"

"We seldom transplant organs any more, Mr. West."

Julian stared at him.

The other said, obviously trying to be soothing, "Some

of the records of your case have been lost. A fire in Pillsbury's files. The man was a charlatan and—"

"Was?"

"He passed away twenty-five years ago."

A finger of ice ran up Julian West's spinal column.

He said finally, "He didn't want to attempt the experiment. I twisted his arm. I was willing to take the chance. It was my only one. He was no swindler."

"I see. Understand, I didn't know Pillsbury. I took over after his death."

"Took over?"

"Yes, through the foundation. Herbert Pillsbury was only partially successful."

"I'm here!" Julian West blurted.

"Yes. To sum it up for you, Mr. West, the techniques required to cure your condition were developed approximately eight years after you were put into what Pillsbury was pleased to call stasis. Shortly afterward you were operated upon, quite successfully. Your organs are now in average condition, if not better."

"What is the date?"

"This is June 3rd, of the year 2."

"You're not making sense. You mean I've been under two years? But you said—"

"No. I meant the year 2 New Calendar."

Julian West closed his eyes before asking the next one. "When did they change the old?"

"January 1st, 2000 A.D. The Gregorian calendar, the Jewish, the Chinese and especially the Moslem were all inaccurate. The year 2000 was considered most suitable for the turn over since—"

"Wait a minute. You mean I've been under for—"

"For over thirty years, Mr. West."

"*Thirty years!* But *why?*"

"Because although Herbert Pillsbury was able to lower your basal metabolism drastically and keep you in what amounted to suspended animation, he had not solved, nor had anyone else, the techniques which would allow you successfully to be revived. Not without danger of a complete, shall we say, psychic collapse. Your mind would not have taken the pressures involved."

28

"I'm not sure it will now."

The other took up the glass again and proffered it. "You'd better finish this."

Julian West, feeling partially dazed now, drank again. A lethargy was coming over him and he could only partially make out the doctor's words.

". . . in desperation . . . resorted to a new development in the psychedelics . . . new departure in psychopharmacology . . . clinical effects of psychotomimetic agents . . . distantly related to psilocybin. . . ."

But Julian West was asleep.

When he came awake again, it was broad daylight in the room which had been artificially lighted before. His strange host was sitting nearby but not looking in his direction. Julian West was able to study him momentarily. The other's face was reassuring, strong, but had an easygoing quality and the wrinkles at the side of the eyes were the result of laughter.

His giddiness was gone and his mind was perfectly clear. This whole thing didn't make sense, now that he brought it back. five years of what amounted to suspended animation? Yes, possibly. But over thirty years, nonsense.

The other saw he was awake. "You had a fine nap of some twelve hours," he said briskly. "And I can see it has done you good. You look much better. Your color is good and your eyes are bright. How do you feel?"

"I never felt better," Julian West said, sitting up.

"You remember your first waking, no doubt, and your surprise when I told you how long you had been in stasis."

"You said that I had, uh, slept, for more than thirty years."

"Exactly."

"You'll admit the story is improbable."

"Extraordinary, I admit, but given the conditions, not improbable nor inconsistent with the trance state imposed upon you by Pillsbury. I suggest, Mr. West, that if you have the strength you go over to the window."

"I'm as strong as I ever was, damn it. I'm beginning to

get the feeling that I've been under no more than a matter of hours, at most, and that you've cooked up this silly story for some reason I can't figure out."

He slung his legs over the side of the bed and came erect. The other took his arm to help him over to the window which dominated one whole side of the room. Julian West, irritated, shook the man's hand away. He was slightly weak, but made it under his own power.

He was seemingly on about the fiftieth floor of what must have been a monstrous building. Below were acres upon acres of parks, woods, lawns, gardens, streams, brooks, ponds. About a mile in the distance he could make out another high-rise building, the largest, he estimated immediately, that he had ever seen in his life. Certainly it had more stories than the Empire State. To his left, and still further away, rose another building, almost the twin of the first. There were paths and walks leading every which way, but no vehicular traffic.

He felt suddenly weak again. Without turning, he said in a whisper, "Where are we?"

"We're in the Julian West University City."

For the moment, he ignored the first part of that name. Instead he said, "What state?"

"We no longer have states, Mr. West, but this is in what was once known as Pennsylvania."

"There is no place like this in Pennsylvania."

"There *was* no such place as this in the Pennsylvania of the time your experiment began."

"But I can see for miles. Possibly this is what Pennsylvania looked like before Columbus but . . . where are the farms, where are the roads, factories, towns? Where in the devil are the cars?"

The other chuckled. "This is a university city. The vicinity isn't particularly suited for agriculture but is eminently suited to residential areas, particularly for those who desire seasonal changes. Factories? Oh yes, in your time they were largely above ground, weren't they? I can remember, of course. I was still in medical school when your experiment began. Cars? They aren't allowed on the surface within city limits."

He took Julian West's arm again, this time without dispute. "Come into the other room. I'd like to get some food into you. By the way, my name is Leete, Academician Raymond Leete."

Julian said, "You know mine."

The next room was obviously a study, although there were only a score or so of books, and they looked on the aged side. The furnishings and decorations were tasteful, Julian West decided, the ultimate in quality but completely lacking in ostentation. It could almost have been a room out of his own period, but not quite. There was an elusive something he couldn't quite put his finger on. He had the feeling that Doctor Leete would have been slightly scornful of the study in the United Nations Plaza terrace apartment once the New York base of Julian West —as though it had been gauche. He felt an edge of irritation.

"What is an academician?" he said.

There was a small table in the room's center. A dazzlingly white tablecloth, a place set for one, several dishes, the utensils with which he was familiar.

"Try some of this broth," Leete said. He picked up a long-necked bottle. "And some of this Riesling." He saw Julian into the straight chair at the table. "We took you off intravenous feeding over a week ago and your digestion should be quite normal."

The broth was delicious, although the flavor was an unknown. In his time, Julian had considered himself somewhat of a gourmet. He had never tasted anything he could remember that came up to this quality. He tried the wine. Superlative.

Leete had taken a larger chair to one side and was observing his charge's food intake with a certain amount of anxiety.

"Academician?" he said. "Ah, yes. The degree had not as yet evolved in the 1960s, had it? As education expanded, we found that the doctor's degree was insufficient."

Julian finished off another spoon of broth and looked at the other. "Insufficient? We used to put four years into a bachelor's degree, two more to take a master's, and usu-

31

ally two more for a doctorate. How many years does a student study these days?"

"His whole life," Leete said simply. "Off and on, that is."

Julian looked at him in disbelief. "You said this was a university."

"Yes, though somewhat different than those of your period."

"I suppose you're one of the professors."

"Not at the time. More of a student, at present."

Julian put down his spoon. "Student! At your age?"

Academician Leete ran a hand over his mouth in rueful humor. "You'd be surprised how difficult it is to have it come back to me, but in actuality, of course, I took my first higher education in your own time. Let me see, how could I explain the changes? Let me take my own field, medicine." He thought about it for a moment. "Back in, say, the 1930s, a young aspirant to a medical degree could emerge from medical school at approximately twenty-five years of age. He could then begin to practice and, if he so desired, never open another book on medicine for the rest of his life. He could practice until the age of seventy or more and never learn anything additional about his profession, save, of course, what he picked up in his day-by-day experience."

"And now?" Julian prompted, taking another sip of the wine. He could already feel the gratifying warmth in his stomach. The broth was finished. He looked at the other dishes. One seemed to be a small steak, though evidently prepared in some manner with which he was unacquainted.

"And now," Leete said, "our physicians are given thorough examinations every two years. If they cannot pass them, they are forbidden to practice. When I was a child, back in the 1950s, there were still many patients who wouldn't dream of going to a young doctor. Families liked an older doctor, one who had been in practice for many years. No more. A doctor today who has most recently come out of the university is most highly prized. You see, today, on an average, we estimate than an education has a half-life of five years."

Julian had taken a taste of the meat. He couldn't place the flavor, although it had a faint familiarity. He said, "I don't believe I get that. A half-life?"

"Yes. Suppose, once again, your field is medicine. In five years, after you have completed your education, half of everything you learned while in the university has become antiquated. In another five years, half of that remaining has become worthless. Obviously, you are through as a physician. Not that our authorities would allow you to practice after that passage of time, without refresher courses. Of course the same thing applies to most sciences, to most fields of endeavor."

Julian was staring at him. "What do you do? You mean a doctor has to retire in five years or so?"

Leete chuckled—he seemed to be a chronic chuckler. "You understate it. No one today would dream of consulting a physician who has been more than five years out of school. Even if so inclined they wouldn't be able to. He would never be able to pass the medical examinations."

"But—"

"Isn't it obvious? We return to school to be upgraded, you might call it. Most often a medical practioner returns to a university city specializing in medicine at least every five years. He spends at least a full year learning the new breakthroughs. Some as an alternative spend perhaps two hours a day at studying the new developments and continue to do this every year of their practicing lives. Some do both."

"That wouldn't be very practical, would it? You can't very easily duck out each day and go to the nearest college for a couple of courses. What in the world is this I'm eating?"

"Heart of chicken. Very nourishing. He doesn't have to duck out to a college, he studies in his own home."

"Oh. Well, that must have its disadvantages. I'm not up on medicine, but don't you have to have laboratories, watch the experts perform surgery in operating theaters, that sort of thing?" He scowled and looked down at his place. "What do you mean, heart of chicken? There was never a chicken born with a heart remotely this size. It's as big as a steak. In fact, it looks like one."

Leete said, "The chicken in whose breast that meat originated possibly lived ten or more years ago. The food you eat was produced in a factory. We have chickens in zoos, of course, and in, well, I suppose you could call them museum-farms, where our children see how the agriculture of the past was handled. But—I'm only guessing—I would suppose that there aren't more than a few thousand chickens in United America."

Julian simply stared at him, then down at the meat he had been eating.

The doctor went on. "Really quite good, isn't it? It's a bit out of my field, but I understand the first experiments took place back in the 1930s or 40s. A chicken heart was kept in a test tube in a laboratory and kept alive. A continual flow of all necessary nutrients needed was pumped through the fluid in which it pulsed. It grew, and from time to time the research scientists who were observing it had to cut back its size. Today, of course, we have sped up the process."

Julian tried another taste. He was astonished. "How about muscle meat? You know, steaks, roasts."

"In my belief, the meat factories don't do quite so well with that. Other problems are involved. But even they are vastly superior to the meat I ate as a boy. There are no such things as tough cuts any more and absolutely no danger of diseased meat."

Julian West shook his head. "This floors me."

The doctor shrugged. "Even in your day such animal food as beef and lamb were becoming prohibitively expensive. It took ten calories of feed to raise one of meat. Chickens weren't so bad, so I understand. By keeping a chicken on wire mesh and injecting it with hormones, you could actually raise one pound of meat from two pounds of feed. Pigs were not quite so efficient as that, but still far less expensive than cattle.

"But to get back to your question about education. Television was in its infancy, thirty years ago, but with the coming of the communications satellites and the computer data banks, it has become practical to study in your own home. But you can go into that later. I see that you've stopped eating. How do you feel?"

"Why, I don't know. I suppose I feel fine. A little dazed with it all."

"How about a bath and a change of clothing?"

"All right." Julian West stood up. "Look," he said to his host. "What's the situation here? What's my status? What am I doing in your home? How do I pay my way? Why should you—"

The other held up a hand to stop him, chuckling. "All in good time. It was decided that in view of the considerable shock you'd go through, a private home and a minimum of persons about you would be most desirable. I've been connected with your case for years, so my establishment here was chosen."

He led the way back to the room in which Julian West had revived. Someone during their absence had laid out a complete set of clothing on the bed.

Leete said, "Here is the bath. I doubt if you'll have much in the way of difficulty. The shower is a bit more automated than you are probably used to, but nothing radical. This is for fineness of spray, this temperature, this is the control for drying and this for soap."

"Automated is right," Julian muttered.

"I'll be in the sanctum," the other told him and returned to the room they had just departed.

Julian West began to strip out of his pajamas.

He deliberately kept his mind as blank as possible as he figured out the workings of the bath. The doctor had been correct. He could slip over the edge if he allowed all the ramifications to hit him at once. He had been in a considerable emotional upset even before going into stasis. Thirty years. Thirty *years* plus. Why, practically everyone he had known would be in their sixties or more—or dead. He blanked out that trend of thought and concentrated on the shower.

When he returned to the bedroom, he had little difficulty with the clothing. Men's clothing of his time had actually changed little from the Civil War days. And an additional thirty-odd years hadn't seen much more in the way of added change. The jacket was without lapels and the trousers without crease. The shoes were slip-ons and made of some material that was most certainly not leather; they were obviously brand new but they had immediate comfort and no stiffness. The shirt was almost identical to those he was used to, save that the collar could not be buttoned nor could the cuffs. Evidently, any type of tie was currently not in, nor cufflinks. The jacket and trousers were tweedlike but most certainly not wool, nor any other animal fiber for that matter. They had a softness and lightness beyond anything he had known, unless it might be cashmere. The fit was perfect.

Something caught the edge of his eye and he walked over to the table beside the bed. There were the personal things he had carried in his pockets when he had submitted to Doctor Pillsbury. Pillsbury! Twenty-five years dead. He hurriedly blanked that thought from his mind and took up the golden pocketknife cum fingernail file, the lighter, the wallet—it still contained the fifteen hundred or so dollars. He wondered what they were worth by now; a third of a century of inflation and devaluation probably hadn't done the dollar much good. He looked at the keys and snorted before tossing them into what first seemed a wastebasket, but then, obviously, was bottomless—some sort of disposal chute. Car keys, apartment keys, so forth and so on. Meaningless, now.

Last of all he picked up the shell briar pipe and tobacco pouch, the latter empty. He stuffed them hurriedly into his pockets, refusing to remember from whence the favorite pipe had come.

He made his way back to what Leete had called the sanctum. The doctor was seated at the desk, looking into one of several screens which sat there.

He looked up. "Refreshed?" he said. "I was just scanning the news accounts of your reviving. I'll have to bring them up to date."

Julian said, "You know, I used to be an inveterate newspaper reader. I couldn't start my day without the *New York Times* and the *Washington Post*. And now here I am, thirty-some years behind on the news. I can't wait to get into the current dailies."

The other made with his light chuckle. "Afraid not, Mr. West."

Julian scowled at him, even as he sank into a chair. "Why not? Is there something you want kept from me?"

"Not at all. It's simply that we don't have newspapers anymore."

"No newspapers! You mean, well, is the country under some all-out dictatorship? No newspapers! Why, not even Hitler completely suppressed all newspapers!"

His host was laughing more deeply now. He waggled a finger in negation, to stem the flow. "You don't understand. I didn't say we didn't have news. Only newspapers. We found them an inefficient method of spreading information. Beyond that, take that *New York Times* of which you spoke. I remember it as a boy. Each day a whole forest was sacrificed to provide the newsprint that went into it, over seven million trees a year. Thousands of persons were employed printing it and then distributing it, and probably thousands more employed at carting it away as trash the following day. And that was only one newspaper among many."

"I don't follow you. You've got to have newspapers."

"Well, Julian . . . I think I'll begin calling you Julian. I've known you a long time, you know."

"Of course."

"Here. Come over here to where you can see this library booster screen."

Frowning, Julian came erect and walked around the edge of the desk. Beneath the screen was a row of three dials that looked considerably like the telephone dials of his own day.

The other said, "It's not as unbelievable as all that, since the first steps took place as far back as the twenties or thirties. I'm referring to first radio and then television news."

The screen was blank at present.

Julian said, "You mean the commentators have taken over news distribution completely?"

"Not exactly. At random, choose some type of news in which you might have been interested before your experiment."

"All right, let's say sports."

"Very well. First I dial current, that is, today's news. The number is eleven." He dialed. "Now we want sub-heading, sports. I won't have to look that up. I happen to be interested in various sporting activities myself. The subheading is twenty-seven, so we dial that. Now then, what sport?"

"I don't know. Let's say, mountain climbing."

"I'll have to look that up." The doctor opened a desk drawer and brought forth what was seemingly a not too thick telephone book. He thumbed through it and found the number he wanted. "Very well, we dial mountain climbing. Now, what area of the world are you particularly interested in?"

"Take Switzerland."

"The Swiss Alps, eh? Very well, we dial that." The doctor did so. "And here we are. Here is all the news that has come in so far today on mountain climbing in the Swiss Alps. Hmmm. Not a greal deal, though it's still fairly early."

On the screen was print, looking not too very different from that of the news magazines of the past. There were several items, each with a headline and a subhead. A new school for tyro climbers was soon to be opened. A delegation of Sherpas from the Himalayas was to be honored at a banquet in Interlaken. Two amateur climbers attempting to scale the Kingspitz without benefit of guide had taken a fall, not fatal. It was expected that abnormally cold weather could shorten the season this year.

As Julian West stared, the doctor flicked a button. The page faded and was replaced by another. There was only one news item on it. A Herr Hans Gottleib was to be honored with a mountain climbing medal as a result of saving his party from an avalanche.

Leete said, "There you have it. All the news applying to mountain climbing in the Swiss Alps today. We can see the films of such events as were photographed, either stills, two dimensional movies, or Tri-Di if you'd like."

"I'll be damned. But suppose I wanted to look up something from yesterday—or last week, for that matter?"

"Or last year, for that. You simply dial yesterday, or whatever date you wish."

"You mean it still remains on file? For how long?"

"Forever, Julian. No news item is ever erased from the library data banks."

"Never! But if all news coverage is as thorough as this, billions of words must accumulate—"

"Trillions, at the very least," the other said.

"But—"

"You must realize the capacity of the international data banks, my boy. All the material that once composed one of those Sunday issues of the *New York Times* can be stored on a data disk smaller than your little fingernail, and considerably thinner."

"But who decides what goes into the news and what doesn't?"

"Nobody actually. All the news goes onto the data banks."

"That's ridiculous. When I was a youngster we used to have these weekly country newspapers filled with such items as, 'Mr. and Mrs. Smith announced the engagement of their daughter Dorothy to Mr. James Brown last week. The little four-page running that news scoop was called the *Far Cry, Nebraska, Bugle* or some such."

"Of course."

"Well, who in Berne, Switzerland, would want to read that?"

"Probably nobody in Berne, unless he was an American tourist from Far Cry, but anyone interested in such news could dial it. *All* of the news goes into the data banks."

"But who supplies it? Who decides what items go in?"

"Aside from reporters, columnists and commentators, anyone who is interested. In that announcement of the engagement you mentioned, probably Mr. and Mrs. Smith submitted the item. In the case of the Swiss mountain climbing items, probably they were submitted by persons or organizations in the Swiss Alps who are interested in mountain climbing. News about the theater is usually submitted by those in the industry, or perhaps by enraged or edified spectators of their work. Today, Julian, you might say that practically all of us are reporters."

"But you'd have to have American reporters there in Switzerland. Or, at least, English-speaking ones. And they must have editors who decide what's news and what isn't."

"Not at all. New communications are international. The computer translators turn them into English and every other written language. Or, for that matter, you can have your news delivered to you orally, in any language." He seemed to be about to add something to that, but didn't.

Julian said, "Then what it amounts to is that all news communications have been collectivized. We would have been up in arms against that."

The doctor looked at him curiously. "Would you have, really? I was reading something on the subject just the other day. Here, let me find it." He turned to his dials and shortly there was a title page of what was obviously a book. He touched the button again and the pages began to flick past. Finally he found the one he wanted. "Here. Read this. It's from Aldous Huxley, a contemporary of yours, long since passed away, I'm afraid."

Before reading the passage, Julian said, "You mean you've still got Aldous Huxley books in your lilbrary"

"Not only all of Huxley, but all of every writer whose books, short stories, magazine articles or other works were available when we began to compile our library data banks. We began with the Library of Congress, the public libraries, the university libraries and then, through arrangements with England, the library of the British Museum. By this time, the banks contain every book and article, every poem, story, novelette, essay or whatever written for the past twenty years or so, and every piece of writing obtainable from before that period, in every written language in the world."

Julian said sourly, "With all that, how in the devil could you ever find anything?"

"It's cross-indexed by author, title, subject, type of work —that is poem, novel, nonfiction, travel, sports, or whatever—and—"

"But who decides what books go into your library data banks?"

"See here, I've just been telling you. Nobody. Everything goes in."

"All right, but suppose I wrote a book?"

"Then you'd submit it to the library data banks and they would record it."

"But I'm not even a writer."

"Then I rather doubt that anyone would read your submission."

"You mean anybody at all can write anything at all, and it will go into your library banks, as you call them. A crackpot poet, a demibuttocked revolutionist, a pot-smoking hippie, a—"

"That is correct."

"But there must be tons of that sort of thing submitted."

"I imagine so. Thank heavens I don't have to read it. Nor does anyone else, for that matter."

"But the expense. What do you have to pay to have, say a novel placed in the data banks? And how does the author get paid if it does go over?"

The doctor was chuckling again. "We've already got more questions than I could answer in the balance of the day. Read this item first, and we'll dispose of this matter of news."

Julian West upped both his hands in a gesture of despair, and bent over to read. The item went:

Mass communication . . . is simply a force and like any other force, it can be used either well or ill. Used one way, the press, the radio and the cinema are indispensible to the survival of democracy. Used in another way, they are among the most powerful weapons in the dictator's armory. In the field of mass communications, as in almost every other field of enterprise, technological progress has hurt the Little Man and helped the Big Man. As lately as fifty years ago, every democratic country could boast of a great number of small journals and local newspapers. Thousands of country editors expressed thousands of independent opinions. Somewhere or other almost anybody could get almost anything printed. Today the press is still legally free; but most of the little papers have disappeared. The cost of wood pulp, of modern printing machinery and of syndicated news is

41

*too high for the Little Man. In the totalitarian East there
is political censorship, and the media of mass communications are controlled by the State. In the democratic
West there is economic censorship and the media of
mass communications are controlled by members of the
Power Elite. Censorship by rising costs and the concentration of communications power in the hands of a few
big concerns is less objectionable than State Ownership
and government propaganda; but certainly it is not something of which a Jeffersonian democrat could approve.*

Julian West came erect again. "All right, but Huxley
had quite a reputation as a nonconformist. Somebody had
to own the mass media."

"No individual does today. It is an international responsibility. We feel it is too important to be left in the
hands of individuals. You see, in your day an editor decided what to submit to his readers. Carrying out the
desires of his publisher, he propagated certain beliefs—
political, religious, nationalistic, socio-economic, even racial."

"Things can't be all that different. Somebody must
affect the presentation of the news even now. You mentioned reporters, columnists and commentators. All right,
they influence their readers or listeners. Who selects
them? Who decides who is to be a commentator?"

"The readers or listeners. In a way, we are all reporters, columnists or commentators. For instance, my field
is medicine and I specialize in stasis, or suspended animation if you prefer. Very well, suppose that some doctor in, say, Japan comes up with a new development in
the field. I would most likely write a paper on his work
and submit it to the news data banks. Anyone interested
would read it."

"As you say, but how would you become a full-time
news writer?"

"Suppose that I wrote a good many medical articles. If
enough people were interested in my views and read my
papers, I could, if I wished, become a full-time commentator on the medical scene, if I so applied."

"But who would decide that you were capable enough
to hold down the job?"

Leete waggled a finger negatively. "Nobody."

"Nobody? You're being ridiculous, Leete. Somebody—"

"Perhaps that's not the way to put it. The readers, actually. Every time one of my papers is read, the computers record the fact. If enough persons read my things and I apply to become a full-time commentator, I am allowed to become one and am free from other duties."

"But suppose you're a wild-eyed fanatic of some sort or other? Possibly you want to overthrow the government."

"We have no objection to a wild-eyed fanatic, necessarily. If some people want to read his material, very well, let them read it."

"Yes, but that can be carried too far, this freedom of speech bit. As has been pointed out, you can't allow someone to stand up in a crowded theater and yell, 'Fire!'"

"Why not? We feel that a few theaters full of people are less important than freedom of speech. Besides, in such a case, the man sitting next to him has a perfect right to stand in his turn and yell, 'He's a liar! There is no fire!'"

Academician Leete dialed one of the other three screens on his desk and said, "Good heavens, I had no idea of the time. Could we cut this interesting subject short for the moment? I promised my wife and daughter to introduce you, as soon as you seemed fit."

"Of course, but frankly I feel more bewildered than before we started. Who in the devil pays for all this?"

IV

. . . I have lived to experience the early results of scientific materialism. I have watched men turn into human cogs in the factories they believed would enrich their lives. I have watched pride in workmanship leave and human character decline as efficiency of production lines increased. . . . We still have the possibility, here in America, of builing a civilization based on Man, where the importance of an enterprise is judged less by its financial profits than by the kind of community it creates; where the measure of a man is his own character, not his power or his wealth.

Charles A. Lindberg
Of Flight and Life

Now.

The two women of the Leete household were in a large living room which led onto a sizeable terrace. Once again, Julian West was impressed by the taste of the furnishings, the rugs, the paintings and other art objects. It came to him that in one respect, at least, there hadn't been much change in the past thirty-some years. Doctors were in the upper-income brackets. This place was as luxurious as his own terrace apartment on Manhattan had been.

The girl—she couldn't have been more than twenty-five—had been bent over a screen similar to Leete's library booster; the older woman, a few years younger than the doctor, perhaps, had been working at embroidery, of all things. They both stood as the men entered, both smiling.

Leete's introductions were simple. "My wife, Martha. My daughter, Edith."

Julian West bent formally over the older woman's hand. "A pleasure, Mrs. Leete." There was a vague something about her that he couldn't put his finger upon, as though he should recognize her, but of course that was ridiculous. Otherwise she seemed a pleasant, down-to-earth type. A middle-aged matron in the best tradition, if a bit on the placid side.

"The pleasure is mine," she told him. "We've been waiting for your awakening for a long time, Mr. West."

Julian turned to the girl and extended his hand. Her eyes were blue, her hair cut boy-fashion, her face healthy, bright and open, her mouth wide and good. She wore no cosmetics whatsoever and, to his surprise, was dressed almost identically to him and the doctor. For that matter, so was Martha Leete. Neither of the women wore jackets, but the slacks and shirts, and evidently shoes, were the same. Not that they weren't attractive. Both women carried themselves with a considerable grace, possibly as though they had professional experience as dancers.

Julian said, "Forgive me, your name is a bit upsetting. You see, my fiancée's name was also Edith. To me, its seems as though I saw her last only three days ago."

Her face expressed concern and there was no connotation of false politeness. She meant it. "I'm sorry. You must be going through an unbelievably upsetting period. Why don't you think of me as Edie? Most of my friends call me that."

The doctor said, "Let's be seated. I'm not at all sure but that I'm allowing Julian too much exercise and excitement."

"I feel all right," Julian said, sinking down onto a couch as soon as the women were seated. "Confused, perhaps, but not at all ill." He looked from one of them to the other. "You see," he said ruefully, "I didn't really expect to awaken again. Not really. I thought it a million-to-one chance."

Martha Leete said, "It must have taken a good deal of courage."

Julian looked at her and shook his head. "No. It was my only chance."

She said, "Well, you can't imagine how glad I am to see you."

"How is that?"

She smiled. "For years not only my husband, but more recently Edith as well, have been immersed in books dealing with your period as compared to the present. It's all I ever hear anything about. Now they can question you to their hearts' content."

Julian turned to the doctor. "But I don't know anything about my period that you don't. You were on the scene."

The other made a negative gesture. "Not in the way you were. Theoretically a person can remember back to his childhood, but in actuality it's a faulty memory at best. You remember things that transpired thirty-five or forty years ago as though it was yesterday. You have the emotions, the prejudices, the viewpoints of the period.

"Let me see if I can explain. When I was in college I had my last fistfight. And practically the first, as well. I'm not the violent type. It was over a girl. The chap had been a hated rival since high school. So we fought. I remember down through the years telling the story and I am honest enough to realize that each time I tell about it, the story changes a bit. Looking back at it now, I can see that very little of the whole, then important, event remains with me. I can't remember his name, nor hers. I can't remember the color of her hair even."

Julian West was amused.

Leete pursued it. "We have men still alive today who are veterans of the Viet Nam war. Supposedly, they can remember it. But can they in any real detail? I understand that you fought in Asia."

"Yes. I was there."

"But your memories are as fresh as though it took place a few weeks ago. When you were a boy, did you ever have a Spanish American War, or even a World War One vet, tell you about his experiences?"

"I see what you mean. They'd usually have two or three little yarns, highlights that they'd tell over and over again."

"Correct. Ah, Julian, you wouldn't be anti-Semitic, would you?"

"Why . . . no. I neither like, nor dislike, Jews as Jews. I try to make a point of judging each person on his own merits."

"That's too bad," Leete said.

Julian West stared at him.

Leete chuckled and said, "That's one of the emotions, the prejudices that it's hard for us to understand any more. We can read about it, we can look at films and photos, but it seems to us so utterly ridiculous. Or any other race prejudice, for that matter."

"Well, you surely still have Jews. Certainly nothing happened in less than forty years."

The doctor said, "Oh, I suppose so. But, well, before you undertook your experiment, how many actual Orthodox Jews did you know?"

"You mean those that really observed Talmudic law? All of it? Darned if I know. Perhaps two or three elderly people. Most of my Jewish acquaintances were either Reformed Jews, or, more likely still, agnostics or atheists."

"And with no prejudice against marrying gentile girls, I imagine."

"No. Quite a few of the people I knew with Jewish backgrounds were married to others with Christian background, or no religion at all. I begin to see what you mean. I suppose it had already begun in my time. Along with the English, Irish, Germans, Greeks, Negroes and everybody else, the Jews are disappearing into the American melting pot."

"It's become a world melting pot now, Mr. West," Edie said.

He looked at her. "Julian, or, better still, Jule."

"Fine."

He turned back to the doctor. "I'm just beginning to get hold of myself. Here we've been discussing education, newspapers, even anti-Semitism. Things I'm not all that interested in. But I've got a thousand questions. I'll answer yours if you'll answer mine. For instance, oh, a thousand things. What happened to the Cold War? What happened to Cuba? Juvenile delinquency, the crime rate. What stage is the space program at? What happened to air and water pollution? What—"

He could see their amusement, so added, "Did Dick Tracy ever get off the moon, and did Snoopy ever shoot down the Red Baron?"

All three frowned puzzlement at that last, and he dropped it.

He said, "I can't wait to see New York, and Los Angeles for that matter. I can't—" He broke it off and frowned at Mrs. Leete. "What's amusing about that?"

She said mildly, "There are no cities any more."

He stared at her. "No *cities*. I . . . you mean, war? The big one?"

Edie said, "There are no more wars, Jule."

He turned on her. "No more wars? You mean you've achieved Utopia?"

Leete gestured a wagging finger in negation. "There is no such thing as Utopia, Julian. It's an unattainable goal. It recedes as you approach it. There is evolution in society, but no end. As each problem is solved, new ones are manifested."

"Wait a minute now. You've got me in a whirl." Julian turned back to Martha Leete who was still smiling. "I think you're all pulling my leg. What do you mean, no cities? They were growing like mushrooms. They were talking about BosWash, a city that would eventually spread from Boston down to Washington. They were even beginning to stretch that into PortPort—Portland, Maine to Portsmouth, Virginia. They were talking about San San, a city stretching from San Francisco to San Diego. And now you tell me there are no cities. Why, when Pillsbury put me into stasis, people were moving into New York, Chicago, Los Angeles like lemmings. The whole country was pouring into the cities!"

Doctor Leete said, "Yes, and they were already beginning to pour out of them, too. Anybody who could afford to."

"But it was one of the strongest trends of the times."

"The existence of a trend doesn't mean that it will continue, Julian. Although cities were still growing in the 1960s, they were already an anachronism and fated to disappearance."

"Look you're not making any sense at all. We've always had cities. As far back as we've had civilization."

Edie Leete nodded. "Yes, by definition you're quite correct, speaking in terms of anthropology. But, you see, Jule, we don't have civilization any more."

He shut up and closed his eyes.

"You're confusing Julian," Martha said mildly. "That's not the way to put it."

"You sure as hell are," he said, before catching himself.

"I'm sorry," Edie said. "I mean, using the Latin original connotation. Our . . . well, our society is no longer based on the *civitas*, the, ah, citizenship in the city state, ah, let's say citizenship in a *state* in general."

"Oh great," Julian West said.

The doctor broke in. "We're still confusing you. What Edith is saying is that we don't have democracy any more. We've evolved to a higher society."

Julian had opened his eyes momentarily. Now he closed them again.

"*What* higher society?" he demanded. "I had my second thoughts about the way the country was run in my time. I was rather laughingly known as a liberal among my usually conservative associates. Basically I thought that government should ultimately be in the hands of the people."

"Oh, don't misunderstand," Edie said. "Government is in the hands of the people. Notice I didn't say *still* in the hands of the people. We don't consider that it was in your day. Now it is. The term democracy, as I recall from my youth, was largely misunderstood. Contrary to popular belief, it did not originally mean rule of the people. What it meant was rule of the *deme*, or what you would have called city ward. The Greeks, when they passed from tribal society to civilization, that is, civil government based on geographic representation rather than kinship, first developed *democracy*. However, it was hardly rule by the people; that temporarily disappeared with the advent of democracy."

"You've got my head swimming."

"Well, think about it. During the so-called Golden Age of Athens rule was in the hands of the male citizens. Neither women nor slaves, and there were many more slaves than there were free citizens, had the vote. Our own United States? Did you labor under the illusion that those patriots who shivered with Washington at Valley Forge were given the vote after the revolution had been won? Only if they were property holders."

"And women weren't granted suffrage until far into the twentieth century," Martha Leete added gently.

"As late as the 1960s, Nixon won the presidential election with a few more than 30 million votes," Leete said. "What was the population at the time? About 200 million? In short, about one person out of six voted for him and less than fifty percent of the registered voters. This is rule by the people?"

Julian said, "Look. Could we get back to your statement that there are no cities any more? Of all the things you've told me—" He let the sentence fade away.

"Let me see, where could I begin," the doctor mused. "I suppose with the nature of the city. Their original reasons for existence were first as a defendable settlement. They were also suitable market centers, handy for trade and usually located at crossroads or at a port on river, sea or ocean. They were also practical as manufacturing centers since ample labor was available, and, through the market, raw materials. They were also centers for education, the arts, and for governmental and religious buildings." He looked at Julian quizzically. "How many of those original reasons for the city still applied by your time, not to speak of the present?"

Julian West thought about it. "All right, you have a point. Obviously they were no longer a defense center. In fact, in case of war they were death traps, even without the use of nuclear weapons."

"And market centers? With the advent of cheaper and cheaper transportation, a market could be anywhere."

"Yes," Julian admitted, nodding, "The supermarkets, department store branches, banks and everything else were moving wholesale out into the suburbs."

"Manufacturing?" Leete pressed. "With the coming of the automobile and still more efficient transportation later, a factory or whatever no longer had to be located in a town where the workers could walk to their jobs, or take streetcar, bus or subway. Who would have been so foolish as to build a factory on Manhattan in the middle of the twentieth century?

"Education? The system was falling apart in the cities of your time. And, besides, with the new techniques that

50

developed based on universal television communication, there was no longer the need to crowd scores of students into classrooms."

"All right. I'd like to know more about that later. But you still haven't given me any indication of how it could have come about. Why, the sheer expense—"

Edie said, "I was just taking some notes on that when you and father came in. Here, listen to this—" She came to her feet and went over to the table on which sat the library booster screen she'd been viewing. She picked up a pad of notepaper.

"In the first seven years of the 1960s the federal government spent on net balance about $1.6 billion for housing and community development, to fight slums and ghettos, and so on, in the urban environment in which seventy percent of Americans lived. The subsidizing of agriculture and the space program both got between twenty-seven and twenty-eight billion. Defense and war got $384 billion."

Julian winced.

Edie said, "Suppose that had been reversed?"

The doctor came in with, "And it was. The revolt against the military-industrial complex went back to your period. Edith, would you mind getting that Eisenhower quotation from his last address, the warning against the unwarranted influence of the military and industrial alliance?"

"Never mind," Julian said. "I'm already acquainted with it."

Martha Leete said, "We seem to be beating you over the head with all our socioeconomics, Julian. Would you like a drink, or some other refreshment?"

"Why, that would be fine. But I wouldn't want you to go to any trouble."

She had risen and was walking toward a piece of furniture set into the wall. She smiled placidly. "You'd be surprised how little trouble."

She touched something, evidently a button on the surface and said to him, "Some wine? Beer?"

He hesitated. "Well, I'd like a Scotch and soda, if you don't mind."

Doctor Leete pursed his lips. "I'm not sure—"

Edie said, "Oh, it will be available."

Martha said, "Raymond? Edith?"

Leete said, "Some of that Moselle would be fine."

"Nothing for me," Edie said.

"Isn't Scotch popular any more?" Julian asked, as Martha Leete dialed.

"Spirits in general have almost disappeared," the doctor told him. "We're more inclined to moderation. Wines and beers, ciders and so on."

Martha came over from what was evidently an automated bar. She handed Julian his drink, her husband his.

"That must be hard on the alcoholics," Julian said, sipping the excellent whiskey.

"There are no more alcoholics," the doctor told him. "At least, if one develops he is cured so quickly that it is hardly noticed. You see, psychotherapy has advanced as much as any other branch of medical science. Alcoholism was a disease of the mind, as were most other addictions."

Julian shook his head ruefully and muttered, "Utopia!"

His host waggled a finger to indicate disagreement. "No, simple progress." He took a taste of his yellow wine. "But to get back to the military-industrial complex. The war you fought in was the last major one, Julian. It was, in many ways, a farce. The actuality of a nation as small as Viet Nam holding at bay the most powerful military machine ever seen for the better part of ten years was ludicrous. Yes, the Vietnamese could have been obliterated by a few hydrogen bombs, but the world would never have stood for that. Peace, perpetual peace, was in the air. The risk of nuclear holocaust was so strongly repudiated by all thinking persons that the trend toward lasting peace was everywhere."

Julian said, "We seem to have gotten away from the cities."

"No, not really. I'll come to that. You see, by then the United States was spending more on so-called defense than all the rest of the world put together. Russia also had a large military budget, of course, but not nearly that of we Americans. They simply didn't have the resources the United States had. Military expenditures by other formerly powerful nations such as England, France and Germany were falling off from what they had been in the past and many of the smaller countries were dependent upon military aid from either America or Russia to maintain armies at all.

"But the thing was, the United States economy was geared to arms production. If the arms budget fell off drastically, something else would have to be found to replace it or there would be depression. Let me see if I have my dates right. Were they already beginning to talk about negative income tax, guaranteed annual wage, guaranteed minimum income and that sort of thing when you were put in stasis?"

"Yes, I recall reading an article on negative income tax. And some of the unions were fighting for a guaranteed annual wage. God only knows where these people thought all the money was going to come from."

Edie said, "It wasn't as expensive as you might think, Jule. Already large numbers of the population were on relief. As many as one person out of eight in New York City. And relief, largely, was very inefficiently handled through city, state and federal agencies which often duplicated each other's efforts. The red tape was unbelievable and literally hundreds of thousands of government workers were involved. When the federal government combined them all, there was a great deal of saving. Social security, unemployment insurance, old age pensions, relief, and all the rest of it was merged into negative income tax. Every family was guaranteed a minimum of $3,500 a year, no matter if it lived in New York, South Dakota, Mississippi, or Puerto Rico, for that matter."

Julian complained, "I still don't see what this has got to do either with military spending or the problems of the cities."

"You haven't thought it out. The reason the cities were growing in your time was that the small farm was disappearing and so were other primary occupations and small industries. Families moved from the South and other distressed areas to the cities for work, or, if that was unavailable, to get on the relief rolls. States such as Mississippi paid a pittance in relief, $8.50 per person per month, but in New York, a sizeable family could get by passingly well on their dole of $71.75 per person.

"Ah, I see what's coming."

"Of course. Nobody loves the city. No one in his right mind would have lived in Harlem, Watts or the South Side of Chicago if he didn't have to. Given negative income tax they didn't have to and the flood turned and started in the other direction. People chose to reside in the more desirable areas of the country, many of which formerly had been losing population.

"The government embarked upon a full-scale housing program, unprecedented in the history of any nation in the world. Every family was guaranteed a home, apartment or mobile home, federally financed. The slack in the economy, once taken up by so-called defense, was now taken up by construction of high-rise apartment buildings, highways—"

"More highways?" Julian protested. "There were already too many of them."

"We put the superhighways and the railroads underground and went about the task of beautifying the country."

Edie twisted her mouth in amusement. "Picking up the beer cans alone was a monumental undertaking, so I understand."

Hardly able to assimilate some of the ramifications, Julian West came to his feet and went over to the window. He stared out. "And this is the present day equivalent of a city." He turned back to the three who were watching him in amusement.

"But what happened to places like New York?"

"Oh, don't misunderstand. Manhattan is still a center —of sorts. It's simply that few people would dream of wanting to live in a cement jungle such as the cities of your day. However, there are still some advantages to a center. For museums, zoos, certain types of entertainment, unique restaurants, some types of hospitals, art galleries—"

"But business offices . . . ?"

The doctor shook his head and gestured to one of the screens the room boasted. "There is no longer need for me to confront a man with whom I am dealing, face to face. I can converse with him, no matter where he might be in the world, instantly. My office is right here in my own home."

Julian stared out again at the other two, no three, high-rise buildings that were within immediate view. "But where are the stores, the shops, the vehicles?"

It was Martha who said, "In a way, you might say that every one of these high-rise apartment buildings is a city. Down in the basement levels are our ultramarkets and the equivalent of your department stores. For all practical purposes they can supply every need. We simply dial, or give a verbal order, and the item desired is sent up through the automated delivery chutes. The same applies to food or drink from the kitchens. Of course, sometimes there are more obscure items that have to be sent for from one of the larger distribution centers."

Edie said, "Vehicles are underground in residential areas. Automobiles were one of the banes of the old cities, what with air pollution, traffic and parking problems, and, actually, was one of the most dangerous devices man ever hit upon."

Julian West had the irritated feeling of need to strike back, as though he were being attacked. Everything was just too damned perfect.

"How tall is this building?" he said.

"One hundred and fifty stories," Leete said. "And, of course, eight underground levels."

"And how many apartments?"

"Some five thousand, I understand. Varying sizes, of course, according to the number in the family, or personal tastes."

"And the same applies to the other buildings in, ah, Julian West University City? By the way, that name surprises me."

"Herbert Pillsbury's research center and hospital which he built with funds from your original foundation grant evolved into a school when the medical education boom began. There didn't seem to be any particular reason to change the name he originally used. Now this university city is one of the largest in United America. But to answer your other question, yes, the other buildings are more or less the same as this."

"Anthills," Julian blurted. "I'd think a good many people would revolt against this sort of packed-in life."

"They do," Leete said. "All of our population do not live this way, in spite of the many conveniences. Some prefer small communities of individual houses. Some prefer almost complete isolation. An increasing number prefer mobile towns."

"Mobile towns?"

"You had the embryo in your time. The trailer came along not long after the automobile. By the late 1960s fifteen percent of all homes built in the United States were mobile homes and already there were whole communities of them. Today they are more elaborate and a mobile town might consist of thousands of moveable homes with auxiliary vehicles containing stores, schools, hospitals, repair units and so forth. It's an interesting way of life, especially for the retired or unemployed. Usually, each mobile community will have some sort of theme. Some follow the sun, north in the summer, south in the winter, and usually park themselves near beaches. Some are hunting or fishing buffs. I know of one consisting of professional and amateur archeologists; they go from one dig to another. And there're even one or two mobile art colonies."

Julian shook his head and returned to his seat. He said, "From all that you've said and implied so far, the thing that sets me back most is the fantastic amount of money involved."

Leete did his chuckle. "Well, when the big changes started there were a good many problems in that regard, of course. However, it's a matter that no longer interests us."

"No longer interests you? Money?

Martha said calmly, "You see, we don't use money any more."

Leete said hurriedly, "I'm afraid that as your physician I'll have to suggest that you retire, Julian. You're beginning to show signs of weariness and this subject could stretch on for quite a time."

V

. . . there are . . . days in which even the mildly critical individual is likely to seem like a lion in contrast with the general mood. These are the days when men of all social disciplines and all political faiths seek the comfortable and the accepted; when the man of controversy is looked upon as a disturbing influence; when originality is taken to be a mark of instability; and when, in minor modification of the scriptural parable, the bland lead the bland.

John K. Galbraith
The Affluent Society

Then

Julian West was a dreamer and had always been. Seldom did he awake in the morning without a lengthy and realistic dream, usually recalling some past vivid experience. And rarely while in dream was he able to recognize the fact; while it was going on he almost always thought it reality.

He was attending a party in a suite at the Conrad Hilton, headquarters of the convention. It was Wednesday but he, in common with the others present, wasn't bothering to participate in the activities at the shabby old convention hall. It was all in the bag anyway and the noisy ridiculousness of the pro politicians repelled him.

So did this party, for that matter, he decided. It was supposedly a celebration, though somewhat premature, of Humphrey's nomination. In actuality, he couldn't care less. The champagne was only semi-cool, and not a very good vintage, probably California or New York, rather than French. He put his glass down and strolled over to Roy London, who was half-interestedly listening to an argument between two Illinois State senators.

Julian said to him, "What do you say we go down and see what's happening in the streets? I understand the damn hippies are gathering forces to march on the convention hall."

London put his own glass down. "Okay, Jule," he said.

They had known each other off and on for more than ten years, since college days. Upon graduation, London had gone into journalism, not being particularly well-off. From time to time they'd meet, on occasion in offbeat places such as Saigon, which the reporter had been covering during the period Julian West was in the military.

He said, "I don't know why the chief sent me here anyway. Nothing deathless is going to occur or be said."

They headed for the door, ignoring one or two voices that called out to them as they progressed.

In the hall, on the way to the elevators, Roy said, "Who's going to win, Jule?"

Julian shrugged. "Why, I don't know. What difference does it make?"

"Well, who are you backing? Whose campaign fund are you sweetening?"

"Both, of course."

"Equally?"

"I imagine. Don't be an innocent, Roy. A few thousand of us in this country make the decisions. It doesn't make any difference if Dick Nixon or Humphrey wins. We're in. We're the boys who got them nominated, we're the boys who'll pull the strings after which ever one wins."

They were waiting for the elevator. The reporter looked at him from the side of his eyes. He said, "Can I quote you? Prominent playboy entrepreneur Julian West, heir of the West industrial fortune, stated today that—"

"You can if you want to be sued," Julian said dryly.

"Whatever happened to honest politics?"

"I doubt if it ever existed. Look, what gives with these kids?"

The elevator came. They entered it and Roy London touched the control for the lobby.

"Well, supposedly a hundred thousand of them were to show up to protest the war, the Establishment and crooked politics. Actually, I doubt if there's more than ten thousand. Mayor Daley, being Dick Daley, has put his whole 11,900 man police force on twelve-hour shifts. Besides that, he's called up more than five thousand National Guards, and they've flown in some sixty-five hundred federal troops. It's already out of hand. He wouldn't let the kids camp in Lincoln Park. If he had, it would have been easier. The cops could have stood guard on the fringes and left them alone unless they tried to parade into town. If he'd had any imagination, he might have welcomed the kids, let them have portable toilets like the government did during the Washington civil rights march in 1963, soothed their ruffled fur a bit. But no, that's not Dick Daley's style. He's got to be rough."

They had reached the lobby and headed through the press of conventioners toward the entrance.

Julian said, "What's happened up to now?"

"For the first three days there were various demonstrations and attempted parades, speeches and so forth. The police used their clubs and tear gas a little too happily. The hippies and yippies yell *pig* at them, and heave a few bottles, bricks and sometimes nail-studded golf balls. There was one pretty bad hassle today when the hippies hauled down an American flag during a rally in Grant Park, next to Lake Michigan. Quite a bit of tear gas was used. I think their idea now is to organize a parade here in front of the hotel and take off for the convention hall. Daley's refused a permit."

They issued forth from the hotel and stood with their backs to the wall, on the sidewalk. There were several hundred spectators, most of them well-dressed and obviously either pedestrians on the way by or guests of the Hilton, participants in the convention. Across the street there was a similar crowd in front of the Sheraton-Blackstone.

In the streets were possibly three thousand youths, practically all of whom were in their teens or early twenties. They wore long hair and those that were old enough, beards; many of both sexes wore granny glasses. The clothes were colorful and some wore war surplus military helmets or motorcycle crash helmets. Possibly one in five had some sort of banner announcing slogans of the National Mobilization Committee to End the War in Viet Nam, or of the Students for a Democratic Society.

They were surrounded by as many as double their number of police and other security officers and the air was tense.

A police captain was bawling something at them through a bullhorn, but even that was drowned out by jeers and chanting. Some of the terminology tended to four-letter Anglo-Saxonisms.

Julian West growled to his companion, "What do they really want?"

The reporter said, "Hear what they're yelling?"

The demonstrators were chanting, "The whole world is watching!"

Roy London said, "That's what they want. To be seen, to be heard. In a way, maybe they've got a point. The Establishment they're against owns the mass media, the newspapers, the magazines, radio, TV, movies, and control even the schools and pulpits for that matter. They watn to be heard and this is one way they can do it. Look at all the TV boys. This thing is going to be covered all the way down the middle."

Julian looked at him. "Whose side are you on? They're a bunch of bums."

London shrugged. "As a matter of fact, most of them are college kids. Most of them have middle or upper-class backgrounds. However, I'm not in favor of them. This so-called New Left has no program. They want to tear down the Establishment but have no real suggestions of what to reestablish in its place. Rebels without a cause."

Several buses of additional police reinforcements rolled up and rapidly disgorged themselves. Whistles blew and the heavyset police moved in, flailing blindly with their riots sticks. Julian West winced when he saw one club literally break over a teenager's head.

The kids for a moment tried to hold, some of them using the technique perfected by the Japanese students, locking arms and snake dancing. But the attackers were merciless. The hippies and yippies tried to break and run for it. Scores, then hundreds of them were on the ground being beaten and kicked. Screams were now mixing with the yells of defiance.

Not all the casualties were being suffered by the youngsters. Here and there individuals or groups fought back, downing their attackers or sending them off with blood streaming down their faces. Which only enraged the others still further.

The TV cameramen were grinding away. A group of the police, their faces grim, riot sticks blurs of motion, waded in. Reporters and cameramen went down before the attack.

"Holy mother!" Roy London blurted.

"Maybe we ought to get out of here," Julian said. "I saw all the combat I wanted in the Mekong Delta."

"Get out how?" Roy London snorted. "We're packed in like salmon."

Some of the hippies, in attempt to break away or hide, had come up on the sidewalk. In a pincer movement, the police were after them. They made no discrimination between hippies and onlookers. One hefty minion of the law bent over a teenager, whaling away on the other's head and shoulders. The youngster screamed in agony. A middle-aged woman attempted to stay his arm and was rewarded with a face full of mace and was then hustled off to a paddywagon by two other police.

"Holy smokes," Roy said. "You know who that was? Anne Kerr, a member of British Parliament here to observe the convention."

In the push and crush, Julian West was hard put to keep his feet. His temper was long gone.

In the street before them, a two-hundred-plus pound brute had leaned over a convertible with three girls in it. He was flailing them unmercifully.

Roy London darted out to him. "Hey," he yelled. "They're just kids! Take it easy and—"

The cop spun on him and jammed the riot stick into his solar plexus. The reporter folded forward, his eyes glazing. The heavyset policeman banged him over the head with the club. Another came up and threw an armlock on the newsman and hauled him away.

A window of the Hilton's Haymarket lounge shattered and a dozen of the entrapped pedestrians and hippies fell through into the lounge in a hail of glass shards. The police followed them, freely swinging, and not even refraining from slugging those who had been having cocktails at the bar or at the tables.

A cop, his eyes wide in violence-lust, yelled at Julian West, "Move it, move it!"

"That just what I'm trying to do, officer," Julian said, in an attempt at placation.

The policeman swung his club in a backhanded swipe, slugging him in the stomach, then turned and swung at an elderly woman who was standing, frozen in terror and making mewling sounds of fear. She collapsed to the sidewalk.

Julian West staggered backward, his face turning gray. He clutched at his heart.

And came fully awake in bed.

VI

Western society has become profoundly materi-
alistic. In contrast to the nineteenth century,
in which saving was a virtue, the twentieth cen-
tury has made consumption into the main virtue.
The aim of life has changed so that the consump-
tion of more and better things has taken the
place of the Messianic vision of a society of soli-
darity and love. While lip service is paid to the
traditional religious ideas, the fact is that these
ideas have become an empty shell. Not perfec-
tion of man, but the perfection of things is the
aim of contemporary society, in the countries
of the West, as well as in the communist system.
The well-fed, well-clad, and well-amused man is
our goal—a man who has much and uses much
—but is little.

Erich Fromm

Now
For long moments he lay there in a dozing state, en-
joying the sensation of bodily comfort. The experiences
of the two days previous, his being awakened by Doctor
Leete and being told that he had been in suspended animation for over thirty years, were a blank in his memory
and he thought he was in his own bedroom in his Manhattan apartment. His half-dreaming, half-waking fancies
going through his mind pertained to his planned marriage to Edith Bartlett, but then to the fore came his
heart condition, and from that, his consultation with Herbert Pillsbury.

Of a sudden his eyes were wide and staring. Obviously,
he was not in his own bed. He sat erect and stared wildly
around the strange room.

He must have sat there for a full minute, glaring about,
before all came back to him. And then in came back to
him like a flood of panic.

Thirty years. Thirty *years* and more! Why, in actuality,

physical appearance to the contrary, he was over sixty-five years old. The world that he had known so well was gone. The people he had known and loved—or hated—were either gone or doddering.

He staggered from the bed and over to the window and stared out, his eyes still wild. It was first dawn but there was no beauty in the morning for him. There was despair, complete collapse of hope, of desire for existence. Suddenly, he had to get out.

He ripped his pajamas from his body, located the clothes he had worn the day before and hurried into them. He had to get out. It was a matter of desperation.

He made his way to the living room, deserted at this time of morning. Obviously the Leete family was still asleep. Good. He couldn't bear the thought of having to see them. He found the front door and left, to emerge into a hall.

There was an elevator bank directly across from the apartment. One of the doors opened upon his approach. He entered and looked about for the controls. There were none.

But this was ridiculous. There had to be some manner of activating the compartment, since it had no human operator.

Built into one wall was a screen which looked considerably like a television screen of his time. He looked into it and, feeling a fool, said, "How do I operate this thing?"

A feminine voice, which had a slight robotlike quality, said, "Where do you wish to go, Mr. West?"

He sighed and said, "Ground floor, please."

"Thank you." The compartment began to drop, accelerating to the point that he had to bend his knees slightly to accommodate himself to the speed. After what seemed a surprisingly short time, it began to slow and he grasped a handrail to steady himself.

It came to a halt and the door opened. He emerged into a lobby that would have been an architect's dream in his own day. But, why not? If advancement in other fields had been a geometric progression, as Leete had described it, why not architecture? It seemed to have somewhat of an ancient Greek motif, complete with statuary, paintings, fountains, columns. It was undoubtedly beautifully done. He hated it.

He wanted to get out. Wanted to get as far from anything that reminded him of the present as he possibly could. Out, out into the open. He hurried toward the entrada at just short of a run.

Out the front, down marble stairs, into the street beyond, across the street to an expanse of lawn that would have done credit to a golf course green. He ignored the various paths and pressed across the grass toward a wood area beyond. He didn't know if he were running or not.

Everything he knew in the world was long gone.

He tore his wallet from his pocket and plucked out the money. Roughly fifteen hundred dollars.

"We don't use money anymore," Martha Leete had said in her complacent way. Smugly? Perhaps smugly. He hated her.

He threw the stuff away in a gesture of despair, and the wallet after it. What securities he had retained before going into his deep sleep, the money he had left in trust, the gold in the Swiss bank. All gone by now. Undoubtedly, all gone. The present world to his mind was a madhouse.

He stumbled on.

Edith. Edith Bartlett. She had said, that very last time he had talked to her—only three days ago, in his mind—that she would wait for him. Wait for him! Why, now she was in her sixties, if alive at all. In her sixties and undoubtedly a grandmother. She'd have sons his age. And what would Julian West be to her? A girlhood memory. Would she even remember his name, for that matter? Leete's story of his fistfight came back to him. After thirty-five years the doctor hadn't even remembered his foe's name, nor the girl over whom they fought.

He dropped to his knees in the shelter of the neatly laid out woods, then to his face. The emotional crisis was fully upon him and with set teeth and laboring chest, he lay there gripping handfuls of grass with frenzied strength and fought for sanity. In his mind all had broken loose, habits of feeling, associations of thought, ideas of persons

65

and things, all had dissolved and lost coherence and were seething together in apparently irretrievable chaos. There were no rallying points, nothing was left stable.

He knew he was on the verge of losing his mental balance. If he lay there thinking, he was doomed. He had to have diversion of some sort, at least the diversion of physical exertion. He came to his feet and started walking briskly.

It was still hardly light. He took off in a straight line. He tried to drum up some interest in what he saw about him.

Evidently, in these pseudo-cities of high-rise apartments, each building was surrounded by what must be the greater part of a square mile of parks, woods, gardens. There were streams, crossed by footbridges, there were playgrounds, deserted at this time of day. There was a lake, obviously utilized for both boating and swimming. Over to his right was a golf course; nearby, tennis courts, a multitude of them. Beyond was an extensive series of swimming pools, wading ponds, an area with diving boards. And everywhere flowers.

It came to him that it must take a host of gardeners to maintain all this, a fantastic number of them.

And then he had to reverse himself. A vehicle about the size of an electric golf cart of his own time went by him, stopped at a decorative shrub and began to trim it. It was unattended, nor could Julian West make out anyone in the immediate vicinity.

No, he took that back. Toward him was toddling a child. It was dressed in an outfit that looked like nothing so much as Germanic *Lederhosen,* though the material wasn't leather. The little one had a ball under one arm. Until she spoke, he couldn't make out if it was a girl or boy. She couldn't have been more than seven and was obviously a fugitive from adult supervision.

Julian West hunkered down on his heels and began to say, "Where are you going this time of morning?"

She looked at him, evidently came to a decision and said politely, *"Kiel vi fartas?"*

Julian West didn't quite place it, although he had

French and a smattering of Spanish and German. He said, "I don't speak . . . uh, Italian, little girl."

She considered that and said, *"Pri kio vi parolas?"*

He took his lower lip in his mouth and shook his head. "We're not making much headway, but I don't think you should be out alone at this time of morning."

Evidently she liked the tone of his voice, whether or not he was getting through to her. She said, *"Kiom da jaroj vi havas?"*

It was possibly some Balkan language. Possibly Rumanian, since there seemed to be Latin elements. But he couldn't put his finger on it. However, the fact that the child couldn't speak English made it still more obvious that she shouldn't be wandering around unsupervised. She must have sneaked out of her·apartment building before her parents awakened. They'd undoubtedly be terrified when they did.

He looked at her in frustration. In these surroundings, he was almost as much at sea as she was. He had no idea of where to take her or what to do with her, but the child couldn't be left out like this alone. But, for that matter, he had no way to attempt her rescue since they couldn't even communicate and he might frighten her by trying to lead her away.

She evidently decided that they weren't hitting it off sufficiently to retain her interest, pointed toward a playground and said, *"Mi iras tien,"* turning on her heel and toddling away. He decided she couldn't be more than six.

Julian West stood and rubbed the side of his face, discovering in the process that he needed a shave. Well, at least he had a purpose now. He turned and retraced his steps to the building which housed the Leete family.

There were a few others about by this time, on the streets and in the lobby. They were so nearly identically dressed, both men and women, that he was hard put to tell the sexes apart except at quite close range, save that some wore beards. Hair styles seemed to have no sexual connotations. Some of the men wore theirs long, as long as down to the shoulders; some of the women wore theirs cut as short as did Edith Leete.

It came to him, as he crossed to the same elevator he had taken down, that he had no idea what floor the Leete apartment was on, not to speak of the apartment number. He hadn't noticed, his mental condition being what it was when he had left.

As before, the elevator door opened before him upon his approach. He stepped inside and, in experiment, said to the screen, "The apartment of Academician Leete, please."

"Yes, Mr. West," the robotlike voice said.

Well, that problem had solved itself. It wasn't too difficult to figure out. Evidently the building was computer-operated and someone, probably the doctor, had fed Julian's name and face into the data banks before his patient had even revived. It probably would have been possible to do in his own time, though he knew of no example.

When the elevator stopped, he emerged and had no difficulty in recognizing the door through which he had stumbled—an hour? two hours?—before.

But now the problem was to reenter. There didn't seem to be a bell and there was no doorknob. However, that problem resolved itself too. The door opened before him when he approached. He went back into the living room.

Edie was seated there before the library booster screen, as her father had named it. She looked up, startled.

"Jule! What's happened to you? Where have you been?" She came to her feet and took in his clothes.

For the first time, he realized that he had soiled his trousers at the knees when he had flopped down in the wooded area. Self-consciously he brushed them.

There was obviously something in his face. She came forward and, perhaps involuntarily, put out her hands and took his.

"Jule, I'm so sorry. We should never have left you on your own. You must be going through a terrible period."

He shook his head and took a deep breath but held onto her hands. "The worst is over but I had my wind up a little. I've been out . . . out in the park."

She said quickly, a bit strangely, "Oh? All by yourself?

Did you talk to anyone?" She led him over to the couch and sat him down, as though he were an invalid.

"That's why I came back." It sounded a trifle foolish now. "There was a child out there, all alone. About six years old. I think she's in the playground now. I didn't know what to do. Evidently from some alien family."

"Alien?"

"She didn't speak English."

"Oh, I see. It will be fine."

"Fine? It's hardly light out. There's nobody around. How will her parents ever find her? She's undoubtedly lost."

"Security has probably already notified them," she said, amusement in her eyes. "But your concern is praise-worthy."

He looked at her unbelievingly. "She could wander off into the woods and, at the very least, frighten herself half to death."

She shook her head. "It's impossible for a child to get lost, Jule. You see, they all have an electronic I.D. tag about their necks. Security can get a cross on any child, at will. There are microlenses scattered about even in the wooded areas. A child alone, at this time of morning, will be spotted, the computers will notify the parents and let them know where she is. Undoubtedly one of them is already on the way."

"You mean you can't get lost these days, even if you want to?"

"Well, it would be rather difficult. Jule, why did you go out? Father intended to keep you under observation for these first few days."

He shrugged unhappily and looked away from her. "Like I said, I got my wind up. It hit me over the head, all of a sudden, all of it. I'm like a fish out of water."

"Jule, you're with friends. Consider this your home. We'll—how did you used to put it—run interference for you."

He snorted self-deprecation. "Before I went under, I tried to make various provisions for when I woke up, but I had no idea I was going to be in stasis for the better

69

part of thirty-five years. I stashed away a considerable amount of gold in Switzerland—"

"We don't use gold as a medium of exchange any more."

"I invested some more in what I figured were the bluest of blue-chip stocks."

"We don't have stocks any more."

"I even put some in a savings account."

"As mother told you—"

"I know, you don't use money any more," he said sourly. "I also put some into gems, diamonds, emeralds—"

She said unhappily, "We seldom wear jewelry. It was a relic of primitive societies."

"So here I am, penniless. Without a profession or even a trade. And currently living on charity."

"There isn't any such thing as charity any more, Jule."

"Damn it," he snapped in sudden irritation. "There doesn't seem to be anything anymore. Everytime I open my mouth—"

She put a finger out and held it to his lips and he subsided, begrudgingly.

She said chidingly, "We aren't barbarians, Jule. You have nothing to worry about. Just a minute, I want you to read something. I'll get it from the sanctum." She stood and left him to return in a few minutes with a book. She handed it to him and said, "This is an old favorite of father's so he has an individual copy of his own. He has a habit of liking to mark passages that particularly appeal to him. Here, read this one. It's from Edward Bellamy, a Utopian writer of the nineteenth century."

He looked up at her, then shrugged and read:

By way of attempting to give the reader some general impression of the way people lived in those days, and especially of the relations of the rich and poor to one another, perhaps I cannot do better than to compare society as it then was to a prodigious coach which the masses of humanity were harnessed to and dragged toilsomely along a very hilly and sandy road. The driver was hunger, and permitted no lagging, though the pace was necessarily very slow. Despite the difficulty of drawing the coach at all along so hard a road, the top was covered with passengers who never got down, even at the steepest ascents. These seats on top were very breezy and comfortable. Well up out of the dust, their occupants would enjoy the scenery at their leisure, or critically discuss the merits of the straining team. Naturally, such places were in great demand and the competition for them was keen, everyone seeking as the first end in life to secure a seat on the coach for himself and to leave it to his child after him. By the rule of the coach a man could leave his seat to whom he wished, but on the other hand there were so many accidents by which it might at any time be wholly lost. For all that they were so easy, the seats were very insecure, and at every sudden jolt of the coach persons were slipping out of them and falling to the ground, where they were instantly compelled to take hold of the rope and help to drag the coach on which they had before ridden so pleasantly. It was naturally regarded as a terrible misfortune to lose one's seat, and the apprehension that this might happen to them or their friends was a constant cloud upon the happiness of those who rode.

But did they think only of themselves? you ask. Was not their very luxury rendered intolerable to them by comparison with the lot of their brothers and sisters in the harness, and the knowledge that their own weight added to their toil? Had they no compassion for fellow human beings from whom fortune only distinguished them? Oh, yes, commiseration was frequently expressed by those who rode for those who had to pull the coach, especially when the vehicle came to a bad place in the road, as it was constantly doing, or to a particularly steep hill. At such time, the desperate straining of the team, their agonized leaping and plunging under the pitiless lashing of hunger, the many who fainted at the rope and were trampled in the mire, made a very distressing spectacle, which often called forth highly creditable displays of feeling on the top of the coach. At such time the passengers would call down encouragingly to the toilers on the rope, exhorting them to patience, and holding out hopes of possible compensation in another world for the hardness of their lot, while others contributed to buy

71

salves and liniments for the crippled and injured. It wa:
agreed that it was a great pity that the coach should b₁
so hard to pull, and there was a sense of general relief
when the specially bad piece of road was gotten over.
This relief was not, indeed, wholly on account of the
team, for there was always some danger at these bad
places of a general overturn in which all would lose their
seats.

It must in truth be admitted that the main effect of the
spectacle of the misery of the toilers at the rope was to
enhance the passengers' sense of the value of their seats
upon the coach, and to cause them to hold on to them
more desperately than before. If the passengers could
only have felt assured that neither they nor their friends
would ever fall from the top, it is probable that, beyond
contributing to the funds for liniments and bandages,
they would have troubled themselves extremely little
about those who dragged the coach.

I am well aware that this will appear an incredible in-
humanity but there are two facts, both very curious,
which partly explain it. In the first place, it was firmly and
sincerely believed that there was no other way in which
Society could get along, except when the many pulled
at the rope and the few rode, and not only this, but that
no very radical improvement even was possible, either in
the harness, the coach, the roadway, or the distribution of
the toil. It had always been as it was, and it always would
be so. It was a pity, but it could not be helped, and
philosophy forbade wasting compassion on what was beyond remedy.

The other fact is yet more curious, consisting in a sin-
gular hallucination which those on the top of the coach
generally shared, that they were not exactly like their
brothers and sisters who pulled at the rope, but of finer
clay, in some way belonging to a higher order of being
who might justly expect to be drawn. This seems unac-
countable, but, as I once rode on this very coach and
shared that very hallucination, I ought to be believed.
The strangest thing about the hallucination was that those
who had but just climbed up from the ground, before
they had outgrown the marks of the rope upon their

hands, began to fall under its influence. As for those whose parents and grandparents before them had been so fortunate as to keep their seats on the top, the conviction they cherished of the essential difference between their sort of humanity and the common article was absolute. The effect of such a delusion in moderating fellow feeling for the suffering of the mass of men into a distant and philosophical compassion is obvious. To it I refer as the only extenuation I can offer for the indifference which, at the period I write of, marked my own attitude toward the misery of my brothers.

Julian West looked up again. He said, "All right. I suppose I was one of those riding on top. Well, there's been a bit of an upset." He looked around the ample apartment. "Obviously, the Leete family has seats today."

She shook her head at him. "I didn't give you that passage to rub in your present status, Jule. I wanted to illustrate the present situation in United America. You see, Jule, that road over which the coach travels is paved now. It's a beautiful highway. And the coach itself is now nuclear-powered, and there is no driver. It's automated. And everybody rides now. There are seats for all."

He looked at her blankly.

She said, "Were you acquainted with the work of the Hudson Institute, headed by a Herman Kahn?"

"Vaguely. Weren't they one of the groups trying to extrapolate in the field of economics?"

"As well as others. However, in his book, *The Year 2000*, which he did with Anthony Wiener, Kahn pointed out that, following the trend that applied in their time, by this period in which we live now the average family income would be over twenty thousand dollars and the per capita gross national product would be more than ten thousand dollars. This if the yearly growth rate was only three percent."

He was still blank.

She said, "They had both the failure of nerve and the failure of imagination, Jule. They understated."

VII

*Some cynics may doubt if any society of human
beings could adjust itself to unlimited abundance
and the lifting of the curse of Adam. . . . Yet
in every age, a few men have known such freedom, and not all of them have been corrupted
by it. Indeed, I would define a civilized man as
one who can be happily occupied for a lifetime
even if he has no need to work for a living. This
means that the greatest problem of the future is
civilizing the human race; but we know that already. . . . So we may hope, therefore that one
day our age of roaring factories and bulging
warehouses will pass away, as the spinning
wheel and the home loom and the butter churn
passed before them. And then our descendants,
no longer cluttered up with possessions, will remember what many of us have forgotten—that
the only things in the world that really matter
are such imponderables as beauty, and wisdom,
laughter and love.*

> Arthur C. Clarke
> *Profiles of the Future*

Now

Doctor Leete entered and said briskly, "Well, you two
are up and around early. Julian, how do you feel?" He
looked at his patient quizzically.

"All right, I suppose. A little punch-drunk. Every time
I ask a question, the answer floors me."

Leete chuckled and looked at his daughter. "You were
the one that was so keen on breaking things to our guest
gently. If the truth be known, you'll be having him in a
relapse. You two haven't had breakfast as yet, have
you?"

Edie stood. "No. At least, I haven't. Jule?"

"I'm starved," he admitted.

"Succor for the starving man," Leete said. "This way, please. Martha read late into the night, I doubt if she'll be with us for a time."

He led the way from the living room into another, which had vague attributes in Julian West's mind to a breakfast nook, though there seemed to be no connecting kitchen. They seated themselves about the table.

The doctor said, "What are your preferences, Julian?"

"Why, I've always been a good breakfast man. Coffee, eggs, bacon or ham, toast, marmalade."

"Excellent. And how do you prefer your eggs?"

"I thought you didn't raise chickens any more."

"We don't, but our food factories produce eggs. The problems were no greater than those involved in manufacturing meat."

Julian West sighed in resignation. "I prefer them shirred."

"Your formula?"

"Why, let me see. My man, Sawyer, usually prepared them but I have on occasion. They were baked in a shallow ramekin. It was heated and a little butter melted into it before the eggs were added to the dish. Then the eggs were baked four inches from a medium broiler flame with a bit of butter on the yolks to keep them moist. The shirred egg dish is made ready with a slice of boiled ham, a rasher of bacon, a slice of salami and one of garlic sausage."

"Excellent. We shall name the dish in your honor. Eggs a la Julian."

He pressed a button set into the side of the table and said, as though not speaking to either Edith or Julian, "Eggs a la Julian," and then recited, word for word, Julian West's recipe for shirred eggs while that worthy stared at him.

He took his hand from the button and said, "From now on your recipe will be on tap in the building's kitchen data banks. You can order it at any time. Edith?"

"I think I'll try the same."

The doctor pressed another button and said, "Three orders of eggs a la Julian, three of toast, three of marmalade, two of coffee, one of tea."

Julian looked about the small room, nonplussed. "You have a speaker system connecting with your kitchen?"

Edie twisted her mouth in amusement. "Surprisingly enough, we do have a kitchen. Very few apartments do, but cooking is one of mother's hobbies. However, our breakfast is being done in the community kitchens on the third basement level. Cooking is seldom in the hands of amateurs any more, thank goodness."

The doctor brought an object from his pocket and pushed it over toward Julian West. At first Julian thought it a silver cigarette case, but for the moment he ignored it to blurt, "You mean cooking is automated too?"

"Why not?"

"It's one of the few arts in which I had any proficiency. I used to pride myself on being an amateur chef. Quite a gourmet, and all that. Automated cooking sounds a little on the cold-blooded side."

"Wouldn't you rather eat the dishes of the most accomplished chefs in the world, always prepared perfectly?" Leete demanded. "Back when I was a boy I recall that you could enter the best possible restaurant and if the chef was having a bad day, as a result of a hangover or anything else, it was just too bad. Today there is no such thing as a chef's bad day. Once a recipe is fed into the data banks, it is prepared perfectly every time ordered. And even an outstanding chef's demise does not mean that you cannot appreciate his specialties. They are on tap forever."

The center of the table sank briefly to return with the three breakfasts. Edith handed them about with the utensils and napkins that accompanied the dishes and cups.

They looked at him questioningly as he tasted.

Julian said, "You mean these eggs were manufactured?"

"That is correct," Leete said.

"I've never eaten better. And this ham as well? It tastes like Polish ham."

"That is correct."

"Fantastic."

They too began to eat. The doctor indicated the object he had pushed toward Julian. "I took the liberty of having

you assigned an I.D. number. There is your transceiver."
"Transceiver?"
"Yes. It is practically impossible for a citizen to operate without one. I believe they were in embryo when you were put into suspended animation. Didn't you have portable telephones?"
"Why, yes. You could have one put in your car. Not very efficient, so I understand." Julian West opened the device. One whole side was devoted to a small screen. "Why, it's television."
The doctor sipped his coffee and nodded. "Ummm. Since the advent of the satellite communications system some years ago, it has become practical for everyone to have a pocket TV phone. But it is more than that, of course. It is also your contact with the international data banks. Through it, also government officials can communicate with you and every other citizen, if necessary. It is also your voting booth at election times. Above that, it is your credit card. When you wish to buy something, you slip your transceiver into the slot of the delivery box and the computers deduct the amount involved from your account."
"Credit card?" Julian West said bitterly. "I have no credit, so far as I know. Evidently a third of a century was ample time to wipe me out."
The doctor shook his head and waggled a finger negatively. "Every citizen has his annual credit deposited to his account. I thought you told me that they were already discussing negative income tax and guaranteed annual income in your day."
"But I have no profession, no trade. Why should I be put on the public dole? I'm worthless! The only thing I could possibly do to earn my way would be a laborer's job and I'm not even sure I'm physically capable of that."
Edie said softly, "There are precious few common labor jobs anymore, and those rather avidly sought after by strapping young fellows who like manual work, especially when it's in the open air."
"See? That's what I mean. I'm unemployable."
"Along with most of the population," Doctor Leete said lightly.

Julian blinked. "You mean a majority of the population today is unemployed?"

Leete pursed his lips. "Julian, at approximately the time you were put into Stasis, Dr. Richard Bellman of the Rand Corporation predicted that by the end of the century two percent of the United States labor force would be able to produce everything the country could consume. And even he underestimated the computerized, automated industry of today."

"Then the majority of our people are nothing but parasites?"

It was Edie who answered him. "None of them are parasites, Jule. And neither are you. Today—forgive me for lecturing—today, in a computerized, automated factory which produces, say, shoes, two or three men on a shift may supervise the production of a hundred thousand pairs of shoes a day. But it is not just the three men who are producing those shoes. It is the whole human race down through the centuries. If they were working alone, without the whole race backing them, it is doubtful if they could produce more than a pair or two of shoes apiece, per day. But they have inherited the efforts of a hundred thousand generations of their ancestors. A million years ago an early man discovered how to use fire. Another devised the first crude stone tool. Many generations later, animals were domesticated, agriculture stumbled upon, the wheel invented, the use of metals begun. Man's background of knowledge increased and increased and soon every generation was contributing. This legacy of invention and development doesn't belong to one man nor to any group of men. It belongs to the whole race. As a result of it, we have finally reached the point where a fraction of our people can produce an abundance for all."

"But this mere handful of people has to do all the work, while the rest do nothing at all?"

The doctor did his chuckle and pushed his dishes to the side. "We didn't say that the rest do nothing. Only that less than two percent of our people of working age are needed to produce an abundance."

All had finished their food. Edie put the dishes in the center of the table and pushed a button set into its side.

The table center sank away to return almost immediately, clean.

The doctor brought several sheets of paper from an inner pocket. He said, "Julian, it came to me yesterday how completely we were baffling you. One difficulty in bringing you up to date and describing your present situation is that we're going at it inconsistently. You ask a question and before it is completely answered, two more have occurred to you. At this rate, it will take forever. So last night I sat down to my voco-typer—"

"Your what?"

"See? That's what I mean. A voco-typer is a typewriter that you speak into and it types out your words. They were already being experimented with in your day. At any rate, this will give you some background in the developments since you were put in stasis. I suggest that you go on into the sanctum and read it. Afterwards you'll surely have questions. Martha, Edith and I will be glad to answer them."

VIII

The future of the industrial system is not dis-
cussed partly because of the power it exercises
over belief. It has succeeded, tacitly, in exclud-
ing the notion that it is a transitory, which
would be to say that it is a somehow imperfect,
phenomenon. More important, perhaps, to con-
sider the future would be to fix attention on
where it has already arrived. Among the least
enchanting words in the business lexicon are
planning, government control, state support and
socialism. To consider the likelihood of these in
the future would be to bring home the appalling
extent to which they are already a fact. And it
would not be ignored that these grievous things
have arrived, at a minimum with the acquies-
cence and, at a maximum, on the demand, of the
system itself.

John K. Galbraith
The New Industrial State

Now

Julian West sank down into a comfortable chair and began to read. He had bathed, shaved—having found a
cream dipilatory in his bathroom—and returned to the
sanctum, as the doctor called it, to find the others gone.
They were evidently leaving him to himself so that he
could read Leete's report.

It began:

FOUNDATIONS OF THE CHANGES
THAT HAVE TAKEN PLACE

When a socio-economic change is pending it is not one
man nor even one group that starts it underway. The
whole trend of society is toward it. Our changes had
their roots far back in the economic history of the country.
By the middle of the century matters had so culminated
that hundreds, even thousands, of persons were inde-
pendently trending toward the new system.

The American Academy of Arts and Sciences established its Commission on the Year 2000, organizing the efforts of scores of experts to pry into the future of the sciences, including the social and political ones. The Hudson Institute, directed by Herman Kahn, plunged full-scale into studies of the future. The Rand Corporation sponsored the Delphi prediction studies of Olaf Helmer and T. J. Gordon. The American Institute of Planners' Fiftieth Year Consultation commissioned several volumes on environment and change in the next fifty years. Such writers as Stuart Chase did his *The Most Probable World*, peering forward to the twenty-first century, and John K. Galbraith his *The New Industrial State*. Even the great fortunes contributed such studies as those of the organization called Resources For the Future, financed by the Ford Foundation.

Nor was America alone. In England, the Social Science Research Council set up the Committee on the Next Thirty Years, and in France there was the *Prospectives* group and the *Futuribles* project. Arthur C. Clarke wrote his *Profiles of the Future* and Michael Young, *The Rise of the Meritocracy*. The British New Scientist Series, consisting of two volumes, was entitled *The World in 1984*. In Germany *The Race to the Year 2000* was brought out by the economic philosopher Fritz Baade. In the Orient, Han Suyin wrote *China in the Year 2000*.

The list could be extended almost indefinitely and possibly should at least include such authors as Margaret Halsey (*The Corrupted Giant*), Robert L. Heilbroner (*The Limits of American Capitalism*), Vance Packard (*The Waste Makers*, etc.) and Fairfield Osborn (*Our Plundered Planet*).

New publications, most fated to last but a few issues, began to emerge and grope toward answers. Student organizations formed, largely in conflict with each other, seeking reply to the problems society presented them with and had thus far failed to solve. There was rioting in the schools, largely on the part of confused rebels not quite sure of their cause. There were riots in the streets against war, against poverty, against political corruption, against the curbing of civil rights and against the race discrimination which split the country.

More minds, in despair of the old society, turned to contemplation of the possibilities of a new socio-economic theory.

Of a sudden, everybody was asking the questions. And the answers began tumbling in.

"What answer?" Julian West muttered. He turned to the next page and began to read again.

THE GOLD DRAIN

At the same time several developments were heading the nation toward a basic change, though many didn't realize their nature.

The means of exchange was in a condition of chaos. In the past, American paper money had been backed by gold and silver. The expansion of business, however, had become so great that there simply was not enough of the precious metals in the world to back the billions upon billions of paper dollars and other currencies. The amount of gold or silver actually supporting such currencies was cut and cut again: a form of devaluation, of course.

Following the Hitler war, the United States found itself with the greatest horde of gold it had ever accumulated. However, through foreign wars such as Korea and Viet Nam, and through aid to Allied countries and the export of capital to purchase industrial and other business holdings abroad, this stock melted away until finally foreign nations held more than thirty billion in paper dollars and there was only a fraction of this in Fort Knox. Had they all demanded gold at once the United States would have been bankrupt.

It was a ridiculous situation. A trillion dollar economy was on the verge of collapse through want of a few billions of dollars in gold with which to back up the national currency.

The solution was finally found. One year the federal government requested that the five hundred largest corporations pay one-tenth of their corporation taxes in common stock of the firm involved. This stock was merged into what amounted to a huge mutual fund which was dubbed United States Basic. Some of this was made available on every bourse, every stock exchange, in the world, to seek its level. United States Basic, of course, paid dividends based on the returns from the stock of which it was composed. Any individual or any nation holding American paper dollars could demand payment in United States Basic shares.

In short, the economy of the whole nation was backing the dollar.

The advantages over gold are obvious. Gold in itself, sitting in strong vaults such as those of Fort Knox, produces nothing. In fact, the guarding of it is a definite expense. Nor, for all practical purposes, was United States Basic limited in amount. Each year the government continued to collect ten percent of corporation taxes in the form of common stock.

This, of course, also led to new revenues for the nation. The stocks drew dividends, and those quantities kept in reserve against paper dollar demands from abroad enriched the treasury. This just in time, since the newly instituted negative income tax was now in full effect, as were the housing and road-building boom, and the medical and especially educational boom.

The government could use all the money it could put its hands on, and while originally this expedient had been expected to be utilized for only a year or two it stretched out and the new tax law wasn't repealed. The conclusion is obvious. The federal government gained larger and larger amounts of voting stock in the top corporations of the nation.

Julian West grunted. "Creeping socialism," he said aloud, turning the next page. It was entitled:
EDUCATION AND THE GROWTH
OF MERITOCRACY
At approximately the same time the education explosion was upon us. In 1968 about forty percent of all youths in America in the age group were going to college. In California, it was fifty percent. But this was simply the beginning.

It had long been thought that the reason the poor

were poor was because they lacked education and the necessary training to hold down jobs in the new industrialized society. In actuality, it was the other way around. They lacked education and training because they were poor. Had they not been raised in poverty surroundings, they would have secured the education and training they needed to hold such jobs. Once our whole nation was emancipated from poverty, the new generations secured the education and training which allowed them to become normal, useful members of society. It is possible for a child born of illiterate, poverty-stricken parents, undernourished and dwelling in a slum with inadequate schooling facilities available, to rise out of it. Possible, but extremely difficult, especially if the child suffers from such diseases of malnutrition as kwashiorkor, scurvy, rickets and pellagra. Few were able to make the break.

New techniques in education were devised to fit in with the demands of the computerized society. Prominent among these was the seeking out of the aptitude quotient of each student. It was, perhaps, a development of the early I.Q. tests. The I.Q. tests, of course, never really measured all-around intelligence since there is no such thing. But the aptitude quotient tests did measure a student's ability to assimilate higher education and indicated the fields in which he could strive best.

From earliest youth each citizen was tested not only for I.Q. but for memory, for digital dexterity, analogizing power, mechanical aptitude, mathematical aptitude, verbal ability and fluency, spatial ability, driving ability, accident proneness, clerical aptitude, emotional maturity, veracity, tone discrimination, taste sensitivity, color blindness, accuracy, persistence, neurosis, and powers of observation. Each year the results of these tests were filed away in the national data banks, their sum total being the citizen's aptitude quotient.

From earliest youth, a child's natural tendencies were carefully noted and he was encouraged along the educational paths for which he had the greatest aptitude. Should a child indicate a strong mechanical ability, his education stressed such fields; should he early in life like to draw or play with paints, he was encouraged to study the arts; should he show an early predilection for music, instruments and instruction were made available. By the time he reached full maturity and his immediate education was completed, he was prepared to go into the field that best suited his nature and abilities.

This alone was a fabulous advantage to the newly evolving socio-economic system. In the past, very often indeed a citizen wound up in a field which he neither liked nor for which he was suited. The son of a small farmer might have been a whiz at math but his father needed him on the farm to help with the chores and hence he "dropped out" as soon as it was legal for him to do so, his mathematical abilities never developed. The son of a banker might have loved to work with his hands and might have had a mechanical aptitude which would have resulted in a full life had he been an automobile mechanic. Instead, he was hustled off to an Ivy League college, and, one way or the other, got through so that he was more or less prepared to go into business upon graduation.

Perhaps, in exploring the origins of our socio-economic system of the present, it can be said that it was the new, universal education that finally tipped the scales. Contrary to popular belief it is not the downtrodden who demand basic reforms. If anything, the *lumpen* proletariat is the most reactionary element in society. Fundamentalists in religion and superpatriots in politics are the first to cry out against the nonconformists. It is not the poor who become reformers, hippies, yippies, radical thinkers, or who in other ways revolt against the status quo. Hippies were college students, artists, members of middle or upper-class families. None were quicker to condemn them than the poor whites, those on relief, those with no real stake in the society the hippies attacked.

In the early days of America a mere handful of scholars such as Franklin, Jefferson, Paine and Madison were able to sway the country. Less than one percent of the population graduated from a university. When that percentage reached above the fifty percent level, then the fat was in the fire so far as social institutions were concerned. An educated man is a dangerous man—he thinks.

And a thinking people would no longer stand for the glaring contradictions of society.

And, on the face of it, these educational developments could not but speed up the managerial revolution, the trend toward what Galbraith called the new industrial state, what Michael Young called the rise of the meritocracy.

During the period of classical capitalism, such as applied in the United States before 1929, the head of an industry, a farm or a business corporation was often the son or other relative of the former head. He inherited the position, or was at least appointed by the owner. But with the growth of the super-corporation and the cosmo-corps this was no longer practical. No one man could possibly make the decisions involved, in the sense that Rockefeller once made them for Standard Oil, or Henry Ford for the Ford Motor Company. Groups of highly trained specialists made decisions.

During the transition period between classical capitalism and our present socio-economic system, our heads of industry, our early men of distinction of the new industrial state, were as often as not poorly selected. Cunning, ruthlessness, social standing, contacts, the backing of the old rich who still owned the corporations, nepotism and skullduggery were often in the saddle. It was pointed out by Vance Packard, among others, that the average ranking official of a super-corporation had a considerably smaller I.Q. than the average scientist or technician in his research department.

But with the coming of the national data banks and the aptitude quotient this situation eroded away. For the national data banks, in the hands of cold-blooded, or rather bloodless, computers, told all. Did a corporation dealing in electronics desire an electrical engineer of a particular specialization? They had only to inquire and the most competent available for employment was immediately revealed to them. Could they afford to be so foolish as to employ another?

The incompetents in our society fell by the wayside. The meritcrats, if you will accept the term, were in the saddle.

It applied, obviously, all the way up and down the line, not simply to managers, top technicians and scientists. There in the data banks was full information not only on aptitude quotient but experience, former positions held, criminal record if any, health, age and everything else pertaining to every citizen of the nation.

If a farmer desired an expert in sexing chickens, he had only to apply to the local employment bureau to find the best available. If a contractor needed a hundred laborers to help push through a new road, the computers would select them from those locally available. If a small restaurant desired a fry cook, a department store a floor walker, a newspaper a general assignment reporter—the computers selected him from the data banks. The best man won.

Julian West growled, "Talk about Big Brother watching you." He turned to the final page.

THE GROWTH OF THE SUPER-CORPORATION
AND THE COSMOCORP

But above all in the changes manifesting themselves during the last decades of the twentieth century was the concentration of industry and agriculture. Nothing was more influential in changing from the old to the new society.

In agriculture, a century before your time farming absorbed the working energies of sixty to seventy percent of the population. By the time you went into stasis, eight percent, working only two-thirds as long, were doing the job and within a decade this was reduced to four or five percent. Today, agriculture is as automated as any industry and the number of persons involved is minute.

In the 1960s, two thousand corporations accounted for eighty percent of all resources used in manufacturing in the United States, but even this does not indicate the concentration. Five hundred corporations had well over two-thirds of all manufacturing assets. Fifty corporations alone had over a third of these, and of them, the five largest possessed over twelve percent of all assets used in manufacturing.

AT&T alone held five percent of all nonbank corporate

assets in the United States. Its income was larger than the gross national product of Sweden. Add two or three more of the American super-corporations and even such countries as France became minor operations.

By 1965 three industrial corporations, Standard Oil of New Jersey, General Motors and Ford had more gross income than all the farms in America. The gross income of any of these three far exceeded that of any single state. The income of General Motors was fifty times that of Nevada, eight times that of New York and slightly less than one-fifth that of the federal government.

And that was just the beginning. Even then, Willard Mueller, chief economist of the Federal Trade Commission, predicted that by 1975 only two hundred corporations would own two-thirds of all American manufacturing assets. The day of the super-corporation, the conglomerate corporation if you will, had arrived with a vengeance.

At first there were elements in the government and in the economy that fought the trend and called for the enforcing of antitrust laws. The small business was being crowded to the wall, as had the small farm even earlier.

However, a new element had arisen. Business was now a worldwide thing, not a local one. With the advent of Common Europe, mergers were taking place abroad that threatened American industry's ability to compete. When the airlines of Western Europe merged into one, the United States was forced to follow with the merging of her own airlines—either that or go under. When Fiat-Renault and Volkswagen, later to include still other European automobile companies, merged, then to compete the remaining American car manufacturers had to do the same. Monopoly raised its head as never before, and a halt could not be called.

But even this was not the end, that is, of national monopolies. What Steiner and Cannon called the multinational corporations and Frank Tannenbaum called the extranational corporate bodies, or the cosmocorps, were emerging. These included such originally American corporations as General Motors, Ford, U.S. Steel, Sears Roebuck, Woolworth, DuPont, Standard Oil and other oil companies, and various banks and insurance companies. They also included such originally foreign corporations as Royal Dutch Shell, Unilever, Fiat, Volkswagen and Philips Lamp.

The cosmocorp was a new phenomenon in the socio-economic world.

Its ownership was irrelevant, for the owners didn't either manage or control it except in legal fiction and it could be owned by people all over the world. Its management was drawn from wherever competence was found, its profits distributed among owners in all nations. Its technical and labor forces were completely international. The cosmocorp was devoted to an international function. Its total commitment was extranational. It had no concern with boundaries, national interest, local cultural pride or regional idiosyncrasies, except only as they favored or hindered the performance of the function for which the corporate body had come into existence.

These cosmocorps were autonomous within the states where they operated. They drew their capital, finance, skill and material from wherever they found it. They were at the service of the local nation, but not of it. Their life would go on when the present government had fallen, or when the state even had changed its character by merger, annexation, defeat, rebellion or whatever.

An international communications corporation, for instance, would go on, no matter what the political map might look like sometime in the future. The functional service was more durable than the political form or territorial prescription. The telephone system operates in both East and West Germany, in both North and South Korea. You could phone as easily from New York to London, or Moscow, as you could to San Francisco. The cosmocorp was extranational and stood indifferent to it. Its personnel thought, planned and operated on a supranational basis.

There is a side issue that should be mentioned here. The coming of the cosmocorp coincided with the repudiation of the military as a means of solving international difficulties. In early wars it was to the advantage of the industrialists to have the industries of the enemy destroyed. They would be competitors again when the war was over. But even as early as the First World War a new element entered. The Germans did not bomb or shell the French steel mills in the Ruhr. Why? Because these mills were owned, usually through Switzerland, by German investors as well as French. They would have been bombing their own property. The situation became even more so with the new cosmocorps. Were the United States of 1980 to have fought a war with, say, a triumvirate of England, France and Germany and have bombed these nations, she would have destroyed billions of dollars of property belonging to General Motors, Ford, IBM and a score of other cosmocorps in which Americans held shares.

For what Steiner and Cannon had predicted when they said, in 1966, "In the light of present trends and future prospects, it does not seem at all impossible that in the next twenty years, six or seven hundred large multinational companies will be doing most of the world's business" had come about.

There is just one other aspect that should be covered here. That is, the extent to which the government was already participating in the economy. Government spending had risen from $10.2 billion in 1929 to $168 billion in 1963; that is, from 9.8 percent of the gross national product to 28.8 percent. In short, federal, state and local government accounted for more than a quarter of all economic activity. This far exceeded supposedly socialistic India, Sweden and Norway. It even exceeded supposedly communist Poland, which was, of course, an agricultural country, and the farms privately owned.

IX

I have never talked or corresponded with a person knowledgeable in Indochinese affairs who did not agree that had elections been held as of the time of the fighting, possibly eighty percent of the population would have voted for Ho Chi Minh.

Dwight D. Eisenhower
Mandate for Change
(In commenting upon reasons why the
U.S. did not support the Vietnam
elections called for by the
Geneva Accords of 1954.)

Then

The dream came through in remarkable vividness. It was far from the first time he had had it.

The choppers bearing Beta Company came in low over the hamlet—the former hamlet—of Ap Bihn Son. It was monsoon season and the valley was soft, beautiful, green and warm in the monsoon wetness.

In the lead chopper, Lieutenant Julian West was facing the possibility of his first combat. However, Sergeant Jake Harkness was an old hand who had seen combat in Korea as well as several years of it here. He suggested they make a preliminary circle of the valley to see if they'd draw any ground fire. He didn't seem overly fearful at the prospect, Julian decided, giving the order to the pilot.

There was no ground fire. They smoothed on in to the edge of the destroyed town.

The sergeant shook his head. "Looks like a picture of the craters on the moon. First the B-52s hit it with five-hundred pounders and seven-fifty pounders from so high the poor bastards couldn't of either seen 'em or heard 'em. Then the A-37s came in low. Napalm and guavas."

"Guavas?" Julian said. That was a new one to him. He was freshly over from the States.

The sergeant was peering down intently. He said to the pilot, "Over there," and to his lieutenant, "Antipersonnel bombs. Little devils, only about two and a half inches in diameter. You're taking out a town, see? First you drop HE on it and that forces 'em into the open, especially civilians. Charlie's too smart, if he's around. He stays in his trenches. They each got about three hundred little steel balls in them. And they pack a whole slew of these guavas into big mother bombs. Got timers on them so the mother bombs spew them all out at a certain height. Then the guavas explode on contact with rooftops, trees or the ground. Each guava's got a maiming area of fifteen yards. Four mother bombs can cover an area of over a mile by two hundred fifty yards."

"Thanks for the lesson, sergeant," Lieutenant West said dryly. He wondered how long he would be considered a novice by his men, a ninety-day wonder.

"Yes, sir."

The chopper came in at a sweep and hit down with a smooth *chunk.*

"Let's go!" the sergeant said to no one in particular, grabbing up his M-16.

They ejected as always from an alighting chopper, piling out in a hurry before it quite touched and then running as fast as they could both to get out of the giant wind and to find cover, on the off chance that Charlie had some snipers about.

Julian West doubted the snipers, even as he ran. There wasn't enough left of the hamlet to hide a good-sized rat. However, his training had emphasized the fact that you stayed alive in Viet Nam by everlasting precaution. Victor Charlie, the Viet Cong, had not remained in continual combat for a quarter of a century by being stupid. They had fought the French, then the Japanese during the occupation in the Second World War, then the French again when they had returned. Now they were fighting the Americans—and each other.

Lieutenant West and Sergeant Harkness squatted in a bomb crater and watched the other choppers come down. One by one they swooped in; the soldiers ejected and dashed for cover. Captain Zerman's chopper came in last.

They climbed to the edge of the crater upon his approach. Captain Zerman walked erect, his air proclaiming that cover was not for him. He sported an RAF-type mustache, bushy and blond, and his sidearm was a World War Two vintage Walther P-38 which he had altered by having a carved ivory butt substituted for the original Nazi plastic one. The story was that he had liberated the gun while a corporal under Patton from a high-ranking Wehrmacht officer. Somehow, Julian West doubted it. Zerman was too fond of reciting the yarn. He had probably picked it up in a hockshop in the States. Julian wondered how he kept himself in ammo.

The captain looked about. He said to the sergeant, " 'Kay. Let's get going on the body count, Harkness."

"Yes, sir. You want we should take ears?"

"Of course. Snap into it." He said to Julian West. "Let's take a look-see." He looked at the lieutenant from the side of his eyes. "You might as well get used to the sights."

"Yes, sir." Julian fell in step next to him. He said, "Ears?"

"You really haven't been around, have you?" Captain Zerman, Julian knew, had an inner dislike of his new lieutenant. It was based, undoubtedly, on the fact that his rich-man reputation had preceded him. He had hope to be able to disappear, unnoticed, into the ranks of the military but he'd been too often in the papers and magazines. Most of his set hadn't been particularly adverse to publicity; in fact, some of them doted on it. The captain wouldn't try anything overt. He'd be afraid of his subordinate's possible connections with higher-up brass. However, the lieutenant didn't relish being under the command of an officer with a chip on his shoulder.

Zerman was saying, "It's always good to have some proof of your body count."

They passed two corpses, both charred so badly that their humanity was all but unrecognizable. There was a sweet odor in the air which Julian West hadn't noticed before when the chopper rotors were still turning. The rotors were stopped now and everything was very quiet.

The ears of both bodies were gone.

Julian said, "That one's a woman."

"Charlie's women fight too, lieutenant. If you ever find yourself wounded and see one of them coming for you, don't get the idea she's a nurse. 'Kay. You blow the top of your head off real quick, friend. Among other little items, they whack off your pecker and stuff it in your mouth."

The men were scattering in all directions, under the instructions of the noncoms, rooting through the litter.

The captain and lieutenant came to the rubble of what had once been a hut and peered inside. The interior was worse than a shambles. The captain grunted, as though in contempt. Few of the occupants were in one piece but it was obvious that they had been a family group—a man, woman, and four children.

Julian West felt the gorge rise in his throat.

The captain grinned at him. "Gruesome, eh?"

"But . . . why didn't they leave I thought we dropped warnings for all civilians to leave."

The captain snickered. "Maybe Charlie wouldn't let them. More likely, Charlie wasn't even around. Maybe some of their crops were almost ready to harvest, so they kept their fingers crossed and stayed on. Crossing fingers wasn't enough. By the time the B-52s came over it was too late to run."

One of the ARVN privates assigned to Beta Company came past them, entered the remnants of the hut and began hacking away at the heads of the bodies.

Julian West said, in protest, "But those are just children."

The captain looked at him. "The colonel likes a good body count. And even if he didn't, the general does."

They continued to stroll about the former hamlet of Ap Bihn Son. There were remnants of bodies everywhere, most of them now earless.

Julian said sourly, "Why not scalp them? Wasn't that the old way?"

"You ever tried to take a scalp, lieutenant?"

"No."

"It's hard, messy and slow. Ears are faster."

Julian said, "So far I haven't seen a single gun, or any other weapon."

"Hell, haven't you caught on? Charlie pulled out before even the B-52s got here. It's the old routine. Somebody —usually a lying fink trying to suck up—reports a concentration of possible battalion strength in yea and so area. It goes through channels. By the time it gets to planning stage, it's been leaked back to Charlie. He slips off into the jungle, if he was ever there at all."

"Leaving these people to take it?"

The captain looked at him in disgust. "You haven't been out here long, West. Most of these people are Viet Cong sympathizers. The young people are with Charlie. 'Kay. If they get wounded they come back home to recuperate."

"But we're only a few miles from Saigon."

"The same thing applies right in Saigon. You can't trust a single gook, lieutenant, and you might as well get used to the idea. The only ones you can trust—once in a while —are those on the top. Those in on the take. But even them. I wouldn't turn my back on any gook."

Julian West decided inwardly that while it was true that he hadn't been out here very long, the romantically mustached Captain Zerman had been out too long. What was the whole war about? They were only some eighteen miles northwest of Saigon. If the Saigon government didn't have control here, where did they hold it?

Sergeant Harkness approached, accompanied by a corporal, two American privates and a couple of the ARVN. The South Vietnamese privates were herding along two bedraggled youngsters who stumbled under their prodding. They wore the single garment of field workers in this vicinity, dirty and in rags.

Harkness said, "Got a couple of gooks out of a bomb shelter, sir."

Julian West looked at the two. They were both obviously in a state of terror and shock. Their eyes were glazed. An ARVN private brutally slugged one of them behind the neck with the butt of his World War Two Garand M-1 and the boy sank to his knees. So did the other, without need of being hit.

95

"They armed?" Zerman said. "Why didn't you bring in their guns?"

"Must've thrown them away, or hid 'em before we got here," Harkness said, shrugging.

The captain looked at the ARVN men, both of whom spoke English, at least well enough to get by. "You ask them where the others went?"

"They're too afraid to talk, captain, sir," one said, giving both of the captives in turn a kick in the side.

The captain looked around. "There's nothing more here. Let's get back to base. Harkness, pass the word." He looked at the captives. "Pretending to be too scared to talk, eh? 'Kay. We'll show them what being scared is. Come along, West, we'll return in my chopper. Corporal, get these two Charlies into my chopper and bring these ARVN men, too." He made a motion with his head at the two South Vietnamese who'd been roughing up the youngsters.

As they walked toward the captain's chopper, Julian said, in mild protest, "They don't look like they're more than fifteen or sixteen."

Zerman said, "You're learning a lot today, lieutenant. That's the age that makes the best Charlie. Too young to be able to think very well, but old enough to handle a gun, and old enough to tramp through the jungles for days on end with nothing more to eat than a handful of rice. When you see a kid that age that's not on *our* side, not in the ARVN, then you can bet your last dollar—and I understand you've got quite a stack—they're with Charlie."

They got into the chopper and the captain gave instructions to the pilot. The rotors started up and the craft bounded into the air and swooped off.

The ARVN captors had forced the two Viet Cong suspects to the floor and periodically gave them a kick or two, sometimes aiming for the groin.

Captain Zerman sat down across the way and eyed them in cold speculation awhile. Their expressions weren't quite so dazed now, but if anything their fear had grown. The chopper's side door was open and they could see down, some two thousand feet or more. Obviously they had never been airborne before.

The captain said to one of the ARVN, "Ask them where the rest of their group went. Ask them how many of them there were."

"Yes, captain, sir."

The South Vietnamese spoke rapidly to the two captives. "*N'gwoy kwa maht chahn ah dow?*" And then, "*Haw bow nee yo n'gwoy?*"

One shook his head blankly. The other seemingly wasn't even up to that response.

The ARVN private looked at the captain.

Zerman said, "Ask them again. Tell them if they don't talk up we throw them out."

The ARVN booted each in turn, then repeated his questions, with the same result.

The captain indicated the duller of the two. " 'Kay. Throw him out."

Julian West shot a wide-eyed stare at his commanding officer. Zerman looked at him and grinned mockingly. "Some war, eh?" he said.

The two South Vietnamese picked up the unresisting captive the captain had indicated and shoved him through the door. He fell, arms and legs going every which way, and at last a long wail of a scream came up over the sound of the chopping rotors.

The remaining captive's eyes grew wider, the fear multiplied a dozenfold, but he remained on his knees, his head shaking now, though whether in negation or the palsy of fear, Julian West couldn't tell. The nausea arose in his throat again. It was the first time he had ever seen a man killed.

The captain said, " 'Kay. Ask him the same questions all over again, and tell him if he doesn't answer he takes the long dive too."

The ARVN private who had been doing the talking turned back to the prisoner. This time he spoke a bit longer.

The suspected Viet Cong had gone back into a glazed expression even deeper than that he had worn when first brought up from the bomb shelter. His head continued to shake, and his mouth worked, but no words came out.

"Oh, he thinks I'm bluffing, eh?" Zerman said in disgust. He came to his feet and began making his way up to the pilot. He said over his shoulder, "Throw him out. The colonel doesn't like us to bring in too many gooks. Takes too damn much time. They only wind up getting shot anyway."

It was then, shaken, as he was always shaken after this particular nightmare, that Julian West came awake in his bed in the apartment of Academician Leete.

X

Anything that is theoretically possible will be achieved in practice no matter what the technical difficulties, if it is desired greatly enough. It is no argument against any project to say: "The idea's fantastic!" Most of the things that have happened in the last fifty years have been fantastic, and it is only by assuming that they will continue to be that we have any hope of anticipating the future.

Arthur C. Clarke
Profiles of the Future

Now

The day before, after going through the papers Doctor Leete had done for him on the developments of the past third of a century, had passed with relatively few major astonishments.

After a quiet lunch, the doctor had suggested that he be checked out a bit and it was not until then that Julian West had understood that his quarters also doubled as a hospital room. He had not realized that it contained the equipment necessary to check his physical well-being. It had few, if any, of the attributes of the hospitals of his own period.

He had difficulty in communicating with Leete on just about every phase of his check-up. He simply was out of his depth, in the technology, the terminology, which more than three decades of medical development had evolved. Which was not particularly surprising. He had been out of his depth in his own day. Even then medicine had been on the racecourse at such a pace that all including professionals had to run at full tilt to keep abreast of day-by-day developments, not to speak of looking into the future.

The doctor, even as he applied various devices and instruments and murmured into what was obviously a recorder for the data banks, explained a bit in terms that Julian could understand.

He had said, "From the first, the medical banks were one of the great successes of the trend to the computerized national data banks. There was considerable outcry against the inevitable institution in the beginning. There should have been, I suppose. Largely they were used to check your tax status and your military record, including whether or not you had registered for the draft. They were also widely used to check your credit rating, and, of course, it wasn't long before your criminal record was fed in, though it might be no more than a few traffic violations."

"I can see what that could mean to the police," Julian said.

"Of course. A citizen might be picked up on an intoxication charge in Colorado. Automatically the local police checked the data banks, using his fingerprints, his photo, his transceiver I.D. number. And, lo and behold, he was wanted for rape in New Hampshire."

"But you were saying about medicine?"

"When everybody's medical record was put into the national data banks and later the international data banks, it was a surpassing advantage. Suppose that a motorist from New Jersey took a vacation and had an accident in Oregon. The local doctor immediately applied for his medical record and had it within seconds. Everything from his blood type to the diseases he had suffered as a child. An account of every time he had received medical care. It could easily make the difference in saving a life or losing it."

Julian West was impressed. The doctor was shining something into his eyes, in instrument his patient had never seen before and which had certain Rube Goldberg attributes.

Julian said, "It sounds good to me. Anytime you want, you can check out any medical information on me for your medical banks."

"Already been done," Leete murmered, still peering. "Did you wear glasses as a boy?"

"No."

"Terrible things. Thank goodness they're an anachronism now."

"How do you mean it's already been done?"

"While you were still in stasis. Your case is celebrated, of course. The first, actually. You've been under constant surveillance for the whole period you were, ah, under. The data banks have a complete dossier on your health, Julian. It's surprisingly good. This afternoon I'm simply checking on some of the symptoms involved in your coming back to consciousness."

It was at the dinner table that his other mild surprise came through.

In the way of a pleasantry, he mildly chided Edie because he hadn't seen her for the greater part of the day and he was a stranger in a strange land.

She was contrite. "But you see, sir, I had to work my shift."

He said, "I don't know why but I had gathered the impression that you were either a student or on vacation."

"Oh no, I put in my full six hours."

"Well, what do you do? I mean—"

"I'm a farmer."

Julian West put down his fork and looked at her. "A farmer!"

"That, sir, is correct. I earn my daily bread by tilling the soil. Shouldn't I add, by cracky? Wasn't that the term?"

"I suppose so. But . . . well, where is your farm? I thought I understand that this area was more suited to residential sections and parks and so forth."

"Oh, we don't farm this area. Not at all suited. The farm I work on is out in the middle West." She looked at her mother as though for confirmation. "I suppose it's all in what used to be the boundaries of Nebraska and Kansas."

Julian West was flabbergasted. "You mean you have to travel all the way to the prairie states to your job? We used to think that seventy-five miles was more than plenty to commute."

"Good heavens, no. I work from here in the house."

"In Kansas! What in the name of anything do you do?"

"I supervise twenty tractors. That is, I do for my six-hour shift."

"You mean you handle twenty tractor drivers from this distance?"

She laughed. "Don't be silly, Jule. The tractors are automated. I simply have to supervise them. It isn't at all arduous. If anything goes wrong with any of them, I'm immediately alerted and take appropriate action working at my control screen."

He was fascinated. "All right. But suppose one of these tractors breaks down?"

"I send out an autocopter from the nearest depot with a replacement and it picks it up and brings the defective equipment back to the repair shop while the new tractor takes over in the line. They don't break down very often any more."

He took up his fork again, shaking his head. "Twenty tractors. It must be quite a large farm."

She said, "Oh, my bank is only one."

He looked at her and said slowly, "Just how big is this *farm* you work on?"

"It roughly corresponds to what used to be Kansas but it also goes up into part of what was known as Nebraska. It's not especially large as farms go. The ones in Canada are really extensive."

"I'll bet they are," he said wryly. "I wouldn't mind owning a chunk of stock in a farm as big as Kansas."

Martha Leete said, "You forget, Julian. We don't have stock any more."

He sighed. "All right. Something I want to go into further given the time, but right now my head is swimming again. Farms the size of Kansas being run by remote control from as far away as Pennsylvania." He looked at Edie accusingly. "Don't you ever go out there—to see if the new crop is coming up, or whatever?"

"Of course. From time to time it's necessary, but not for anything as routine as plowing the fields. In actuality, it's not as far out as it might at first seem. Most of the developments you see now had their germ in your own period. A third of a century sounds like a long time and in some respects it is, but in others it's very short. A technological breakthrough is years in the working before it's usually in everyday use. I'm sure that in your day you had the beginnings of remote control of agricultural tools, the ability to utilize television to supervise an operation from a distance, and the beginnings of agriculture on a truly extensive scale."

"The small farm was disappearing," he admitted.

The doctor pursed his mouth. "It seems to me you were already utilizing what they called *Waldos* with which a technician could handle tools at a distance in such dangerous situations as, say, work performed in a nuclear power plant in an area that was hot."

"I did read something about that," Julian admitted again.

Leete nodded. "Today we've carried that to the point that it is quite possible for a specialist in Australia to perform a delicate surgical operation on a patient in a hospital in Denmark." He added, "It has cut down on transportation admirably."

Martha Leete commented upon the excellence of the dish they were eating and for a while the talk turned to food and wine, and here, at least, Julian West was temporarily on home ground.

Most of the balance of the evening was spent on their asking him questions about his youth which to them had taken place some sixty-five years before—even the doctor hadn't as yet been born—and about his experiences in the war. Edith Leete, sitting there, lips slightly parted, eyes a bit rounded at some of his words, gave him what he inwardly considered a childish gratification. The more he saw of the girl, the more her basic attraction came through to him. He had been somewhat disconcerted at first at her lack of concern with dress or make-up. In fact, her clothes and her hairdo as well had seemed to him absolutely masculine and he had even gone to the extent of wondering if she liked men. However, her mother attired herself in the same manner and so had the few women he had seen that morning.

It must have been the discussion of the Asian War and the part he had played in it that brought on his dream, at the time he couldn't have realized that would result. Both the doctor and Edie had been fascinated by the psychological factors involved in the average man at work killing his fellow man, not to speak of the noncombatant civilians who had fallen in such numbers in the bombings and the guerrilla warfare.

They had finally brought it to a close when his host caught him in a yawn.

Leete said, "You're tired. It's to be expected. Your muscles are flabby, in spite of all we have tried to do in the past year or so." He pursed his lips. "We must plan on more exercise."

Julian said, "I was going to mention that. For the past three days I've been cooped up in the apartment here, largely sitting around and talking. It's been fascinating, of course, and I couldn't thank you more for your time and hospitality. However, I wouldn't mind getting out a bit and seeing this world you've been telling me about."

Edith Leete darted a look at her father.

The doctor said slowly, "Why, I don't suppose there is any reason why you couldn't take a drive tomorrow. Especially if Edith accompanied you to run, ah, interference."

"I wouldn't want to intrude—"

"Not at all," Edie said quickly. "Couldn't bear the idea of you being out on your own, like a babe in the woods. Why, you're not even checked out on your transceiver."

"I think I could make my way around," Julian said. "It's not as though I can't speak the language, and I'm sure people are still courteous enough to answer questions from a time-traveler such as myself."

For a moment there was an awkward silence but Edie said, "I'd love to be your guide. Let's say a drive about at dawn's early light, or at least, immediately after breakfast."

Doctor Leete was evidently having some second thoughts. "You'll have to be careful, Edith. To, ah, avoid —" He let the sentence fall away.

She shot him a strange look. "I'll avoid Jule having any upsetting . . . excitement, father."

"Yes, of course."

XI

A social order that cannot reaffirm its aspirations,
goals, values and also revise and reconstruct its
institutions must succumb to increasing disorder
and conflict or decline as the torch of human
advance is taken over by the new nations.
Lawrence K. Frank
Daedalus, Toward the Year 2000

Now
In the morning when he awakened, after his dream
of the Asian War, Julian West stared at the ceiling for
long moments. This time he realized immediately where
he was and was fully aware of the developments of the
past several days. However, there were small blisters of
sweat on his forehead—the dream was never an easy one.
What had they told him? There were no wars any
longer.
Fantastic. There had always been wars, there would always be wars so long as man were man.
There had been periods before when there had been
relatively little warfare, supposedly. The so-called Pax
Romana, the peace of Rome, when that empire had kept
the Mediterranean relatively free of war for the better
part of half a millennium. Which didn't mean that it
wasn't done at the cost of tens of thousands of legion-
naires always on the alert at the borders. Or the era
between Napoleon's defeat in 1815 and the outbreak of
World War One in 1914. There was relative peace in
Europe during that period with a few exceptions such as
the Franco-Prussian scrap. However, elsewhere there was
fighting aplenty, including the American Civil War.
No, he decided, even as he climbed from the bed. War
we would always have with us.
He went through the routine of showering and shaving.
The depilatory cream was fascinating. You simply
smeared it on your face and rubbed it off with a towel.
He supposed that if you wished to grow a mustache or

105

beard you simply avoided those areas where you wanted the hair to grow. Well, chalk one up for progress. He had always hated to shave.

A towel around his middle, he returned to the bedroom and came up abruptly. Edith Leete was there at his closet. She had the trousers, jacket, shirt and underclothing he had worn the day before over one arm and was turning even as he entered.

She smiled cheerfully at him and said, "Morning, sir. It occurred to me that you didn't know how to order fresh clothing."

She walked on past him into the bathroom and threw his clothes into what he had already figured out was a disposal chute and then returned.

"Let me have that towel," she said, "and I'll toss it away too."

He looked down at his sole garment and then up at her and cleared his throat.

She flushed and said, "Sorry, I'd forgotten."

"Forgotten what?"

"You were still, uh, *modest* in your day, weren't you? Bathing suits on the beach and all that sort of thing."

She was a damn attractive woman and, he reflected in a wry inner humor, it had been a long time. Thirty-plus years, to be exact, and he had never been less than lusty when it came to sex.

"Well, yes and no," he said.

She smiled and returned to the closet. "You have a delivery chute here and an order screen. I should have checked you out on this yesterday, or mother or father could have. You put your transceiver in this little slot here to have the amount involved deducted from your credit account. If you already know what you want, you simply dial clothing, like this, and ask for the items verbally. If you don't, you can dial catalogue and . . . come over here and I'll show you. Don't hesitate to dial information if it gets complicated."

He came over and she checked him out on how to order fresh clothing.

He said, curious, "How long will it take the others to be cleaned and laundered?"

She looked at him as though vaguely surprised. "Oh, we don't clean or launder clothing. Not usually, at least. Some old favorites, or sometimes imports of special materials."

"Don't clean clothing?" he said. "What do you do, just throw it away when it gets slightly soiled or out of press?"

"Yes."

He looked at her. "You must be even richer than I thought."

"Oh, no. It's not that. It's just simply easier, more economical and more hygienic to throw away yesterday's clothing. It saves a good deal of storage space, too."

"Just flush 'em down the drain, eh? And start all over again."

"Well, not exactly. Most textiles are reclaimed and made over again." She frowned at him. "I thought that materials had already become so cheap in your period that, had you eliminated the various middlemen between the manufacturer and the consumer, and eliminated such overhead as advertising and sales forces, you could have disposed of clothing had you wanted to rather than going through all the rigmarole of laundering and cleaning and pressing."

"Eliminated the middlemen and advertising?" he said. "Do you mean to suggest that you don't have advertising any more, not to speak of wholesalers and sales forces? Next you'll be telling me you don't have delivery men to supply—"

"That's right," she said brightly. "Delivery, of course, is automated, the others antiquated."

He gave up. "Look," he said. "I want to go into it later. But could I get dressed now?"

"Why not? Oh, sorry, I forgot . . . modesty."

She turned and left him, closing the door behind.

He looked after her and muttered, "I wonder what would have happened if I'd asked her to crawl into bed with me for a quick friendly roll in the hay." Then he grunted in self-deprecation. He had no call to bad-mouth her. Having no sense of modesty had nothing to do with sexual promiscuity, necessarily. And she was obviously a fine girl.

She had put the things he carried in his pockets on the table next to his bed. After he had dressed, he picked them up and put them in the pockets of the fresh clothes that had come up into the delivery box in the bottom of the closet. The clothes were all but identical to the ones he had worn the day before.

The shell briar was the last item. He felt a twinge as he tucked it away. He remembered the occasion on which Edith Bartlett had given it to him. She had been anxious, knowing a man's taste in pipes to be a personal thing and not easily chosen by someone else. However, it had immediately become a friend.

Edith Bartlett, Edith Bartlett. It was still seemingly less than a week since had had last kissed her.

He decided that this was as good an opportunity as any to check out using his transceiver to order something from the ultramarket in the building's basements. He brought out the pocket communicator *cum* credit card *cum* a dozen other things and put it into the slot on the order screen.

He seemed to be able to locate just about any category of products save a supply of tobacco. Finally he gave up and dialed information.

A robotlike voice said, "Yes, Mr. West."

He was impressed, all over again. Evidently the computers immediately recognized his I.D. number and answered him by name. And obviously the same would apply to everyone in the building. He recalled that the elevator screen had also named him.

He said, "I'd like to order some pipe tobacco." He scowled, realizing that the brand names of his time were probably gone with the snows of yesteryear. He added, "Preferably a rough-cut aromatic with a Latakia base."

"We are sorry, Mr. West, that item is not stocked."

"Well, any pipe tobacco will do, I suppose."

"We are sorry, Mr. West, that item is not stocked. You might try Central Warehouses."

He hadn't the vaguest idea of how to order from Central Warehouses, whatever that might be, so gave it up and followed Edith Leete into the breakfast nook.

She looked up and said, "I took the liberty of ordering for both of us."

"Good." He sat down across from her. "How do I go about ordering pipe tobacco?"

She seemed mildly surprised. "I understood from father that you had been cured of the nicotine habit."

"I have?"

"I believe so."

"Now that you mention it, I haven't any particular desire to smoke. I simply noticed my pipe and decided to give your present-day tobaccos a try."

"I . . . I'm not sure there are any anymore, Jule."

"You mean nobody smokes any more?"

"Well, there may be a few old diehards that still do. Leftovers from the past. But not the new generations."

"Something like prohibition? The government stepped in and outlawed tobacco?"

"Oh, nothing like that. The, uh, government has no power to forbid a citizen to conduct himself as he will, so long as it doesn't interfere with the prerogatives of others. However, our medical research people long ago—" She hesitated and frowned. "It seems to me it must have begun as far back as your time."

Julian said, "Yes. However, they were having a hard time putting their warnings over. It seems as though billions of dollars were invested in the industry, and tens of thousands of people working for it."

The center of the table sank down and then returned with their food. Edie had evidently ordered him a ham omelet and the various breakfast basics to accompany it. She served the dishes.

Before tasting her own, she nodded and said seriously, "Yes, that was one of the factors in your society. The profit motive. It made no difference that nicotine was a deadly poison responsible for a great deal of lung cancer, among other things. Profit was involved, so the tobacco industry expended hundreds of millions in lobbying, hiring experts to deny that cigarettes were injurious and in advertising, so that their profits would not be disturbed."

Julian tried his egg dish, and found it to be excellent. Now that he thought of it, he had never tasted food in the Leete household that hadn't been excellent.

He said, a bit miffed, "As you say, as you say, but I'm not so sure but that I don't think a bit of escape from reality such as is afforded by tobacco, alcohol and such isn't desirable. You can go too far in the search for perfect health. Do you deny all candy to kids, just because too much of it is bad for their teeth?"

"Oh, candy isn't bad for children's teeth any more. I had forgotten that it once was. We no longer produce the type of candy that developes cavities."

He said sarcastically, "I suppose teeth don't have cavities any more."

"Of course not. But to answer your point. We're not fanatical. We still have such minor narcotics as chocolate, tea, coffee. And, as you know, we still appreciate alcohol, particularly in fermented drinks such as wine, cider and beer. It is simply that we are educated from earliest youth to avoid excess in any of these. If you wish tobacco for your pipe I am sure we can acquire some either from our Central Warehouses of this area, or, if not, through one of the major centers. If there is any demand at all for a product, it is available."

"Look" he said. "What happened to cavities?"

"Oh." She frowned slightly again and Julian West decided that on her it looked provocatively good.

"I continually am set back by the fact that things I thought had already been developed in your time, you are not familiar with. Surely fluoride was being utilized to prevent tooth decay before you went into stasis."

He sipped some of his coffee before nodding grudgingly. "They were beginning to use it. It was on the controversial side."

She nodded. "Well, that was the beginning, fluoride. Dental science has progressed as rapidly as any other branch of medicine. As a matter of fact, it has progressed to the point where it has all but eliminated itself. There are precious few dentists anymore."

He grunted sour humor. "Why couldn't I have been born in a day when dentists had become redundant?

When I think of all the hours I've sat in a dentist's chair. And you tell me this isn't utopia."

She made a humorous *moue*. "It's as father told you, Jule. Utopia is the perfect society. There is no such thing. When one set of man's problems have been solved, two more take their place. Society evolves but it never reaches perfection."

When they had finished breakfast, Julian West followed her to the front door. She hesitated for a moment, looking up and down the corridor before emerging, for some reason he couldn't make out. No one else was in the halls.

They crossed to the elevator which he had taken the day before and, as before, the door opened for them and they stepped into the compartment.

Edie said to the screen, "Car pool, please."

"Thank you." The compartment began to sink and this time Julian West was prepared for the acceleration.

Edie said, "I don't think it's advisable—until father approves—for you to be leaving the building alone. However, if the occasion arose, this would be the elevator to take."

He looked at her. "Oh? Why? Suppose this one is at some other floor, occupied?"

"It won't be. It's temporarily assigned to our apartment." She explained. "You see, due to your presence we've had certain privileges extended to facilitate, uh, your recovery."

"I'm just beginning to get the feel of this. I'm evidently a minor celebrity."

"Yes. There is a great deal of interest in your case. As we've said, you are the first of the long-term stasis patients. Interest is very widespread."

He snorted. "I'm surprised there hasn't been a flock of reporters turning up. In my day, even most minor celebrities soon got fed up with public interest."

She shook her head. "No, no. It would be unthinkable to intrude on you. Particularly until father decided that you were in perfect health and, uh, adjusted."

There didn't seem to be anything further to say about

that, so he said, "You know, you called this a university city, whatever that is, but thus far I haven't seen anything to indicate a university. Where do you have your classrooms, your lecture halls, all the rest of it?"

She had to twist her mouth in amusement at that. "I'm afraid, actually, that within a decade or two the university city will have become antiquated. Originally the idea was excellent, but every year that goes by they become more redundant. We don't have lecture halls any more, or, at least, very seldom utilize them. Nor classrooms, for that matter, for higher education."

He said dryly, "Some university. What *do* you have? How do the professors operate if--"

She said hurriedly, "Oh, don't misunderstand. We have laboratories, of course. And equipment that wouldn't ordinarily be found outside a university city. However, the lecture hall is *passé*. Sitting in a crowded, noisy hall, packed shoulder-to-shoulder with hundreds if not thousands of others, was never a way to take in a professor's lecture. Now, you can listen to the lecture in your own chosen time, in the quiet and comfort of your own study."

She elaborated. "Today, a professor, of whatever subject, cuts a lecture."

"I bet I know," he muttered. "And it goes into the data banks and is then available for the rest of all eternity."

"Of course. And you can see various advantages. A professor who repeated, time after time, the same lecture, must surely have had days—when he was tired, ill, or possibly just bored—when the lecture was not at its best. But when he records such a talk on a screen and it is filed away in the banks, then he will record himself at his best."

She added, "There's another advantage. Suppose he covers a subject that isn't quite clear to the student. The pupil retraces the lecture to the point where the matter began to lack clarity and plays it again, and again, until it is understood."

"But suppose a student wants to ask some questions?"

"Then he simply calls the professor on the phone screen."

112

"Why have a university city at all? Why not just tune in from wherever you happen to live?"

"Many do. However, there are some advantages to being in residence at a university city. For one thing, as I said, the laboratories and other advance equipment. Then too, some students like to have at least occasional personal contact with their tutors. There is also the personal association with fellow students. Informal get-togethers to discuss, argue, debate." She smiled. "Or to have beer busts, dances, all sorts of student type brawls that have come down to us through the ages. But here we are."

The elevator had come to a halt and now the door opened.

Edith Leete stepped forth into a corridor and he followed her. She cast her eyes up and down the hall. One couple, chatting away earnestly, was approaching.

Edie took him by the arm and turned in the other direction. She said, "We can go this way."

He had the damnedest feeling that she was avoiding the others. He inwardly shrugged. Possibly someone with whom she was carrying a feud. Things evidently hadn't progressed in the past third of a century to the point where you didn't have neighbors you detested.

They entered a larger room that vaguely reminded Julian of a king-sized underground parking area of his own day. Edie stepped before one screen among many that were built into the wall and said something into it.

He looked about him. "So this is where you park your cars. For a building this size, you must need one monstrous parking area."

But she was shaking her head at him. "There are very few personally owned vehicles any more, Jule."

That stopped him. "You mean with all this obvious affluence, people can't afford cars any more? Why, in my day—"

"Yes, I know. In your day even supposedly poor people had cars; many, two or three to the family. Thank goodness that day is over."

XII

No nation can afford to divert its ablest men into such essentially noncreative, and occasionally parasitical, occupations as law, advertising and banking. Nor can it afford to squander indefinitely the technical manpower it does possess. Not long ago Life *magazine published a photograph which was a horrifying social document; it showed 7,000 engineers massed behind the car that their combined efforts, plus several hundred million dollars, had just produced. The time may well come when the United States . . . will have to consider freezing automobile design for a few years—or, better still, revert to the last models that were any good, which some authorities date around 1954.*

Arthur C. Clarke
Profiles of the Future

Now

A rather small, two-place four-wheeled vehicle smoothed up to the curb before them. It was driverless, covered with a plastic canopy, and practically the whole interior seemed devoted to passenger room. Julian West could make out no area where fuel tank or engine might reside. The canopy slid back so that they could step over the side and into the bucket seats. It was obviously this day's equivalent of a sports car.

As Edith Leete took her place in the driver's position, Julian walked around to the other side and slid in beside her.

"Where's the engine?" he demanded.

"There are four of them," she explained. "One in the hub of each wheel. Various advantages. It eliminates the transmission system, as you used to know it, and gives maximum torque at minimum engine speed. It also allows for the designer to fit the car around the occupants rather than the engine."

"But where's the fuel tank?"

"There is none."

He looked at her.

"Electric," she explained, even while dialing. "The power is picked up from the road. I understand the Russians pioneered the method in Kiev. It became more practical with unlimited power."

"*Unlimited power!*"

"Well, practically unlimited power. Nuclear fusion. They're working on tight power beams, so that a vehicle could go anywhere and pick up power on its antenna. As it is now, only the automated roads can be utilized by vehicles without fuel cells or power packs. This particular model runabout has a power pack under each seat."

The canopy slid back over their heads and the little car smoothed forward and headed for an entrance. Her hands weren't on the wheel, which made Julian uneasy, in spite of the fact that he had seen the vehicle come up to them without a driver. They emerged into an underground highway, brilliantly lit and with considerable traffic of a score of different types of vehicles ranging from little two-seaters such as they were in to what he assumed were buses. He was somewhat reminded of the car tunnels that had run under the Hudson from New York to New Jersey in his day.

"All automated, eh?"

"Yes," she said.

"All right, but with this traffic, zipping along at this speed, what happens if the automation equipment breaks down? Within split seconds you'd have a pile-up such as never dreamed of on California's speedways."

"The equipment is in triplicate, each independent of the other and with their own power sources. If one set broke down, another would instantaneously take over, while it was being repaired. If, unbelievable upon unbelievable, the second broke down, the third would take over. I don't believe it has ever happened, that is, a situation where the third had to take over. If it did, every vehicle on the road involved would be alerted and the occupant readied to take over manually, in the almost

115

impossible case of even the third set of automated equipment going out."

"That seems to cover it," Julian said dryly. "Where are we going?"

"Out of the city."

"I had rather looked forward to seeing the town."

"Cars aren't allowed above ground in city limits."

"Well, how do you get around in town?"

"You take the underground to the metro stop nearest your destination and then walk."

"You must do a lot of walking."

She looked over at him. "I wouldn't think any more than in your days."

"We could take a taxi right up to any building, or to any other spot we wanted."

"Every building has a metro entry."

"But what if you wanted to go shopping, a lot of stop-and-go stuff, in and out a dozen—"

"We don't go shopping anymore. The shopping comes to us."

"I forgot. Look, don't you people ever like to *see* the things you're buying before you order them?"

"Of course. We can see them on the screen on the order box."

He felt frustrated. "In my day, women, in particular, liked to shop. They liked to look at the stuff, possibly finger it, consider it in more detail, compare it to other items as to quality, as to price."

"Quality?"

The frustration was growing. "Look. Suppose you want to buy a sweater. You look at two. One is of inferior quality to the other, so you buy the best one."

"We don't manufacture items of inferior quality any more," she said brightly.

He gave up.

Edie said, "If you wish to acquire some item that you prefer to examine first, you have it delivered to your home. If you don't like it, you send it back. There is no particular reason to go all the way to the ultramarket to examine it. For that matter, it would be rather difficult, since there are no display cases, salespeople, and so forth.

The ultramarkets are largely storerooms and control offices."

"No salespeople any more, eh?"

"That's right."

He said, "Look, this is fascinating and I want to go into it in more detail some time, along with a hundred other things you and your parents have brought up and we haven't been able to complete. But right now I'd like to go back to something you said a little earlier. About cars."

"Fine. Oh, just a moment, Jule. Here we are."

The little vehicle had swerved off onto a side road, smaller than the underground highway they'd been on, and now had turned off still again and was on its way up a ramp. A red light flickered on the dash and Edie took the wheel in her hands. Obviously they were now under manual control.

They emerged into the countryside.

In his younger days, in particular, Julian West had on many occasions taken drives with his parents through back areas of New England and other parts of the country where the superhighways, of the six and eight-lane variety, had yet to penetrate. The two-lane roads, not even always paved, had dipped and turned, ever presenting new vistas: streams, woods, lakes, fields of crops or pastures, stone fences, orchards, haystacks, farm buildings, cows, horses, sometimes even sheep or goats, occasionally, particularly in the early morning, a covey of quail, a deer, a rabbit or other representative of wildlife. Julian had loved it.

As he had grown older, it had largely changed. Traffic had increased, the roads had improved in that they had been straightened, were invariably paved and were more apt to have three lanes at least. The little farms had largely folded, the buildings either abandoned or turned into residences of those who worked in the nearest town or city and were refugees from the smog, pollution, traffic and other urban disasters.

This, now, brought him back to his youth.

"Where's all the traffic?" he demanded.

"Largely underground."

"Who in the world would want to be driving underground with scenery like this up above? What is this, a national park?"

"Not exactly. Not unless you want to think of the greater part of the nation as one big national park. If your purpose is to *get* somewhere, preferably fast, you stay on the underground automated highways. If you want to enjoy your drive, go on a picnic, or whatever, then you surface and drive manually."

She thought about it. "I can remember, when I was a girl, the last of the type of traffic of your day. I would say that nine-tenths of it was composed either of commercial traffic, trucks, buses, and so forth, or private drivers in a hurry to get to their destination. They weren't interested in scenery, or driving along slowly. The commuters going to or coming from work; the housewife going down to the supermarket; the student going to school.

"Today, all freight, either truck or our present equivalent of railroads, is underground and automated. And public transportation is so efficient that few would wish to drive from their homes to their place of employment in a private vehicle. At most, they would summon a car such as this one we're in. For instance, if I had to go out to the farm where I work, I wouldn't dream of driving out on the surface. I'd take an express, the equivalent of your train or perhaps bus."

"How fast do your automated trains go?"

"About eight hundred kilometers an hour. If you're in more of a hurry, you can always fly, of course. But we don't make a fetish of speed."

"Kilometers?"

"We've adopted the metric system. The old inches, feet, yards and miles, not to speak of ounces and pounds, and pints and quarts, were ridiculous."

"I suppose your planes are supersonic."

"Only over the oceans or on other really long hops. There's seldom call to go over fifteen hundred kilometers an hour. As I said, we don't make a fetish of speed, we're more inclined to stress safety. I rather doubt that we have any more air traffic today than you had—perhaps less. Your system of driving out to an airport, on the outskirts of town, getting into a plane, flying to your destination city and then driving into town to wherever you wanted to go was frustrating. You spent more time going to and coming from the airport that you did in the air. As it is now, I can summon a car in our apartment building and dial it right through to, say, New Denver, to the exact building I wish to go to."

Julian nodded acceptance of that. He continued to appreciate the countryside as she expertly tooled the little roadster around the bends, hills and alleys. She touched a control and the canopy slid back to allow the fresh air to swirl about them.

"You mean to tell me that in this short period of time you built all these underground highways, turned the old superhighways back into woods and fields, and even relayed all the railroad track underground? It's impossible."

"Not at all, sir. If you'll remember the amount of capital and manpower you used to plow into such items as the Asian War and World War Two, and so-called defense in general, can you begin to see what a garden we were able to make of this country when we began putting our resources into beautifying and improving?"

Julian had been feeling something nagging at him and finally realized what it was. He said, "What in the world ever happened to all the scrap that used to litter the country? All the piles of junked cars, all the tin cans?"

"We cleaned it up, reconverted it. It's just short of a phobia with us now not to throw away anything that can be reconverted. We husband the world's resources for following generations. Possibly we're overdoing it in this field, but it's good for the soul if nothing else. Waste is an unhealthy attribute."

"Why overdoing it?" He looked over at her. "It was one of our major worries. That fellow Vance Packard your father quotes—I read a book of his called *The Waste Makers*. He pointed out that the once rich resources in zinc and lead in the United States had become so low that they were approaching the point of being uneconomic to work and that the country had changed from being the world's leading exporter of copper to being the world's largest importer. And I recall another interesting comment he made. At the time, everybody was talking

119

about industrialization of the whole world to the point that the West had already achieved. But he stated that there wasn't enough tin, copper and lead left in the world to allow for its industrialization."

She laughed. "He was quite an exposer of the status quo, so I understand from father; however, when it came to extrapolating he sometimes made mistakes. For one thing, he didn't foresee the coming of the laser-mole."

"The what?"

"Another field in which the Soviets pioneered, even before the full development of the laser."

"We were just beginning all-out experimentation with masers and lasers when I went into stasis. But what's a laser-mole?"

"Well, let me give you the background." She came to a momentary halt by the side of a small lake and turned to him.

"Back in the '50s and '60s the Russian mining engineers developed a man-carrying mechanical mole for tunneling at shallow depths. They solved the problem of soil disposal in much the same manner as the mole or gopher —that is, the earth loosened by the drilling head was compacted and tamped to form the tunnel wall. Those early experimental moles were slow-moving, possibly a kilometer or two a day. They were hindered both by the large amounts of power needed and the rapid wear and tear of the drilling mechanism, but, of course, those problems were solved. They used high-frequency electric currents to blast through rocks by sheer heat. But the laser revolutionized the mechanical mole.

"What you have to realize, Jule, is that in your day the very deepest that man drilled into the earth was about five miles, on the part of petroleum engineers. So far as mining was concerned, your deepest mines were about seven thousand feet. Nothing at all when you consider the earth has a diameter of eight thousand miles. I'm using feet and miles, rather than meters and kilometers, to make it easier for you to visualize."

"All right," Julian said. "So now how deep do you go?"

"We mine more than five miles deep and advanced probes have made it down to ten."

LOOKING BACKWARD, FROM THE YEAR 2000

"Ten *miles!* Can a man live and work ten miles down?"
"He doesn't have to. The mechanical moles are operated by remote control. With mines going that far down,
there is no shortage of any mineral or other element. But,
of course, even if this wasn't so, we wouldn't be short of
the elements we need to conduct modern industry."
"Why not?"
"Jule, with the coming of nuclear fusion power, we can
exploit sources impractical before. Let me see if I can
remember a quotation we had to almost memorize back
when I was studying geology. It was from Harrison
Brown's *The Challenge of Man's Future* and went:
'One hundred tons of average igneous rock such as
granite contains eight tons of aluminum, five tons of iron,
twelve hundred pounds of titanium, one hundred eighty
pounds of magnesium, seventy pounds. of chromium,
forty pounds of nickel, thirty pounds of vanadium, twenty
pounds of copper, ten pounds of tungsten and fouɪ
pounds of lead.'"
She twisted her mouth in amusement at being able to
quote it so well. "The big requirement to extract these
was power, a problem no longer with us. Nor is this the
end. You've probably read that a single cubic mile of sea-
water contains about one hundred fifty million tons of
solid material, mostly, admittedly, salt, but the remaining
thirty million tons contains just about all the elements,
including approximately twenty tons of gold. One of the
most valuable is magnesium, about eighteen million tons
per cubic mile. That's enough to supply the world at
present rates of consumption for centuries."
"All right," Julian said. "I surrender. There's no longer
shortages of the basic minerals. That's a beautiful lake.
Would there be fish in it?"
"Of course. Well stocked. We don't hunt much any
more—most of us. At long last, man treasures the remnants of wildlife on the planet. But I'm afraid fishing is
another thing. Personally, I love it."
She started up the car again and they went on.
Julian said, "To get back to something we got sidetracked on—you said people don't own cars any more.

121

Why not? If there was anything the average American prided himself on, in my day, it was his car."

She nodded. "Yes, I know. It's difficult to understand from this perspective in time. Evidently it was the status symbol *par excellence*. A youngster hadn't arrived until he bought his first jalopy. As he grew older, he strove to upgrade his car both in year and make. The tops, of course, was the Cadillac, or, even more so, some very expensive foreign makes. And, as soon as possible, the thing to do was to buy a second car, and ultimately a third, for each family. It didn't apply only to the pyramid-climbing middle class. Right in the urban and rural slums could be seen late model Detroit dinosaurs parked bumper to bumper. Poor families would sometimes expend as much as a quarter of their annual income on their automobile. Which isn't hard to believe when you consider insurance, car payments, tags, tolls, parking fees, tires, repairs and gasoline at thirty cents plus per gallon for overpowered monstrosities that gulped the stuff.

"It was amazing, the degree to which the people allowed Detroit to get away with planned obsolescence. The average American car was built with the expectation of going about thirty thousand miles, say three years, before it began to deteriorate and the owner began to consider a new one. As a contrast, the German Volkswagen was expected to do a hundred fifty thousand miles and the Mercedes was constructed with three hundred thousand in mind. Even the Russians, much as we laughed at their backwardness in styling, turned out much more rugged vehicles. Style, ha!

"Above all, our cars were murderous. Not only through accidents, in which they killed and maimed more persons than all of the country's wars, but in the pollution of the air. Our medical researchers are still estimating the number of deaths that the internal combustion engine was responsible for."

Julian nodded. "A howl was beginning to go up, but it was hard to see an answer. It was by far the nation's biggest industry; billions of dollars were involved and millions of persons were working either directly or indirectly for it. The whole economy was an automobile-orientated one."

It was her turn to nod, very seriously. "Once again, the profit motive. The answers were available but not under a profit-orientated economy. Both the auto manufacturers —with all their satellites—and the petroleum industry were on full-time guard against anything that might attack their position."

"So, how do you handle it now?"

"Every community has a car pool. You dial for whatever type of vehicle you wish, and it comes and you utilize it for as long as it is needed and then it returns to the nearest car pool. One advantage is that you have at hand any type car you wish. If only one or two persons are involved, take ourselves now, you dial a small runabout, such as this. If there are four or five of you, you request a sedan. If you're a sizeable family, with several children and possibly a dog or two, you get a stationwagon, or even a small bus. Suppose you're driving up to your summer place and have a good deal of luggage, or are carrying something else bulky. You dial for a light truck. If you're going off on a vacation, possibly you wish a camper or even a car and trailer or mobile home. If your trip involves going into areas where there are no roads, you might want a hovercar.

"In the past, a one-car family would have the use, usually, only of a sedan which would seat as many as six persons. Most often, only one person at a time utilized it. If you drove into a city, it was unwieldy to handle in the traffic and difficult to find parking space. On the other hand, people who owned smaller cars were limited in space when they did have occasion to carry several persons at a time, and when they drove long distances they had neither the speed nor comfort desirable."

She thought about it some more and came up with, "There's still another advantage. In your day, a privately owned car was usually kept going until it stopped, or in other manner indicated something was wrong and had to be taken to a garage for repairs. Poorer people kept a tire until it blew out, with all the danger involved, both to themselves and other motorists. Today, a vehicle

123

never leaves the car pool unless it is in top mechanical condition, computer-mechanic checked. And every six months it is returned to the factory for a complete rejuvenation, restoring it to like-new condition."

They passed through a small community of perhaps forty homes. In some respects it didn't differ too much from a well-to-do suburban settlement of Julian's time. There was at least an acre of lawn and garden about each establishment, but the architecture of the buildings held few surprises.

They were through the settlement before it came to Julian West what was missing. He said, "Where do they shop?"

"The ultramarket is almost invariably underground, along with the car pool."

"And each house has a, what do you call them? A delivery chute?"

"Of course."

"Look. With this distribution system you have, what happens if you order something too large to be whisked through to your home delivery box?"

"Well, in our case, living in a high-rise apartment building, there is a larger delivery box on each floor. Or, if the item is too large even for that, it comes to the delivery room, down on the third sub-level floor and is brought up on the freight elevator. But in a small individual home community, such as this, delivery is made to the community building, town hall, or whatever you wish to call it. These smaller settlements always have at least one public building, which usually includes a restaurant, possibly a bar or some sort of night spot, and various community rooms for cards, chess, ping pong and so forth. They're usually also connected with the town's tennis courts, golf course, swimming pool, that sort of thing."

"But look. Suppose that you're the type that doesn't even like that big a town. You want to be off by yourself, somewhere in the boondocks. Don't tell me you run a delivery chute arrangement for miles, just for one isolated house."

"No. Not as yet, at least, although possibly some day that will be done. If a home is too remote, then the inhabitants have to depend for their supplies on the nearest community such as the one we just passed through."

"Have to drive in for their shopping, eh?"

"Oh, of course not. They use their phone screen to order and an automated delivery vehicle brings whatever they require."

Julian shook his head ruefully. "But they do, at least, have to *unload* it, don't they?"

Her mouth twisted in her characteristic moue of amusement. "Well, yes. I'm afraid they have to put up with that terrible imposition if they wish to live off in the boondocks, as you called it."

The wind was in their faces as they sped along through the calm, solitary countryside. Chestnut and oak, beech and locust were posted like sentinels along the gray, winding road. From time to time there were small ponds in the rolling green meadows, shining like glass in the morning sun, winking in the sunlight.

He looked again about the vehicle in which they rode. "You know," he said, "this is even smaller than a Volkswagen. The last time I rode in a car, it was a Bentley. You could have made six of this out of it."

She said, "I've often wondered about the American romance of your time with the automobile. Each year, each company would bring out a new series of models, supposedly antiquating everything that had gone before. In actuality, the changes were usually meaningless. More, or less, chrome; wider or narrower; longer or shorter; differences in bumpers and bumper guards; one tone, two tone, or even three tone in color; tail fins, or no tail fins. I recall reading about a period in the late 1950's, when General Motors got on a light binge. In the past they had been able to do with three lights, two in the front, one in the back, but now they began to carry up to fourteen outside lights. The designers evidently couldn't decide just where all these should be located, largely in front, or largely in back. The Chevrolet Impala had eight in the front, while some of the others carried most of theirs in the rear. But the amusing bit is that some of the lights were dummies. That is, they weren't hooked up to the battery; they were just for pretty.

"In actuality, the Detroit designers weren't particularly interested in improving the automobile, only in selling it. The changes they made were largely cosmetic, rather than in engineering."

He was amused. "All right, as you say. However, it kept the economy going. The automobile industry, with all its satellite industries, was the single biggest in the country."

She flicked a sardonic glance at him. "Are you acquainted with a writer named Dorothy L. Sayers?"

"British, wasn't she? A mystery writer."

"She wrote more than mysteries, particularly toward the end of her life. At any rate, in her book, *Creed or Chaos*, she said, 'A society in which consumption has to be artificially stimulated in order to keep production going is a society founded on trash and waste, and such a society is a house built upon sand.'"

"Then I'm afraid our society was one built on sand," Julian said sourly, "because I suspect that sales promotion, advertising and its various related industries such as most entertainment, probably was almost as large a business as the automotive."

He thought about something and changed the subject. "It occurs to me that there isn't any payment slot here in the car for your transceiver credit card. From what you say, it's something like a taxi, or, more like an auto-rental deal. How do you pay up?"

"Oh, transportation is free."

"Free! All transportation?"

"That's right, sir. We found it saved considerable labor and red tape, and this is one of our big drives, that is, eliminating all tedious or arduous jobs that we can."

"But good *grief*."

She thought about it. "You know, I believe that's another field in which the Russians pioneered, and in your own time at that. They first began by eliminating fares on buses and streetcars in the city of Kharkov, I think. That immediately cut in half the crews of such vehicles by eliminating the conductor and saved the city considerably in payrolls. At any rate, you can see the saving in labor. Take the subways of New York in your day. Thousands of persons were employed in sitting in change booths making change, selling tokens. Thousands of more guards were employed checking to see that no one sneaked past the turnstile without payment. Still more thousands were employed collecting the coins and tokens, counting them, doing the statistical work involved, the banking and so forth and so on."

"But look—"

"City transportation was first, but later we also made transportation free on buses, trains and last of all aircraft."

He closed his eyes in despair. "Who *pays* for it?"

"Oh, it wasn't practical until after we had given up the use of money."

"But free transportation!"

She frowned at him. "It isn't as far out as all that, even given your viewpoint. In your day, the highways, the streets, the bridges were free and kept up by local, state and federal government. Of course there were some toll roads and some toll bridges but largely these services were free. We've just gone a step further and now provide free transportation over them. In your time the roads and bridges belonged to the nation as a whole. Now transportation does."

She looked over at him. "How do you feel?"

"Wonderful. This is great. Reminds me of my childhood. There were still parts of the country like this when I was a boy. Not many, but some. How much of the countryside has been reforested and remeadowed, I suppose you could call it?"

"All of it."

"Oh, now really. You mean the Arizona and Utah deserts as well, for instance?"

"Don't misunderstand. There would be no reason why we couldn't pump irrigation water from the Pacific to the desert areas, if we wished. Given unlimited power, desalination of water is no problem. However, deserts have their own beauty and great numbers of our people like to live there. What we attempt to do is restore those areas of the nation not utilized for agriculture to the state in which they were found when the Europeans first came over. These northeastern states are reforested and remeadowed, as you say. The rivers, streams, lakes and ponds have been cleaned up. In some of the Western states, on the other hand, we've brought back the buffalo grass—and the buffalo, for that matter—in gigantic game preserves. On the west coast, reforestation again; we're bringing back the big trees."

"I understand that it takes hundreds of years to get a redwood well under way."

"Oh, there's been considerable progress in forestry too, you know. We can speed up the growth of trees." She said, a bit worriedly, "I think we'd better head on home. Father doesn't want you to overdo these first few days."

"All right."

She made a turn and headed back in the direction from which they had come.

XIII

In the society of sexual equality that is coming, there will be a blurring of artificial distinctions between the sexes, a blurring that is already on the way. But so what? A particular boy will know who his particular girl is and vice versa, and if someone else is not part of the relationship what does he/she care which is which? . . . I say we can't beat the trend and we should join it. I say it may even be the most wonderful thing that has ever happened to mankind.

Isaac Asimov

Now

Edith Leete said, "Well, now that you've been in the land of the living again for several days, what is it you find most strange?"

He had to laugh at that. "Everything." He considered it for a moment and looked over at her. "You know, one thing that's set me back are you women. Aside from you and your mother, I've only seen a few and at a distance at that. But no jewelry, no cosmetics, no elaborate hairdos, clothing just about identical to that worn by men. What happened to fashion, to styles?"

"Status symbols," she said contemptuously. "Did jewelry ever really make a person look more attractive? Nonsense, it made her—or him—look gaudy. Take gems. How many of them were really beautiful? Not even an expert could tell the difference between a diamond and a rhinestone from across a room. Oh, opals and pearls had their beauty. But rubies, emeralds, sapphires? You had to have a lapidary or jeweler with a magnifier to tell the difference between a good stone and a poor one and the layman couldn't tell any of them from a cleverly faceted piece of colored glass.

"Cosmetics? An attack on half the human race. Have you any conception of what powder, rouge, eye make-up and all the rest of it did to the feminine complexion? Un-

comfortable to wear, dirty, unhygienic, and actually un-
attractive, though generations of conditioning taught us
differently. Have you ever seen a woman past her prime,
trying to maintain a pretense of youth by painting herself half an inch thick?"

"Yes," Julian said. "However, in younger women—"

"Nonsense," she said, a few calories in her tone now.
"Besides that, it was contemptible that a woman should
have to strive to attract a man by painting herself up like
a harlot. Do you know the origin of the use of lipstick?"

"I don't think so. I thought it went way into the past."

She said contemptuously, "It was originated by Phoe-
nician prostitutes who painted their mouths red to re-
semble the vulva. It was an advertisement that they performed fellatio."

He was somewhat taken aback. It wasn't a statement
that he would have expected from a well-raised girl who
was, after all, a comparative stranger. Evidently youth
didn't pull many punches these days. Well, the tendency
had started back in his own time, he supposed.

"Fashions, styles," she blurted bitterly. "A woman's face
and figure were supposedly her fortune, while a man's
fortune didn't depend on his physical appearance. Take
the fact that the men's magazines of your period continually displayed the nude female figure, while the equivalent opportunity was not to be found in the women's
magazines to view the male figure. Such magazines as
were devoted to the male figure were usually for the
benefit of homosexuals. The women, in short, were offering their bodies for exhibit, and, vicariously, the bodies
of all their sex. A form of prostitution and the editors
of these magazines were the pimps."

"Look," Julian protested. "Don't take it out on me."

She was not placated. "Why in the world should I
wear high heels and totter around so that my figure can
supposedly be more alluring to a man? He doesn't wear
high heels, cosmetics, girdles or other uncomfortable af-
fectations to attract me. It was an indication of the in-
equality of the sexes. Why should a woman have to put
on supposedly pretty plumage to attract a man while the
man could remain drab? In fact, the really successful

man sometimes made an absolute point of being careless in his grooming. An Einstein, an Edison, a Hemingway or a Picasso, a Bing Brosby or Marlon Brando, or a Howard Hughes or Onassis, for that matter, couldn't have cared less about his clothes."

He grinned at her. "You're quite a feminist. However, you still haven't told me what happened to styles and fashion."

She drew in her breath, as though to blast, but then looked over at him and gave a chuckle reminiscent of her father. "Okay," she said. "There is no more fashion in the old sense of the word. Fashion was a status symbol. It drew the line between the rich and the poor. Skirts were one day two inches below the knee and tweed was all the thing. A few months later, tweed was out and the skirt two inches above the knee. Very well, the rich could immediately swing over and abandon the whole wardrobe which was now out of style. The poor could not and continued to wear their out-of-fashion clothing. They tried desperately, altering hems and so forth, but it was simply out of the question. The very rich could journey to Paris, Rome or New York and be part of the new style before it ever filtered down to the moderately well-to-do. The greatest acclaim a woman might achieve, far above being awarded the Nobel Prize, in excellence in the arts, sciences or whatever, was to be named one of the ten best-dressed women of the year. That she might be an idiot otherwise had nothing to do with it. Her name was on a hundred million lips. She was one of the best-dressed women in the world."

Julian said wryly, "I gained the impression that women loved it."

Edie snorted her rejection of that opinion. "It was a desperate game the ordinary woman had no chance of winning, but practically impossible to resist without becoming a conspicuous nonconformist. The wife of the professor, the scientist, the artist, the supposed intelligentsia of the nation, also had to keep up with the con game. Such persons as the duchess wife of a retired king would be offered free models of the latest designs of one or more of the top dressing houses in Paris, by way of surreptitious advertising. She'd wear these gifts and a hundred million helpless women would dash out to emulate her, spending billions in the attempt."

Julian West was amused by her venom and she noted it.

She said tartly, "Oh, it didn't apply to women alone. Each year or so the lapels on men's suits would grow wider or more narrow, ties narrower or wider, with knots bigger or smaller, pants legs cuffed or uncuffed, tight or bell-bottomed. And who would dare be seen in his office, or anywhere else, in last season's styles?"

"You couldn't afford to be branded a hippie," Julian laughed.

"As a matter of fact, your hippies were among the first to have the courage to revolt against conforming to the fashion racket. They dressed as they pleased, wore their hair long or short as they pleased, regardless of sex, and even went barefooted if they felt like it and the weather allowed."

Her companion was still amused. "We were flabbergasted by the fact that you couldn't tell boys from girls."

"Why should that be necessary? Why should you be able to tell a male from a female at a distance? Why should a girl who likes the comfort of a short haircut have to wear it long? Or why should she have to wear a skirt during the winter months when pants are obviously more sensible? The slave master has always taken steps to make sure he isn't mistaken for his slave. In Egypt the slave went nude or, at the very most, wore a brief loincloth. In China, the underclass wore the pigtail."

"Wait a minute," Julian protested. "Are you suggesting that in my day, women were slaves to men?"

"Exactly."

"Oh, come on."

"The end was already in sight, in your time, the struggle for freedom already well under way. But so long as a person is dependent upon someone else for food, clothing, shelter and the other needs of life, that person is not free."

"I'd say you were putting it strongly."

"No. I am not saying that the relationship between many men and their wives was not on a very high level. But a benevolent slave master doesn't change the status of his slave. He is still a slave, even though his master might be Jesus himself."

He grunted deprecation.

"You think I exaggerate? Look at the Greeks. Even during the so-called Golden Age, they considered women little more than animals. So contemptuous of them were they that they resorted to homosexuality for their real romances, figuring that there couldn't be true love except between equals and women certainly were not equal to men. Take the Jewish Ten Commandments. *Thou shalt not covet thy neighbor's house, thou shalt not covet thy neighbor's wife, nor his maidservant, nor his manservant, nor his ox, nor his ass, nor any thing that is thy neighbor's.* In short, she is listed with the rest of her husband's property."

"I suppose you could also point out the harems of the Mohammedans and the other Asiatic and African societies," he begrudged.

"Of course. And the Christians weren't any better. Remember in Ephesians? *Wives, submit yourselves unto your husbands, as unto the Lord.*"

"Well, by the twentieth century we'd come a long way in the emancipation of women."

"Not so far as some evidently thought. For instance, would you have married a woman you knew was smarter than you were?"

That set him back. "Why, I don't know—"

"Or had you need for employment, how would you have reacted to having a woman as your immediate boss?"

"I . . . don't . . . think . . . so . . . well."

"Of course not. It would be a blow to your masculine pride. Women were second-rate citizens. In the lesser jobs they were not paid as much as a man holding down the same position. In the better jobs, very few made it to the real top, no matter what their ability. I understand that many a corporation executive's personal secretary knew considerably more about his job than he did. It was something like the slaves of some of the Roman emperors, who actually governed the empire."

In the distance, Julian could make out the high-rise apartment buildings of the university city.

He prompted her. "So now?"

"So now a woman is no longer dependent upon a man. She no longer has to do her utmost to make a *good marriage*. She chooses her man for other qualities than holding down a good job, or the amount of money he has. For the first time we have true equality between the sexes. We no longer have to be cute, or pretend to be silly and helpless, or to look up to men. We no longer are taught that it's ladylike to squeal at a mouse and to be unable to total up an account accurately."

He said wryly, "In my day, women were considered the gentler sex. A gentleman protected—"

"Well, forget about it," she said tartly. "We're not. That was a cultural trait, and had nothing to do with reality. Women are no more gentle or delicate than men, and our I.Q. and aptitude quotients are just as high. The only differences between us are physiological ones. Women become pregnant and have children, men don't. Men are on an average bigger and stronger than women, which is partly countered by the fact that on the average women are more deft, which is, if anything, more important in modern society. Faster, more slender fingers are often of premium value."

Julian said, "So now we're completely equal. Tell me, do you women, these days, sometimes take a lumberjack's job?"

"Of course."

"You *do?*" He'd thought he had scored a point.

"Jule, Jule. Trees are no longer cut down by lumberjacks with axes in hand. They're cut down by machines. The whole operation is automated. There are so few jobs left today that can't be handled by either sex that they're meaningless. I'm an example. I'm a farmer. Not a milkmaid, or the hired girl who feeds the chickens out in the barnyard. I'm a farmer. I can handle any job on a modern farm that a man can."

She gave her tart laugh again. "Back in the old days, you made quite a to-do about men's jobs and women's jobs. When Americans would take trips to the communist countries they were invariably horrified to see women digging ditches, or sweeping the streets. But here in our own country they would work in the harvest, picking fruit, digging potatoes, and so forth. They would also work in steam laundries There is no harder, rougher work than that. Happily, we've eliminated the hypocrisy now."

They were coming up to the point where entry could be made to the underground highway that led into the city.

Something she had said earlier came back to him and he laughed lightly. "When the time came that women no longer had to worry about making a good marriage or finding some man with as much money as possible—there must have been a real rash of divorces." She said, "Oh, no. You see, we don't have divorces any more."

That one really stopped him. "No divorces any more! Under *any* circumstances? In my day they were getting so common you could almost get them by mail. In fact, I think you could in Mexico."

"Don't misunderstand, Jule. It's just that you don't need divorces if you don't have marriages. We don't have marriage anymore."

XIV

There seems little need to demonstrate, by marshaling evidence, that a mongrelization of ethics has taken place in the United States since the end of World War II. Everyone, or almost everyone, is already aware of it. The institution of payola, the rigged quiz shows, white-collar employees matter-of-factly stealing from their corporate employers, the admittedly universal prevalence of cheating on exams, the evidence of proliferating corruption in the world of sports, teenage behavior reaching "the point of alarm" as reported in Darien, Connecticut . . . these and other circumstances make up such a clear pattern of deteriorated morals that the New Testament seems almost sentimental in depicting eleven apostles and one Judas. In our bailiwick, one cannot help thinking, the ratio would be reversed.

Margaret Halsey
The Corrupted Giant

Then

Her revelations on the marriage relationship in the year 2, New Calendar, hadn't been as block-busting as all that. Edie had given him a rundown as they reentered the city and finally wound up again in the car pool in the basement of the building housing the Leete apartment.

The relationship between the sexes was now considered a private matter. It was no longer a legal contract which could be broken by divorce, but a personal agreement between adults who had decided to live together. Either could break it upon desire. All children were legal—if that were the term. Upon birth, they took the family name of both parents, or only the woman's if the father was unknown. Since neither mother nor child was dependent upon the father financially, there was no such thing as alimony or child support. Julian West had some questions at that point but they arrived home before she had time to answer them.

The religious question? She had shrugged. Anyone who still followed the old rligions could go through the marriage ceremonies under priest, preacher, rabbi or whatever. That too, was a personal matter. If the church to which they subscribed forbade divorce, then it was up to their own individual conscience whether or not to obey. It was simply that it was no longer a civil contract; no laws applied.

He had gotten the feeling, once again, that in returning to the apartment she avoided his coming in contact with, or even getting very near to, any other building occupants. He couldn't figure out the reason why, finally deciding that her father had probably suggested that for the time he be kept from the excitement of new acquaintances. It didn't seem to make too much sense to him, but there it was.

At lunch they carried on the discussion with Dr. Leete and Martha. Martha Leete was more amused than anything else at his instinctive rebellion against the new arrangement. She admitted that she and the doctor were married and had even had a civil marriage back in the old days. It no longer applied now, of course, and if either of them had wished to split up, there would be no hindrances, certainly not legal ones. It would be merely a matter of coming to agreement on dividing what little community property they had, which consisted largely of art objects, a few old-fashioned hardcover books and that sort of thing, mostly items with sentimental connotations.

Edie, the new generation, had stronger opinions. Her belief was that the ancient Greeks had been quite right in turning to homosexuality for their highest emotional expression. A true love could only be maintained between peers, between equals. As long as woman had been the undersex, dependent upon a man for her living and that of her children, real romance was largely a farce. Love cannot reach its heights between inferiors and superiors.

Now, for the first time in history, at least, true heterosexual love was possible.

It came to Julian West, even as he debated with her, that the flush of argument certainly became Edith Leete.

Following the meal, Leete decided that his patient had had enough activity for the time and prescribed a rest.

Julian was impatient at that. He had the feeling that thirty-some years of rest were enough. He wanted to be up and at this new world, this far-out world of which the more he learned, the more confused he became. It was as the doctor had said the other day. Every time he asked a question, he had two more to fire at them before they were halfway through the answer. What was this about not using money any more? How in the hell could a modern society operate without money?

He went on into what the Leetes called the sanctum and found one of the old books that the doctor collected in the way of a hobby. He sprawled out on a couch to read.

He was more tired and had fewer resources than he'd been tellin himself. Before he had gotten very far beyond the title page, he had dozed off into a half-reverie.

The dream-memory came to him as vividly as if he had been fully asleep.

Her name—at least her theatrical name and the one she used as a model—was Bobby Storm and she was a tiny, bouffante girl with an hourglass figure of the type so highly prized in the days of Diamond Jim Brady. She had a cream complexion all over, a pile of blue-black curls and the black eyes that are seldom achieved except in the Greeks; there was a sex-flash in them. There was also a defiance, a chip-on-shoulder quality in her face, except when she was in bed and her expression turned slackly animal.

She was, briefly, a sexpot such as Julian West had never met before in his amorous adventures, not even in the Orient. He was not prone to professionals, desiring intimacy in the act of love beyond what the most accomplished of prostitues were able to manufacture. In his day, of course, he had made exceptions, particularly when he was younger. There had been a two-week leave in Tokyo, one week in Bangkok, and for a time he had kept a full-time mistress in Saigon.

He wasn't sure why Bobby Storm was an exception. Possibly it was because she so loved her work. She was insatiable and the only girl he had ever met who could actually climax while still in the process of getting out of her clothes and before penetration had occurred. She simply couldn't wait. If there were anything less than desirable about bedding Bobby it was her haste to get into action. She was absolutely aggressive in preparing her lover for the act, and was as apt to mount him, at least for the first bout or two, as to submit to the passive role.

He had met her, the first time, on an alcoholic evening that had developed spontaneously upon running into two former buddies of the Asian War days. They had bar-hopped the Village, knocking the drinks back with a regularity far beyond his usual consumption. At about midnight, the fog had rolled in temporarily and when it rolled out again he found himself in a small Go-Go spot on Bleeker street. Somewhere in the past hours one of the buddies had disappeared and two youthful willing-and-ables had taken his place. His was Bobby Storm and he had finished off the night in her walk-up apartment on East 58th and Second Avenue. That had been the first time. Over the next couple of years he had phoned her and made a date on two or three more occasions. It was before he had met Edith Bartlett.

Bobby Storm was a typical outrider on the entertainment scene. Her name was legion. She was a model who never quite made the covers, with an exception or so on the cheaper men's magazines. She was a "special extra" on occasional TV shows, who seldom got more than a line or two, seldom made more than a hundred dollars for her bit parts. And, in common with her sisters, she picked up enough to get by by putting out to selected well-heeled admirers.

Her difficulty, which she had never figured out, was that Bobby Storm did not come across at all in clothes. Dressed, there was a vaguely drab quality about her.

139

And, in actuality, she didn't really come through in the nude for the baffled photographers, especially baffled if they had ever bedded her, which they often did, at least those of them who liked girls. Photographers specializing in nudes often don't. The fact was, in person Bobby Storm projected raw sex, which somehow didn't come off in a photo.

And now Julian West was paying one of his rare calls on Bobby.

Her fourth-floor walk-up, a few doors down from Second Avenue, was a studio apartment, one room in actuality, with kitchenette and bath and surprisingly well done, considering Bobby Storm. Feminine, of course, with suggestions of perfume and scented soap in the air, but not so feminine as to make a male uncomfortable. There were various blown-up photos of her on the walls, specimens of her more profitable jobs. There was one studio shot of her with Ed Sullivan, another with Red Skelton. She also boasted three paintings, two watercolors and an oil, gifts from artist friends, all three on the ultra-abstract side, all three horrible to Julian West's taste.

There was a somewhat sad effort at the light approach she adopted to match her attempt to present a defiantly gay outlook on life. On one of his earlier visits, Julian had bent down and picked up a dime from where it had fallen slightly under the bed, with the intention of putting it on her dresser, but in picking it up had spotted still another further on. She had explained. Sometimes when she had completed a modeling or extra assignment she would take her check to the bank, convert it into dimes and return home and toss them helter-skelter all about the apartment. She'd then go about on hands and knees and pick them up again, invariably missing some which had rolled to inaccessible spots, gotten under couch cushions or whatever. Julian had been mystified.

"Don't you see?" she had said gleefully. "Then when I'm dead broke, I get down on my hands and knees again and search. The first time or so, I'll come up with as much as a dollar, then it falls off, but no matter how many times I search, I can always find twenty or thirty cents, enough for coffee and sinkers at the automat."

On this occasion, he had met her at a nearby bar and even on his entrance her black eyes were already sloe behind the very dense, very long black lashes. He ordered drinks but they never finished them. She had put a hand on his wrist. "Let's go," she said, her voice low, husky and urgent.

On the third flight of stairs of her walk-up her hand snaked up her back and unlatched the little hook-and-eye at the top of her dress. On the fourth flight, just before reaching her door, he stripped the zipper down.

She moaned, "Oh, God."

Inside, he pulled the dress from her shoulders, let it fall to the floor, fumbled the brassiere off. As usual, she wore no pants. He stood up against her and put his hand down on her plump pudendum. She had an unusually abundant thatch of pubic hair and it was already moist with her Bartholin secretion. She groaned as she pressed her heavy lips to his and spread her legs slightly. He ran a finger inside her labia minora and to her clitoris, and her face paled beneath her make-up and her eyes rolled upward without the lids completely closing.

He realized she was already on the verge of orgasm and picked her up bodily and carried her to the bed. He dumped her there without bothering to pull back the pink bedcover and began fumbling hurriedly with his own clothings. This was her thing, this was what she offered beyond the usual accomplished pro. There was no faking, she was at the height of heat.

He mounted her in lust. She received him in frenzy. Initially she demanded more than was possible, squealing, moaning, sometimes issuing suppressed screams as she climaxed and climaxed again. Later, she would taper off slightly and be amenable to different positions, slower techniques. Bobby Storm had the ability to bring from a man repetitions which he would have thought beyond him: had the ability to, and did. By early dawn her lovers were sometimes inclined to wonder why it was they who wound up paying.

141

When they knocked off for a spell, he fished pipe and tobacco from his topcoat pockets, pushed two pillows behind his back and sat up, almost straight, his back against the headrest. She was stretched out on her belly, temporarily satiated, her superbly rounded buttocks satin smooth. As he enjoyed his smoking, during that period when tobacco is at its best, he slowly and lightly stroked the smooth contours of her back from the deep curve of her waist and the swelling of her hips to the moist warm of her shoulders.

For a time she issued forth low moans and murmerings of satisfaction and then she eventually rolled over on her side and said, abruptly, "Honey, do you know Johnny Carson?"

He blew smoke from his nostrils and gave up fondling her body. "Somewhat. Met them at a few parties. Johnny and Joanne live in the same apartment building I do, the United Nations Plaza."

"Gee, that's a woodgy place. I'd love to take in a bash there."

He said nothing to that. He could just see himself bringing a Bobby Storm to a soiree in one of the three hundred and thirty-odd, ultra-swank establishments in the United Nations Plaza. And the thought irritated him. He wasn't particularly a snob, or, at least, didn't think of himself as such. But here he was, indulging in the ultimate intimacy with a fellow human whom he must then slap in the face by letting her know that he couldn't be seen in public with her.

She said, "Honey, would it be possible for you to put in a good word with Johnny for me? His show is the living most right now. I'd sure like to make that scene."

He shook his head in reproof. "Bobby, I'm not in show business. David Susskind lives there too. I know him slightly. However, I'm in no position to corner him down in the lobby and say, 'Look, Dave, I've got this little girl friend—'"

"No," she grumbled, without rancor. "I guess not. How in the hell do you make the right contacts in this business?"

"Out of my line, Bobby. Sorry. How are things going these days?" He tried to pretend interest.

"Oh, okay. I got a dog of an agent. Ever heard of Ted Fern?"

"I don't believe so."

"Small time." She let out a whoosh of air in disgust. "I had to pony up the money to join Sag, last week. Believe me, *that* put a hole in the bankroll."

"Sag?"

"Screen Actor's Guild. Two hundred and fifteen bucks. That's a lot of bread for a working girl, man."

"Why don't you let me—"

"Gee, that's awfully sweet of you, honey."

It was usually like that. You never made a definite monetary commitment before going to bed with Bobby Storm, but before the night was out something came up. And now he knew what was coming next.

She said, anxiety in her voice, "You think I'm a tramp."

Every time, and, he suspected, with each of her lovers, she had to be reassured.

He said, making only minimum effort to make it sound sincere, "Look, Bobby, just because you go around doing what everybody else is doing doesn't make you a tramp. You're a nice, sweet, clean little gal doing what comes naturally."

It was then that the first scream welled up from the street below.

She shot upright. "Holy Jesus, what was that?"

Another shrilling topped the first.

He swung his legs over the side of the bed, put his pipe on the side table and hurried over to the window. He pushed the curtain back and stared down. The screams were coming in a lower pitch now, but were still audible even at this distance.

Bobby came up beside him, nude and barefooted. She grabbed his arm and hung on.

He said, "It's coming from that doorway there. Right across."

They could hear several windows going up, one of them in their own building. The cries were for help now, and gurgled off into stillness.

Julian turned and headed for his clothing. "I better get in there."

She stared at him, aghast. "Are you putting me on? You can't go down there."

"Why not?" He reached hurriedly for his pants.

"You don't want to get involved. It's probably just some drunk hustler getting herself a piece she wasn't expecting."

He hesitated.

She said urgently, "Listen, you can't afford to be hauled down to the pokey as a witness."

He came back to the window again. He heard one of the windows slam shut.

She said reasonably, "The fuzz'd want to know who you are, and what you're doing in this neighborhood. What could you tell 'em? What would all your classy friends say when some smart-assed reporter picked it up?"

Down below a male figure had appeared at the entry to the building opposite and was looking, obviously anxiously, up and down the darkened street. Bent over, almost double, he scurried up the street away and down into a cellarway. Sobbing, gurgling noises were still coming from the hall he had just deserted.

"I'll phone," Julian said.

"No. Don't get involved, Jule, don't stick your neck out. They can trace a phone call. They'll come with a thousand questions. What'd my husband say if he found out I was entertaining a gentleman friend here?"

"Your husband? I didn't even know you had a husband."

"Well, I have, and if I got into something like this, he'd have divorce grounds and I wouldn't get a cent out of the bastard."

Even as he stared down, he could see the furtive male figure returning to the scene. It ducked into the hallway and the screams came again.

"Help! Help me! He's killing me . . . !"

Bobby Storm had him by the arm, urgently. "Somebody else'll come. Somebody else's already phoned the cops. They'll be there before you could get down anyway. Don't get us involved, Jule. We can't afford it."

He suffered her to lead him back to the bed.

Down below, there was one last piercing scream. Julian West winced.

There was no more sex in him. He finished smoking his pipe, staring into a far corner of the room, and rejecting her attempts to interest him. Half an hour or so later, he left, leaving two hundred-dollar bills on the side table.

There were police cars across the street. He turned sharply right and hurried off.

His apartment building was ten or eleven blocks away on the East River across the way from the United Nations headquarters. He could have called a cab at the first all-night cafeteria on Second Avenue, but decided to walk. He felt both sexually depleted and upset at the violence that had taken place so nearby. A newspaper account of a mugging, a rape, or even a killing was one thing, being a witness was another. He knew damn well he shouldn't have listened to the pleas of Bobby Storm. You had some civic duties to your fellow man, even in the Manhattan jungle. He was a heel . . . a sonofabitch . . . a conscience-less bastard.

He crossed Second Avenue and made his way down toward First.

In the very early morning the city was asleep with a silence uncanny. For some reason it seemed all but smog-less; possibly the ocean breeze had temporarily cleansed it. Well, that wouldn't last; in a few hours the vehicles, inching along, packed bumper-to-bumper, would vomit up new tons of pollutants into the suffering atmosphere.

He was cold sober but too caught up in his thoughts to have detected them before they jumped him. It was pure luck that he had just shifted his line of walk further out toward the curb when they popped down from the porch of a brownstone, one of them attempting to throw a ragged blanket over his head.

Combat-trained, he ducked, crouched, did a quick shuffle of avoidance. He felt something slash through top-coat and jacket.

There was a small neighborhood grocery store, well locked up and steel-shuttered. He got his back up against the door.

145

There were four of them, three whites and a black. Kids. The oldest was possibly seventeen, the youngest no more than twelve or thirteen; all wore feral animal snarl. And he was close enough to catch the hot glaze of eye. Marijuana, he hoped. You had a better chance with someone on marijuana than you did a crazy who was mainlining horse. Two of them had switchblades, one an ice pick, the other, the Negro, a bicycle chain.

The seventeen-year-old, switchblade extended toward Julian as though it were an Italian small sword of the Florentine period, said, "Okay, baby, toss over the wallet and the watch."

They had formed a semicircle around him and were moving in.

The youngster, the twelve-year-old with the ice pick, had taken in his clothing. "A goddamned sterling. Let me slip this to him couple times."

Julian dipped his hand quickly into his right topcoat pocket and came up with the Colt Cobra, .38 Special. It was a handy, two-inch barrel, lightweight version of the well-known Detective Special and, at short range, just as deadly. He flicked it in a half-circle, covering them all.

"All right, kids. Take off. I'm an old veteran infantry-man."

They came to at least a temporary halt.

The black snarled, "Let's hit the motherfucker square. He's afraid to shoot, or he already been doin' it. We get his bread and the gun too. We could use a gun."

Julian directed the revolver in that direction. "You get the first one, pal," he said.

Whatever else they were, they weren't afraid. Possibly it was the marijuana—or heroin. Possibly, slum-bred, they'd seen so much violence they simply didn't give a damn. They spread out a little more, so that his gun had to cover a wider arc. He had six shots and there were four of them, close enough that at best he would be able to drop two before the others were on him. They were shuffling in, the knives extended, the bicycle chain swing-ing.

"Better you should just toss us the wallet, the watch and the gat, baby," the leader hissed at him.

He didn't want to shoot, damn it. In his time he had killed kids no older than this, guerrillas so young they were hard put to carry their Chinese supplied auto-rifles. He hadn't liked it, ever. He had thought killing behind him. Never again. Besides, these were just kids, American kids. The youngest out of his mother's arms only a few years.

He swept the gun in the arc again. He was going to have to gut-shoot them. He didn't have the time to try for a leg or other less vulnerable targets.

"I wouldn't advise it, boys," he growled, trying to sound both tough and confident.

However, they were gaining courage from his hesitation. The bicycle chain swung pendulum-style. He knew what the colored kid had in mind. He was going to make his play for knocking the gun from Julian's hand.

The showdown was avoided when a red-light flashing police car swung in from First Avenue. For a moment, all froze in the headlights.

The leader of the gang yelped, "Take it on the heel and toe!" and they were gone, in every direction.

The squad car zoomed up to the curb where Julian West stood; doors banged open and two huskies erupted, revolvers in hand.

Julian West began to return his lightweight gun to his pocket.

"Hold on there, buddy," one of them snapped. "What d'ya got there?"

The other, who was standing back and to one side, covering his companion, snapped, "What's goin' on here?"

Julian West's voice took on the accent of the Ivy League college from which he had graduated. He said mildly, "A group of juvenile delinquents just tried to, ah, mug me. You arrived quite in the nick of time, officers. Thank you very much."

The first of them came closer, his gun still at the ready, while the other covered him. He said, "You never heard of the Sullivan Act, maybe?"

However, they were taking in his five-hundred-dollar suit, his homburg, his hundred-dollar tie from Rome, his custom-made shoes from London.

He said gently, nonchalantly, "I do suppose I should
have gone to the bother of asking my friend, the com-
missioner, to have a permit issued me, but I simply didn't
get around to it."

He handed the gun over to the suspicious cop and
reached for his wallet. He brought forth two fifty-dollar
bills and extended one to the first of the duo. "I really insist that you officers have, ah, a beer on me. Over-
whelmed with gratitude, you know. And here is my card.
I'm over in the United Nations Plaza apartments. The
next time there's a police benefit, you simply must call
on me for a check."

The other cop came up and got his fifty. "Well, thanks,"
he said.

The first one handed the gun back. "I guess you know
how to handle this," he said, apologetically. "But I think
you're right, Mr.—" he looked at the engraved card. "West.
You oughta get a permit."

"Of course, officer. And thanks again."

"Maybe we ought to run you over to your apartment
building."

"Why, thank you."

He sat in the back and murmered under his breath,
"New York's finest. A couple of twenties would have been
plenty."

He entered the cavernous, cathedral-like main lobby,
and nodded to the night-desk captain as he made his way
toward the elevators. That worthy beamed unctuously.
Good staff at the United Nations Plaza: valets, seam-
stresses, luggage carriers, caterers, on tap twenty-four
hours a day, not to speak of the six uniformed security
guards who patrolled the building.

At the elevator he nearly collided with a noted neighbor who was currently taking kudos in the literary field.

"Morning, Truman," he murmered, as he sidestepped
the other to enter the compartment.

"Why, top of the morning, Jule," the other fluttered.
"What in the world are you doing out this time of day?"

It was a rhetorical question. Julian West passed on.

In the morning, he read about it in the *Times*.

More than thirty-five persons had heard the girl's

screams, over a period of half an hour, as the sex maniac was first assaulting and then killing her. He had raped her, performed various sexual perversions, and finally cut out her sex parts. No one who had heard her cries had even so much as telephoned the police. Their responses had been the same; when reporters looked into it, they hadn't wanted to become involved.

God save him, he thought, neither had he.

XV

. . . for the first time since his creation man will be faced with his . . . permanent problem—how to use his freedom from pressing economic cares, how to occupy the leisure, which science and compounded interest will have won for him, to live wisely and agreeably and well. . . . I see us free, therefore, to return to some of the most sure and certain principles of religion and traditional virtue—that avarice is a vice, that the extraction of usury is a misdemeanour, and the love of money is detestable, that those walk most truly in the paths of virtue and sane wisdom who take least thought for the morrow. We shall once more value ends above means and prefer the good to the useful. We shall honor those who can teach us how to pluck the hour and the day virtuously and well, the delightful people who are capable of taking direct enjoyment in things, the lilies of the field who toil not, neither do they spin.

John Maynard Keynes
Essays in Persuasion

Now

Someone was saying, anxiously, "Julian, are you all right?"

He opened his eyes and shook his head for clarity. It was Martha Leete. He put the back of his right fist to his forehead and rubbed. He could feel the tic at the side of his mouth.

"I must have dozed off," he told her.

"You seemed upset," she said gently.

He came to his feet and shook his head again. "No. I'm all right. A nasty memory came back to me."

She had some of her inevitable needlework in her hands and settled down into one of the oversized chairs. She said, "We don't seem to be able to decide whether we intrude on you too much, that you'd rather have more of your hours to yourself, or whether we should spend more time with you, since things are so strange and your friends are . . . so far away."

"You're all being wonderful," he said. "It's just that I'm continually confused. Look, a couple of things I was dreaming about. What came of the juvenile delinquent problem?"

She cocked her head slightly to one side in thought. "That's right, it was quite a problem, wasn't it. Literally millions of frustrated young people. I recall, when I was a girl. Well, I suppose you could say that time solved it. One big factor was the ending of the slums and ghettos, and, for that matter, of the suburban slums. Another element was the coming of adequate education to all. The end of poverty was still another."

Martha Leete thought about it some more. "But it seems to me that possibly most important of all was the change in the social climate. A good many of these young people had nothing to *do*. When the big changes began, a great number of them were swept up in the emotion of it all, they wanted to participate. They got into the spirit of the search for a better tomorrow."

"It's hard to believe that the typical slum kid of New York, or wherever, could get onto an idealistic binge. Their binges were more apt to be based on pot," Julian said wryly. He sat down opposite her and rubbed his forehead again. Her placidity had a calming factor; his mouth tic was gone.

"Oh," she said. "I don't mean that all of the juvenile delinquents of your period turned overnight into little saints. It took a whole generation before the problem was solved. And now that you mention it, the ending of the narcotic thing helped a great deal."

"I'd think it would. How did they go about that? A ruthless crackdown?"

"By making narcotics legal."

"You have to be joking."

"Not at all. You see, back before the First World War you could walk into any drug store and purchase such items as opium or morphine without even a prescription.

151

And there was very little addiction. It was when narcotics became illegal that the first great upsurge in use came. Criminals took over and deliberately campaigned to spread usage. And that was the source of much of the juvenile delinquency. They needed the money because of the high price of drugs. When narcotics became legal, the syndicate and other crime rings were dealt a real blow. There was no profit in it for them. Drugs were cheaper in drug stores."

"All right, but good God, addiction must have soared."

"No, no. To the contrary. You see, at the same time we went into an unprecedented educational campaign against their use. All the mass media were involved, TV, movies, radio, the newspapers, the magazines, the church pulpits, and especially the schools. Courses in narcotics were obligatory and they involved at least one field trip to an addict rehabilitation institution where students could see the ultimate ravages of the more extreme drugs. That, by the way, was another phase of our attack on the use of narcotics—a crash program in the medical field to find cures for addiction, not only to the opiates but a dozen others as well including even tobacco and alcohol. It was largely a matter of psychotherapy, of course."

Julian shook his head in amazement. "It must have been quite a blow to the syndicate, the Cosa Nostra families."

She studied the work she was at critically before saying, "It's not the only blow to which those gentlemen were treated. I imagine the ending of gambling was the final kiss of death which finished organized crime."

"Oh, come now. Man is a gambling animal. Don't tell me there's no more gambling."

"Ummm. However, you end it commercially, at least, when you do away with money as a medium of exchange. With the coming of the checkless-cashless society it becomes very difficult to steal anything worth stealing and very difficult to, ah, con a person out of his credit account or to gamble it away from him. I suppose we still have a certain amount of gambling but it's on a small scale with picayunish stakes, certainly not worth a professional gambler's time."

152

"There's something I'd like to come back to there, but first tell me the present status of prostitution."

"It's disappeared."

"Completely? We've had prostitution as far back as the early books of the Bible. I'm not denying that in some societies they cracked down on it so hard as to drive it underground, but it was always ready to raise its head again."

She nodded in her placid way and went back to her work once more. "Edith should be the one to go into this for you. She's the amateur anthropologist of the family. However, if I understand it correctly, prostitution is a fairly modern development. They didn't have it in ancient society, before the advent of private property, man's domination of the female sex and a woman's reliance on a man, or men, to survive. And today, once again, women no longer depend on men. We wouldn't dream of degrading ourselves by offering sex to a man to whom we actually had no attraction."

The memory of Bobby Storm came to him. He said, uncomfortably, "Not all prostitutes disliked their customers. Some enjoyed the act for its own sake and were attractive enough to be able to pick and choose their men."

"Don't misunderstand. We're not prudes today. I suppose if one is overly sexed he can find his counterpart or counterparts. However, it is no longer commercialized. A promiscuous person, either male or female, is no longer so for financial reasons. I understand that in your day a good many prostitutes were actually lesbians and hated the men they serviced for a fee. What was it they called them?"

"Johns," Julian said dryly.

"Of course. And prostitution wasn't entirely a matter of a girl selling herself to a man. You also had the gigolo. Can you imagine the contempt that a young handsome beachboy on Hawaii or the French Riviera must have had for the elderly rich women who paid him for his services?"

"I've known a few of the type," Julian said. "All right, so now that everybody gets their negative income tax and can make out without having to peddle themselves, you no longer have prostitution. However, I'd think there'd be some women on this basic income who would be ambitious for more. Even if they couldn't get cash from a . . . John, they'd be able to get him to buy them presents. A fur coat they couldn't ordinarily afford, or whatever."

Her eyebrows went up. "But you've got the wrong impression, Julian. We no longer have negative income tax."

Doctor Leete entered from behind them. He made with his usual, good-natured, quizzical beam and said, "Hello, everybody. What goes on?"

"Ulcers," Julian said bitterly, "if these conversations continue the way they've been going."

"Oh, we don't have ulcers anymore," Leete said, missing the sarcasm.

"I might have known," Julian said. "From most of what I understand you don't have anything I used to know, anymore. Look, do you still have headaches? Because if you say no, you're having me on. I'm developing one by the minute."

They caught his mood and laughed.

The doctor said, "It's still possible to get a headache but if one did it would quickly be analyzed and eliminated."

"Great, at last I've found something still with us. You get a headache and pop an aspirin into your mouth."

There was an almost apologetic note in the doctor's voice for contradicting him. "Aspirin," he said. "It's been a long time since I've heard that word. A somewhat primitive drug, though, of course, effective in its time. It was a painkiller. We seldom use painkillers any more."

"What do you do?" Julian demanded, exasperated. "Just sit around and suffer?"

Leete waggled a finger in negation. "No. Certainly not. We find the reason for the pain and eliminate it."

"Oh, everybody goes around in rosy good health and the least thing that happens you check it out and immediately cure it. No more aches and pains."

"Yes," Leete said simply.

Julian West gave up. "And you keep telling me this

isn't utopia," he grumbled. "At least I've finally come up with some field that you haven't automated and computerized out of existence."

"What would that be?" the doctor said curiously. He wandered over to the automatic bar. "Drink, anyone?"

"I suppose I'll have a sherry," Martha said.

"Scotch for me," Julian said. "The medical field."

The doctor dialed the drinks and returned with them, handing them around before sinking down onto the couch. He nodded. "We currently have more people in medical research than ever before, but so far as practicing medicine is concerned I would imagine we have fewer medical doctors than in your own time."

"Oh, come now. We had a terrible shortage. Large numbers of doctors had to be brought in from abroad, but we were still short. Of nurses and other medical personnel too, for that matter."

"Of course, but you must realize that we've eliminated such illnesses of your time as cancer, the heart and other organ diseases, the common cold, flu, the venereal diseases and various others. Besides, you were erroneous in thinking that automation hasn't come to the profession. You see, almost every home has what we call an auto-doctor."

"Oh, *no.*"

"Oh, yes. In the past, four visits out of five made to a doctor were for minor or even imaginary reasons. The auto-doctor eliminates these. If you feel a bit ill, you sit down before your auto-doctor. I'll show you the one in this apartment later. It takes your temperature, your blood pressure, your pulse. It takes a tiny sample of your blood and analyzes it. If necessary it requests a sample of your urine or feces. It makes various other tests which, as a layman and particularly unacquainted with recent developments, it would be difficult to explain to you. It has available, of course, your complete medical record since birth and those of your parents as well, and, for some of our younger people, the medical records of their grandparents. It makes a diagnosis and prescribes."

"But suppose it's something *serious!*" Julian demanded. "Or, for that matter, suppose it's something like a broken

leg? Don't tell me this damned auto-doctor can set a leg
in splints."

Leete sipped at his wine and chuckled. "No. If your
ailing is such that the auto-doctor is incapable of dealing
with it, then it informs you what particular specialist you
should call upon. Or, if you are quite ill, he calls upon
you."

"You can't select your own doctor, eh?"

"No, certainly not. You aren't a professional yourself;
how should you be in any position to know what doctor
is needed for your particular case?"

"In my day, that was one of the highly debated issues
in the socialized medicine fracas. The right to a doctor of
your own choosing."

"That would be like allowing a child to chose its own
diet. Suppose that surgery was required upon me. Do you
think I am so foolish as to wish to decide what surgeon
should perform the operation?"

"You're a doctor. If you don't know, who would?"

Leete was shaking his head negatively. "I wouldn't begin to know as well as the computers of the medical
branch of the international data banks in which is deposited all the medical information, past and present,
available to the human race. It includes, once again, my
complete medical record in such detail that it would take
a human long hours, perhaps days, to read it."

"Suppose the particular surgeon who is tops in the specialization needed is too busy? How is it decided who will
have the advantage of his personal attention? Does it go
to whoever can swing the highest fee?"

Leete was still shaking his head negatively. "We don't
have fees any more. One element you must keep in
mind is that there is no longer that much difference between individual doctors. All information is available to
all. All specialists are just about equally qualified. You
see, possibly only one tenth of our graduates from medical schools ever practice. They are, of course, the top
tenth selected by the computers on the strength of their
aptitude quotient."

"One *tenth*! What happens to the others?"

"Some are suitable for research or other projects in

the medical field and are given appointments there. Some return to school in the hopes that additional studies will up their aptitude quotient to the point where they will be selected later when openings occur in the profession."

"And what happens to the others? Or what happens to those who go back to school but never make the grade?"

Leete shrugged. "As we told you, only two percent of the population is now needed to produce what we need and do all other work necessary to society."

"You mean this applies to every field? A man might study all his youth to become an engineer and then, when he graduates, the computers say, 'Sorry, Jack, your aptitude quotient just isn't high enough.'"

"How else would you handle it? Would you put incompetents into key positions?"

"Not necessarily key positions, but surely some junior opening should be available to them if they really want to work."

"The difficulty is that just about all positions in our economy are key positions. We've largely automated junior positions out of existence."

"A man must have a tough time working his way to the top in this world if he's only got one chance in ten of landing a job at all."

"Once chance in fifty, on an average," the doctor said. "But what do you mean, working his way to the top?"

Julian West made a gesture of the obvious with his two hands. "To where the pay is better. To where the power is."

The doctor finished his drink and put the glass down on a cocktail table. He was frowning, as though not quite sure how to handle the subject.

He said finally, "I don't think that we are quite as obsessed with what you call power as people were inclined to be in your day. So far as pay is concerned, there is no such thing as higher pay."

Julian was blank. Finally, he looked at Martha. "You said earlier that you no longer have negative income tax."

"Of course not," she said reasonably. "We no longer have taxes, for that matter. Negative income tax was an early step in the changes that have been doing on, but we've evolved far beyond that."

Julian went back to the doctor. "You mean to tell me that the, say, head of a gigantic corporation gets paid no more than, say, a janitor?"

Leete said, "He gets paid no more than the janitor's one-week-old child."

"Now that makes no sense at all. You're trying to make a fool of me. Why should a man work if he gets nothing extra whatsoever for working?"

"Because he likes to."

Julian West was stopped, all over again.

The doctor said, "See here. Suppose early in a young boy's education it becomes obvious that he has a bent for math and science in general. He is encouraged to develop in that direction. By the time he is in his early teens it has further developed that he is particularly inclined toward chemistry. That is encouraged and he is given every opportunity to expand in that direction. By the time he enters the university—a science university, of course—it is the big thing in his life. As he continues to study, it is found that his particular bent is to this sub-division of the science, or that. By this time, he eats, sleeps and dreams of his particular branch of research chemistry. He can't wait to graduate and get into advanced aspects of his field. Very well, Muster Day comes and—"

"Muster Day?" Julian said.

"I'll tell you about that later. When at long last he graduates, believe me, he is chewing his fingertips for fear that the computers will pass him by. He *wants* to work. He is frantic with desire to be chosen and be able to continue in his life work. Everything else is ashes in his mouth."

"All right, then if he's so capable, such a whiz kid of a chemist, doesn't he deserve more than, say, one of his classmates who turned out to have considerably less ability? In my day, the best man got paid the most."

The doctor looked at him quizzically. "Are you sure? I recall reading of the time Albert Einstein was offered a position to join the Institute for Advanced Study at

Princeton. He was asked by Dr. Abraham Flexner, the director, to name his price. Einstein was, as he put it, 'flame and fire' for the position and suggested $3000 a year. Flexner quietly set the pay at $16,000. Even this is ridiculous in view of the fact that the man was possibly the greatest scientist of the century. A salesmanager of a moderate-sized company made more than that.

"It was not an isolated case. I happen to be a bit up on the subject because it particularly irritated me when I was a young man and a bit on the nonconformist side, if the truth be known. According to the National Science Foundation of the time, in the 1960s the pay of scientists in the United States was in the range $6,000 to $15,000 per annum, about the average for a successful plumber. And Paul Woodring, educational consultant to the Fund for the Advancement of Education of the Ford Foundation, pointed out that there were dozens of liberal arts colleges which paid average salaries as low as $3000 a year and minimum salaries much lower still."

Julian said, slightly miffed, "If you had it on the ball, you could get to the top financially and otherwise."

The doctor ran a hand over his mouth ruefully. "Could you? Have you ever heard of the case of Professor Edwin H. Armstrong, inventor of ultra short-wave super-regeneration, the superheterodyne circuit, wide-swing radio frequency modulation and the regenerative circuit for vacuum tubes? All these were cold-bloodedly infringed upon by leading well-heeled established companies. He sued and spent the better part of a lifetime trying to protect his discoveries. Even when he won, he collected only a percentage royalty. The infringers claimed that what they earned through their promotional efforts they should be allowed to keep—and did. Their voice in the courts was considerably stronger than that of a lowly scientist."

Julian said, "Well, what did he wind up with?"

The doctor said simply, "He wound up with death. He was so overwrought he committed suicide."

Julian West was quiet.

The doctor said, "There are endless examples. Thomas Edison himself died leaving only a minute estate. No,

Julian, by your time it was no longer the best man who was at the top. It was the cleverest man, perhaps, the most ruthless, perhaps, or the slyest. Above all, those at the top were those who had inherited great wealth. With few exceptions, the ultra-wealthy families had inherited their positions and that was where the ultimate power resided. The DuPonts, the Rockefellers, the Mellons, the Fords, the Pews, Hughes, Getty and almost all the rest inherited their basic fortunes. What were their true abilities? Have you ever heard of one who excelled in any of the arts or sciences?"

Edith Leete entered, tossed a tennis racket to the couch and fell exhausted into a chair, arms and legs sprawled out.

"Does the marathon quiz show still go on?" she laughed.

"That it does," Julian said, taking time out only long enough to notice that a sweaty, exhausted Edith Leete looked, if anything, more attractive than ever. She projected enjoyment of life, enthusiasm for living. It came to him that she would undoubtedly be a superb bed companion, and wrenched his mind away from that. To him, Edith Bartlett was still less than a week in the past.

He turned back to his host. "To return to what you said a little earlier. I simply can't see why a top manager in an industry, or wherever, should get no more pay than a janitor. It would take all initiative away."

"Let's continue the same example," the doctor said. "Suppose in your day that manager stepped out into the hall and drank a glass or two of water from the cooler. Shortly afterward the janitor came along and also drank. Now, would the manager have minded if the janitor drank twice as many glasses as he had?"

"Why no."

"Would he have cared if the janitor breathed twice as much air?"

"I don't get your point."

"Had they been in the middle of the Sahara, with a desperate water shortage, I can see where your manager might exert what influence he could, or the leverage of his money, to acquire a greater supply of the precious fluid. Or, if they were in a submarine or spaceship, with a shortage of oxygen, he might have attempted to get a greater share to breathe. But, otherwise, why in the world should it make any difference how much the janitor drank or breathed?"

Julian West was scowling.

Martha said, gently always, "In your day, there was a shortage not only of the luxuries and good things of life, but, for some people, even the necessities. That day is over. Today we can and do produce an abundance for everyone."

"All right," Julian insisted. "Then what motivates a man to take a position involving responsibility and added effort, when, if he wished, he could fluff off? From what you say, he wouldn't have to work at all if he didn't want to. He could deliberately fake a few of his tests and the computers would never pick him for any job."

The doctor was nodding complacently. "You make the mistake of thinking that the only thing that motivates men in their field of endeavor is pay. Indeed, it is probably the least esteemable of motivations. Perhaps it didn't apply considerably in your time, and particularly in those jobs in which a man could hardly take pride. A man of genius, working in the advertising business, or in sales, particularly when he doubted the value of the commodity he sold, must have been frustrated indeed and only high pay in a world which evaluated a man by his income must have kept him from resignation.

"However, even in your time, the great achievers were seldom the money-grabbers. Once again, your Einsteins and Edisons and scientists in general; your great painters, writers, musicians and other artists. Yes, they were glad to take the money, when and if it came along, but it was not what basically motivated them. Nor did it only apply to scientists and artists. Take public figures, back before politics became contemptible. Do you think for a moment that Washington, Jefferson, Lincoln, to name only a few, were motivated by high pay when they took the presidency?"

"They had power, public acclaim."

The doctor fingered a small red ribbon worn on the left lapel of his jacket. "You are acquainted with the French Legion of Honor?"

"Why, yes. Originally instituted by Napoleon and a civil decoration, rather than military."

"Originally most decorations were military; today they are civil and can be awarded for outstanding service in any field. We make almost a fetish of honoring those in our society who bear a white, blue, red or gold category ribbon."

For the first time, Julian noted that Martha Leete wore a blue ribbon over her left breast.

"Who decides who is awarded a ribbon?" he asked.

"The people. The people who think I should be awarded a red ribbon, the highest national award, cast a vote for me and it is recorded in the data banks. If enough so vote, I achieve the award and am notified. White ribbons are local, blue for a wider area, somewhat similar to your states, and red is the national. Gold ribbons are international, and extremely rare."

Edith evidently had recovered from her exertions somewhat. She said, "In your day, a girl did her utmost to marry a man of wealth. His other attributes were secondary. Today, she is highly impressed by his achievements. It works both ways, of course. Today, a girl's face and figure are not nearly so important to a man as her abilities. She is no longer a status symbol for him to display, if she is merely beautiful."

"You mean that these days, the only thing that counts when you seek out a mate is whether or not he's been decorated?"

"No, of course not, Jule. Under classical capitalism a man was evaluated by the money he made. But even during Galbraith's new industrial state, skill, educational standards and technical intelligence took over top prestige. When all the problems of production of abundance were solved, a fresh element appeared. For the first time possibly in the history of the race, a man began to be evaluated by his sensitivity, charm, generosity, sympathy and imagination. These qualities were given lip service in the past but they had never taken precedence over money and power before."

Julian shook his head. "It still doesn't come through to me. I can't see why the average man would take on a really tough job when there's no special remuneration."

Leete waggled a finger. "Don't forget, he *likes* the job. His education and training have been preparing him for it all his life. If he didn't like it, he would never have been selected for it."

"You mean the men for even the top jobs of the country are selected by the computers? Suppose one of these confounded machines blew a fuse?"

The doctor chuckled. "Not entirely. In such matters there are human elements that thus far, at least, the computers cannot handle. Before a man is eligible to be considered for a position of authority the computers must check out his aptitude and training for it, but the final say is in the hands of his fellows. The position is elective."

"I'm not following."

"Well, in one of our early discussions Edith used the shoe industry as an example. Let's carry on with the example. Suppose that you worked in the clothing industry, in the subdivision shoes. Suppose you worked with a group of ten other technicians in one department. Very well, it is necessary to have a foreman. You elect one of the group to hold that position, and, if the computers agree that he has the qualifications to handle the job, he becomes foreman. Each day, as a foreman, he works with the other foremen in his division, say ten foremen in all. From their number they elect a divisional supervisor who, once again, must be found competent for the job by the computers. The supervisors of all the factory's divisions also work together daily. They elect from their number a plant manager, who also represents that plant in all affairs pertaining to all the shoe factories of the nation and who also sends a representative to the final council of the Clothing Guild, which has representatives from all other branches of the clothing industry."

Julian said, trying to assimilate all this, "What's the final top of the heap?"

"The Congress of Guilds: representatives from every guild in the nation, agriculture, mining, transportation, communication, distribution, various manufacturing, even health, entertainment and education. The Congress of Guilds is a planning body, of course, rather than a legislative one. It coordinates the production and distribution of the national product."

"And the ultimate head, the president, or whatever? He must have more power in his little finger than—"

"No. No. There is no ultimate head. The Congress of Guilds works through various committees."

"Look, these elected representatives. How long is their term in office? Four years? Life?"

"They have no set term. Any official, if you wish to call him that, can be removed immediately, as soon as the majority of those who elected him wish his recall, to be replaced by someone else."

"It's considerably different from elections in my time."

"Yes," Martha Leete put in, mild deprecation in her voice. "In your day the electorate voted for persons of whom they had no real knowledge. The candidates were nominated by political parties that were dominated by the rich. A great farce of a campaign was then entered into to sell their personalities and the ignorant electorate chose between them. Even the highest office might be held by an ex-general who knew nothing of governing, by an ex-haberdasher who was the tool of a corrupt political machine, or by a multimillionaire whose ambitious father literally bought him into office utilizing the latest Madison Avenue techniques."

Julian looked from one of them to the other. "The whole thing is just beginning to clear up for me," he said, a strange quality in his voice. "Look here, just when did the revolution take place?"

"Revolution?" Doctor Leete said. "What revolution?"

XVI

We can less and less afford to limit ourselves to routine repair of breakdowns in our institutions. Unless we are willing to see a final confrontation between institutions that refuse to change and critics bent on destruction, we had better get on with the business of redesigning our society. We must dispose of the notion that social change is a process that alters a tranquil status quo. Today there is no tranquility to alter. The rush of change brings a kind of instant antiquity. That human institutions require periodic redesign (if only because of their tendency to decay) is not a minor fact about them. How curious it is, then, that in all history no people has seriously attempted to take into account the aging of institutions and to provide for their continual renewal. Why shouldn't we be the first to do so?
  John W. Gardner
  Secretary of Health, Education and Welfare

Now

Julian West said, "When I went into stasis, the United States was a capitalist country. Whatever it is now, it is no longer capitalist. So when did the revolution take place?"

The doctor grimaced. "I suppose that the changes we have seen in the past thirty-some years have been revolutionary in actuality, but you must remember that revolutions are not necessarily abrupt. For instance, although in France feudalism was overthrown and capitalism inaugurated overnight and in a sea of blood, in England this change took place over a lengthy period. In fact, there were still vestiges of feudalism such as the royal family and the House of Lords right up to modern times. Capitalism was in the saddle and had been for a couple of centuries, but there had never been a revolution in the sense of Lenin's overthrow of czarism in Russia."

"You seem to be evading my question."

"Not really. There simply is no one date you could pick out as the exact time a revolutionary change took place in the American socio-economic system of your day, in the way you can point to July 4, 1776. It simply evolved and was largely upon us before most realized it. Possibly the first obvious seeds were sown by President Roosevelt, back in the 1930s."

"I vaguely remember his administration as a child," Julian nodded. "In my family's circle he was thought of as a wide-eyed radical."

"Well, he wasn't. He was a conservative pushed by developing events. As he himself pointed out, a true conservative is a liberal because he realizes that in order to conserve the old order you must reform. Roosevelt was elected on an economy platform, but that very shortly went by the board. He instituted new devices such as social security, the germ of today's cradle-to-grave income for all citizens. He instituted the Work Projects Administration, the Public Works Administration and the Civilian Conservation Corps, the first seeds of our present system of working for the nation as a whole rather than for individuals or corporations.

"But these were early steps in the changes from classical capitalism to what Galbraith called the new industrial state, and still later to our present socio-economic system which the more starry-eyed like to call the Republic of the Golden Rule. You see, classical capitalism died in 1929 with the big crash. For ten years the world stumbled along trying to right itself and couldn't. The Hitler War brought it out of the doldrums, but when that war was over almost all the western countries had a socio-economic system possibly best described as state capitalism."

"Then there wasn't any bloodshed, bringing in this new society of yours?"

"Not in the sense that you're probably thinking. Scattered riots, demonstrations against war and the military, poverty and racial discrimination, yes. You must remember the riots in the cities, in the universities, and the ghettos in the 1960s."

"Yes, of course, but at the time I didn't think of them as manifestations of revolutionary changes."

"Well, they were. They were the stirrings of revolt against the status quo. Don't forget that those students in revolt were going to emerge from their schools in a few years and, more mature, become the new executives, the new writers, newspapermen, community leaders and whatnot. Nor that the soldiers of the time, drafted to fight the most unpopular war in the history of the country, were going to return in hundreds of thousands to make demands that such military adventures never be resorted to again."

"But there was no civil war, in the sense that the Americans under Washington fought the British and Tories, or Lenin's Red Army fought the White armies in Russia?"

"No. There was no one to fight such a conflict. There weren't two clearcut sides. Everything blended into a conglomerate of interests. It was to the interest of the big corporations to become still bigger and to exert more pressure on the government to their own advantage to obtain super-contracts with profits guaranteed. It was to the interest of the government to exert more control over the super-corporations and the cosmocorps. It was to the interest of the employees to work for a super-corporation with the security and good pay involved. It was to the interest of the aged, the poor and the unemployed to receive a guaranteed annual income and to the interest of all who didn't want the boat rocked that they receive such a stipend, so as to keep them from revolt and retain them as consumers. Extremists of the right and extremists of the left and crackpots in general ranted and raved but it was to the interest of the overwhelming majority to establish the new society—and it was established."

Julian West bit his underlip. He wasn't satisfied with the answer. He said, "What would you call the present socio-economic system—communism? I can't imagine the American people I knew ever resorting to communism."

"Possibly it's hard to label it, in the sense that you're asking me to. Certainly not communism, if you mean by

167

that what the Russians, the Chinese and the other Soviet states meant. You had an absolute mania for labels in your day. You had built up mental taboos against such terms as socialism, government control, social medicine, social ownership and collective ownership, although in actuality there were so many of these—at least in embryo —that by the end of the 1960s that you couldn't describe the system as classical capitalism any longer. In the same way that we almost instinctively reacted against terms like socialism, we absolutely drooled over terms such as free enterprise and private enterprise, although in actuality there was precious little free enterprise left in the old sense of the word. The established super-corporations took every precaution that there be no risk involved in their enterprises, and in increasing measure the government helped insure that."

"But what *would* you call the system you have now?"

"Well, if the truth be known, it is in a condition of flux and evolving as rapidly as any of the sciences, social and physical. There are elements of socialism, in the various senses of the word, since the term is so elastic. There are elements of collectivism and of syndicalism and perhaps technocracy. It might even be said that there are elements of anarchism, if you mean by that the anarchism of the nineteenth century Proudhon and of the poets Shelley and Blake. Elements too, of meritocracy."

The doctor was finding difficulty in putting over the reality. "We're in a condition of flux. You see, in the past a social system could take millennia to change. Primitive communism, clan society, lasted for hundreds of thousands of years before the socio-economic system of slavery replaced it. Slavery lasted for millennia and remnants of it persisted into the twentieth century. Even the United States didn't completely abolish chattel slavery until the second half of the nineteenth century. Feudalism lasted several centuries before capitalism dealt it its death blow, but then things began to accelerate. Classical capitalism was with us only for a few centuries, and state capitalism, if that is the term, only a few decades. Leninism was even briefer in duration, in those nations where it appeared. In fact, it never did jell into a system of any permanency. It began to change almost as soon as it was achieved in its various backward countries. Its paramount aim was to industrialize, and as rapidly as it succeeded it antiquated itself. Its terminology, its slogans, its labels they tried to hang on to, but the actuality behind them quickly faded. Marxism it never was, though they gave lip service to that nineteenth century economist."

"All right," Julian said. "I suppose I'm beginning to get the picture. These super-corporations finally squeezed out just about every other enterprise in the country, and at the same time the government was taking over increasing amounts of their common stock, both to float a backing for the national currency and to raise money for such projects as negative income tax, slum clearance, anti-pollution drives and the rest. So finally the government just took over the corporations."

It was Edie who protested that. She said, "Not exactly. It's rather moot whether the government took over the corporations or the corporations took over the government. They . . . well, they just sort of merged."

He looked at her.

She twisted her mouth in sour amusement. "You might say the corporations, or rather the guilds as we call them now, *became* the new government. If you can call it a government."

"Oh, brother," he protested. "My mind was confused before, now it's in a state of chaos."

The doctor moved in again. "You see, various different developments were coming to a head, centering in on the needed changes. With the advent of really universal education, and of the aptitude quotient arrived at by the computers, a change took place in management of the nation's productive forces. Under classical capitalism, the owner was the ultimate head of a corporation, no matter how large. After the managerial revolution and the coming of the new industrial state, the heads of industry became the top executives—usually, but by no means always, highly competent men. They were appointed by the owners, or by each other. But even this gave rise to nepotism, favoritism. The computers ended that with

169

their aptitude quotient. No longer could the top managers of a corporation be less than the best men in their field. The most important factor in a socio-economic system is the production of the products needed by the people. What finally emerged was a, well, you might call it a dual government—the government of the former super-corporations on the industrial side and, on the other, the civil government which grew increasingly less necessary as the threat of war fell off and the need for courts, police and prisons largely disappeared. Many of the departments of the civil government simply atrophied."

"Such as what?"

"To name a few, the various departments concerned with defense and war. The Veterans' Administration, all the various offices involved with pensions and relief, commerce—"

"Don't tell me you don't have international commerce any more."

"A great deal less than in your day, and it is handled through the Congress of Guilds, through what we called the cosmocorps when they first appeared."

"But I'd think that with all the new production in the world, there'd be more trade than ever."

"No. A great deal of it was really unnecessary. For instance, hundreds of thousands of Volkswagens would be shipped over from Germany. Why not make them here? Shiploads of Scotch whiskey would be sent over from England. Why not make it here? Iron and petroleum were sent up wholesale from Venezuela. Utilizing the laser-mole we now produce all we need of the former, and with the coming of fusion power we no longer need the latter."

"But if you don't buy things from abroad, they won't buy from you."

"Which was a big problem in the old days when each nation tried to achieve what they called a favorable balance of trade. That is, they attempted to sell more of their products than they imported of the other fellow's. Each nation wished to dispose of its surpluses. Well, we don't have surpluses anymore. Each nation consumes what it produces."

"But you can't produce everything in any one country."
"I didn't say international trade was eliminated, just that we don't have the fantastic amount of it you had in your day."
"Without money, how can you have any trade at all?"
"Money was always an awkward method of exchange, particularly in international matters. Today we trade, even-steven."
Julian West simply stared at him.
The doctor said, "We no longer evaluate products in dollars and cents, or pounds and pence, francs and centimes. We now utilize the hour and minute."
Julian waited.
The doctor said, "It is rather basic economics that the exchange value of a product is determined by the amount of labor power expended to produce it."
"That's Marxism! You said you weren't—"
Leete waggled a finger negatively. "No. Karl Marx subscribed to the Law of Value but he by no means invented it. Various of the great economists hit upon the Law of Value before Marx came along, including David Ricardo. Marx himself gave credit to Benjamin Franklin who outlined the theory in his first essay, published in 1729 and entitled *A Modest Enquiry into the Nature and Necessity of a Paper Currency.* Franklin pointed out that if equal quantities of labor be fixed in one bushel of wheat and one ounce of gold then their exchange value is equal."
Julian said disgustedly, "That's great if you're dealing with a farmer on one hand and a miner on the other, both common laborers. But you can't contend that the time of a top nuclear physicist and that of a ditch digger is identical in worth. You can't evaluate the product of one's hour with that of the other."
"Possibly you couldn't in your day, but we can now. In the past, when there was a shortage of brain and an abundance of brawn, a thinker's time was seemingly of considerably more value than a laborer's and the ethics of the matter were ignored."
"Ethics?"
"Julian, to say that all men are created equal is non-

171

sense. Obviously, no two men are ever created equal, not even identical twins. However, in one respect *all* men are created equal. They are endowed with twenty-four hours a day. No one has ever been born who has had either more or less. It is the basic of life. And it is just as precious to one person as it is to another, since once a moment of your life has fled, it is gone forever."

Edie murmured, *"And all your piety and wit can't lure it back."*

Martha said gently, looking up from her needlework, "They used to say that life was cheap in the Orient." She shook her head. "No. Life has never been cheap, anywhere. It is as precious to the Chinese coolie as it has ever been to the Roman emperor, or the American billionaire. And time is the unit of life."

The doctor said, "You see, we are getting back to our earlier discussion. You were insistent that the manager of a plant be paid more than its janitor. But the fact is that once both the manager and the janitor . . . by the way, we don't have janitors anymore—"

"Of course not," Julian said under his breath, "the computers are out there handling the brooms."

The doctor chuckled at that but didn't bother to answer. "Once they both have all they need or want, then there is no longer a selfish motivation for judging one's time worth more or less than the other's. At any rate, that is how we handle the international transactions. Everything is valued by the amount of necessary labor power needed to produce it."

"Then if you have a seminaked savage—as you say, as you say, you don't have seminaked savages any more—but for the sake of example. A savage in South Africa scrabbling for diamonds wants to trade his smidgeon of second-quality diamonds for an American-produced vehicle. His time is considered on a par with a highly trained technician's in this country?"

"That is correct. The fact, of course, is that the diamond mining industry is also highly automated in this age."

"Suppose he deliberately lies down on the job, takes

twice as long as needed to produce a given number of diamonds?"

"You're nit-picking. The necessary amount of labor required to produce a product, is the way I worded it. In South Africa, as elsewhere, they have adequate methods of determining the required amount of labor. Featherbedding we no longer have with us; it was a product of a class-divided society, and a dog-eat-dog economy."

"I'd like to go into that further, but first, something else. Who does the dirty work? You have the manager, the scientist, a professional such as yourself, all bucking for your decorations and honors. But who takes the undesirable jobs?"

"I see what you mean. For one thing, there is precious little dirty work—"

"As you say, as you say. But who takes the hard jobs? Who takes the dangerous ones? Like the miners who still have to go underground, in spite of the fact that the mines are largely automated; the divers who have to go down into the ocean for whatever reason. The explorers still plowing through the snow down in the Antarctica, or, at least, I suppose they still are. The spacemen sent out to the moon, or wherever."

Edie said, as though mystified, "Why, the people who like that sort of work."

"There are some kinds of work that *nobody* would like."

"You'd be surprised. With a working force of over a hundred million to draw from, the computers are never at a loss to find a suitable employee. Take your examples. A mining engineer, willing and able to go down into the depths for some special matter the machines can't handle. There have always been men who loved mining, who actually liked working below ground and pitting their muscles against nature. Divers who go down into the depths? There are so many people who love being under the sea that hundreds of thousands of skin-divers take it up as a sport. Explorers in Antarctica, or spacemen on the moon? Those anxious to take such adventurous jobs are far more than required. Ditch diggers?

It is quite true that such hard physical work is largely automated, but there is still some and hundreds of thousands of young men and women who glory in hard physical work. They are the same type of people, often, who go in for the more strenuous sports." She shook her head. "Even if this didn't always apply, there are many among us who would volunteer for a job that was particularly dangerous, or rugged, because of high idealism and desire to serve the community and perhaps win decorations and acclaim as a result. These, of course, we have always had in any system. They particularly abound today, when society is more worthy of serving than it has usually been in the past."

Martha Leete took out her transceiver, dialed for the time, looked at her husband and said, "Good heavens, Raymond, we have that date with Jean and Harold."

He came to his feet. "I'd forgotten. What time is it?"

"Eighteen hours." She stood too.

The doctor said to Julian, "We're going to have to leave you to the tender graces of Edith for the evening." He chuckled. "You can take out some of your irritations about the way the world has altered on her."

Julian West looked at the girl ruefully. "I suppose I'm somewhat of a pest."

"As a matter of fact, sir, it's quite educational. How would you have liked the opportunity to have discussed with someone of Washington's time the politico-economic system that prevailed, the way he saw the world, the dreams he had of the future?"

"The differences between your time and mine are hardly as great as my time and that of Washington."

Martha Leete said, "In some ways they are greater, Julian. As all four of us are finding out."

XVII

*Two hundred years after we declared our ca-
pacity to achieve freedom for all Americans, we
have the capability of making that freedom real
and operational. The nation has developed
through several historical stages during that
brief period. We passed through the vestiges of
the agrarian-preindustrial era, led the world
through the industrial age of cities, and are now
emerging into a still uncharted era when few
men will pursue the manual occupations and
most will devote their energies to serving others
and to learning. The next gentration of middle
class Americans is destined to enjoy the un-
precedently rich life that the post-industrial,
national urban society will offer. Our central
domestic task now is deliberately to invent ways
of extending those opportunities to those groups
that future history threatens to exclude.*
                                    Professor Melvin M. Webber
                                    The Post-City Age

Now
  When her parents were gone, Edith Leete looked at
him and said brightly, "Well, sir, we're on our own.
You've been dropping hints that you used to consider
yourself quite a gourmet, quite an amateur cook. In fact,
you project an air of dissatisfaction that the art of the
chef has been so automated. Very well, this apartment
sports a kitchen. I challenge you to whomp up a home-
cooked meal."
  He was taken aback. "I haven't even seen your
kitchen. Besides, I'm not sure you'd have the ingredients
for—"
  "Ha!" she said. "Trying to weasel out."
  "That does it," he told her. "You're on. But just one
minute. There was one thing I wanted to ask your father,
and got sidetracked."

"What was that?"

"I still don't get this paying a top scientist or a manager of a large industry no more than the most common laborer. You answer by saying that there's abundance for all. But that can't be true. Suppose, for instance, that your plant manager wants a large establishment where he can entertain. He wants servants, a special cook, maids, a gardener or two. He wants a yacht, and the necessary crew to service it. He's willing to work for these luxuries, to contribute more than the janitor does. Then why shouldn't he be able to? Don't tell me the janitor can have these things too. Obviously, that's ridiculous."

Something came to him and he looked about the room, scowling. "By the way, I haven't seen a single sign of a servant here. But obviously an establishment of this size requires them. I suppose a man of your father's prominence, with his red ribbon decoration, and your mother with her blue, rate a place like this and the servants to take care of it."

She was amused. "No servants," she said. "Even in your time they were rapidly disappearing. Who but the very rich could afford them any more? Besides, in a status-symbol society such as yours, where plumbers called themselves sanitary engineers, rat-catchers called themselves rodent officers, and no worker called himself that, but a technician: who but the most incompetent was going to take a servant's job? On a national poll, way back in the 1940s, when asked if they belonged to the working class, the middle class, or the upper class, over eighty percent of Americans claimed to be middle class. And who, in the middle class, would demean themselves to a position as a servant?"

"But you can't run an establishment like this without—"

"Yes you can. We've simply gone far beyond the equipment you had, and you already had quite a bit of it. Dishes are returned to the auto-kitchen to be washed, sweeping, mopping, dusting and window washing are automatic. Your room is somewhat different, due to special requirements involving your convalescence, but in the rest of the bedrooms of this apartment the bed slides into the wall during the day, and when it emerges, to your order, it is made up—with fresh bedding, of course. Oh, I don't mean that there aren't little odds and ends to be done around the place. When some such comes up, whoever is handy does it, and it might well be father, rather than mother or me.

"Servants were all very well when you had to wash laundry by hand, do the dishes, cook, mop the floors and all the rest of it. Now they'd be a bother to have around. Even gardeners. The true lover of a garden wants to do it himself. Those gigantic estates in Victorian England gave more pleasure to the gardeners than to the owner."

"Such gardens were a pleasure to behold, believe me. I'm sorry to see them disappear from the world."

"They haven't disappeared. They're more lavish than ever, but now they're public and everyone can appreciate them, not just some duke who inherited his title and estate, or a millionaire who inherited his wealth."

"All right, so you have no more servants—"

"Just a minute. No personal servants. A scientist, a hi-ranking engineer, various different important officials or professionals, have assistants. Obviously, a doctor needs nurses and other technicians, a scientist needs lab workers, the engineer needs junior engineers for some of the more routine work, and perhaps all of these need secretaries—"

"You mean in this whole building, some five thousand apartments, there isn't a single servant?"

"No personal servants. There are quite a few maintenance workers, various specialists and technicians down in the restaurant division, nurses in the building's hospital, that sort of thing."

"All right," he said. "So the manager of an industry neither has nor wants servants. Suppose he wants to throw a big bash?"

"Fine. We have automated bars, auto-tables to produce any food required; any music he wishes comes through

Tri-Di depth screens. What is the need for a handful of flunkies—other than for the ostentatious display of wealth?"

"But the yacht and its crew?"

"If a citizen likes yachting, he can join a yachting club and participate, sharing in the work as well as the pleasure. Surely that's not new to you. When you were a boy, didn't you used to have yacht clubs? Weren't the yachts often crewed by enthusiasts who came from ultra-wealthy families? You might well have a multimillionaire's son pulling on a rope, setting the jib, or doing the cooking down in the galley. It was an indication of reality when it came to such things as sports. Even your billionaires, your top executives, the President of the United States himself, used to take fishing trips up into Canada, or wherever, and glory in being completely away from their flunkies. They loved to do their own cooking, make up their own beds, wash up the dishes, sweep out the log cabin in which they were staying."

"All right," Julian sighed. "For once, I largely agree with you. My grandfather had an estate out on Long Island that must have been staffed by more than a hundred. There comes a point of diminishing returns. You have to build a new wing, or a new building, to house the servants of the servants. More than ninety percent of the food and drink consumed on that estate was put away by the servants. It was like an overgrown resort hotel. God only knows what the old boy got out of it. Probably the satisfaction of knowing his place was larger than that of one of the Vanderbilt family who lived across the road."

Edie said, "Well, into the kitchen, chef." She stood to lead the way.

He followed, protesting. "I'm used to all my own equipment. You can't work in a strange kitchen. It throws you off. Why don't we eat some of this canned food of—"

She turned her head in indignation. "Canned! Do you think we're barbarians?"

"Well, frozen, or whatever."

"Ha," she said. "Some gourmet you turned out to be. Didn't your taste tell you? Everything you've eaten in

178

this house, sir, came out of the kitchens freshly cooked and piping hot, split seconds after you ordered it."

He couldn't help taking in the feminine narrowness of waist, the roundness of haunch, as he followed her. She was a superbly proportioned young woman.

He said, "Some dishes, most dishes, can't be cooked in split seconds. A fine roast—"

"You'd be surprised at the evolution of cooking, with the new electronic devices," she said, pretending huffiness. "However, those dishes that still require time you order in advance and they are served when you are ready."

The kitchen actually held few surprises for Julian West, though it did hold a few. For instance, though there was an extravagantly wide variety of spices and herbs, readily at hand, there was no refrigerator and no pantry. There was an unbelievable collection of pots, pans, skillets and all the rest of the paraphernalia of the chef, but except for a few specialized mixing bowls, olivewood salad bowls and such, no dishes. The collection of knives, cooking forks and spoons, and wooden salad and stirring spoons was excellent, but at first there was seemingly not even a garbage can, though he soon came upon the disposal chute.

He took his time looking about. The monstrous range was obviously electric and he supposed that he would have little difficulty in mastering it.

However, he said grumpily, "I don't like to cook on electricity. I prefer gas, or better still, a wood range burning hickory. The heat—"

She interrupted mildly. "We practically never use gas, kerosene, gasoline, oil, nor especially wood for heat, Jule. However, the electric stove has probably evolved since last you poked around in a kitchen. I'll be able to instruct you."

"All right. But what am I supposed to cook? Where's your deep freeze, your refrigerator?"

"Hold it, chef," she said, raising a hand. "You cook your specialty."

He had her now. He turned and put his hands on his

179

hips and narrowed his eyes. "Great. My specialty is couscous," he said triumphantly, and stretching a point.

"Couscous?"

"Couscous."

"What's it made of?"

"Couscous."

"Very funny. Just come over here to the delivery box."

The kitchen's delivery box was about the same size as
the one in the closet of his room. She touched the dial
and said, "We might as well order verbally. Now, what
do you need?"

He dug into his memory. It had been some six months
since his last visit to Morocco and some three months
since he had last cooked up a Moroccan repast for . . .
for Edith Bartlett and several others. No, he took it all
back. It had been more than thirty years.

"For only two of us I can cut the recipe in half. Say
one pound of couscous, dried, of course."

"Of course," she said, and into the order screen, "One
half-kilo of dried couscous."

The screen repeated it back to her in a somewhat
metallic voice.

Julian said, "You mean that they have such unusual
items as the Moroccan national dish on hand in your
ultramarket, or whatever you call it?"

"If not, certainly in the more elaborate central warehouses of the Julian West University City," she told him.
"You must realize that with five thousand apartments
in this building alone, among the exchange students I
imagine there are quite a few with North African and
Near Eastern backgrounds. Good eating is a great hobby
these days, sir. I rather doubt if you could name a food
ingredient we couldn't dial. Now, what else?"

"About a pound of mutton."

"A half-kilo of mutton," she repeated into the screen.

He looked over at the array of spices. "Salt, ginger,
pepper and wood of saffron, you have. Your mother
is quite an amateur. But we'll need a tablespoon of parsley, and one of chervil. I can chop them myself. Then
about five small onions and a couple of ounces of butter
and a loaf of dark bread."

She repeated the order into the screen and then looked at him.

"A steamer," he said. "I have to steam the couscous. But I see your mother has one, over there. Then I'll need a large, fairly flat bowl, preferably wooden."

"That's all?"

"That's all. How long do we have to wait for it?"

"Moments. Nothing else? What kind of utensils?"

"You eat it with your fingers. The fingers of your right hand, to be exact, if you don't want to run afoul of the rules set down by Mohammed in the Koran."

"Paradise forbid," she said. "What goes with it?"

"Well, actually, a good many things if you wish to have a real Moslem feast."

"Fine. Why don't we order the other dishes direct from the kitchens to save time?"

"Right you are." He again figured he had her now. "I'd say, start with Herrera soup, then Bistaela, pigeon pie, and we'll finish up with almond braewats for dessert."

She said, "You'd better order those, I'm not sure of the pronunciation."

He repeated into the screen and the screen acknowledged.

She said, "How long will it take for you to do the couscous?"

"About two hours."

She instructed the screen to deliver the ingredients immediately, and the prepared dishes in two hours, then turned back to him.

He shook his head in surprise and went over to the side table to select a chopping board, then a deep pot. Martha Leete had several steamers. He selected one.

She stood beside him and watched.

The things he had ordered were delivered and he began chopping the parsley and chervil and quartering the onions.

As he worked, he said, "I've been thinking over this everybody getting paid the same, and it occurs to me that even if I did agree that it makes sense in basic industry, there are some fields where it comes a cropper."

"Oh? What field, for instance?"

"Take the arts."

She looked at him.

He said decidedly, "Your whole setup doesn't apply to the arts. This method of evaluating everything by the hours of time required to produce it. All right, this is fine when you're dealing with wheat, iron, lumber, manufactured things, so forth and so on. But do you evaluate a Picasso's hour of painting with some young kid's who is still in art school? A John Steinbeck, after spending a lifetime learning his field, does a short story which takes him six hours to write. Does some tyro, fresh out of college where he edited the class magazine and who has about the same amount of talent as I do when it comes to literature, deserve the same recompense as Steinbeck?"

She was shaking her head in despair. "Jule, Jule."

He said in irritation, "It's a valid question. How do you pay a great artist, writer, musical composer, or whatever?"

"We don't."

He put down the chopping knife and remained in silence for a moment while he took up a butcher knife and cut the mutton into small chunks. He put the meat, the ginger, pepper, wood of saffron, parsley, chervil, the onion and a teaspoon of salt into a deep pot.

Then he said, "How do you turn the stove on? I want to boil this for about an hour and a quarter."

She showed him.

She said, "How can you pay an artist?"

He turned back to her. "That's what I'd like to know. If you tell me that he gets paid the same as everyone else, the same as the janitor, ditch digger, lab technician, or junior engineer, then why in the devil should he bother to beat his brains out producing masterpieces? Why not just sit back, and hope the computers will never tap him on the shoulder to assume a job, and go through life taking it easy?"

She paused a moment, as though trying to find words with which to express her thought. Finally, she said, "Fine. Take your Picasso. Under your society when he was a boy he lived in garrets and shacks having problems raising enough money to buy paints and canvas. Largely he was sneered at as a bohemian, an unacceptable, probably not quite clean crackpot, too stupid or lazy to go out and take a conformist factory, office, or sales position. He was lucky if he ate regularly. Very well, as he became successful, financially and otherwise, the attitude changed. Toward his last decades of life, his paintings, which he once could hardly give away, began to sell for tens and then hundreds of thousands of dollars. In his old age he was a millionaire and the darling of the intellectuals, pseudo and otherwise. Much the same story could be told of Steinbeck."

While she talked, he turned back to his task, saying, "Go on."

He took the plastic packet of couscous, noting that it looked like any other couscous he had never seen: based on semolina flour, of course, and somewhat resembling rice in appearance. It was the basic cereal of the Moslem world. He knew how to make it himself from the flour, and could have, but it was a time-exhausting process. He washed it by pouring a little water over it and running it off at once, which would cause the couscous to swell a bit. He let it set and waited on the mutton.

Edie was saying, "It's just as unacceptable to pay a young Picasso nothing as to pay an arrived Picasso millions. Art can't be evaluated in terms of dollars and cents, nor even in terms of man-hours. It's something transcendent. Cro-Magnon cave artists who accomplished some of the greatest paintings the world has ever seen, were not motivated by profit. They probably weren't even excused from the hunt and other tribal duties. They painted because they had to paint. Or take the ancestor of Steinbeck. He sat at the fire at night, this tribal storyteller, and told stories to the young—and to the old, for that matter. Stories about the tribe's heroes, their past disasters and triumphs, their religious myths. He was a storyteller by nature and it simply came out."

Julian was exasperated. "But look, what do you mean an artist isn't paid?"

"Simply that. He isn't paid for being a painter, a writer, a sculptor, a composer, or whatever. He does, of course, get his share of the national product, just as does everyone else, but he gets neither more nor less."

"Who decides whether he's an artist or not? Or whether he's a writer or not? In my day if an artist was successful the quality of his work came out in the sale of his paintings and in the price he received from them. A writer's popularity was easily estimated by the number of books he sold, a composer by the number of times his work was rendered."

"Nobody decides. Or possibly I should say everyone does."

"Oh, come on now, that makes no sense at all."

"Fine. Be quiet for a moment and I'll explain. A citizen has a feeling for painting and does it. He, or she, paints with metallic-acrylic paint, or with ink, pencil or watercolors having the same properties, on a presdwood-duplicator board. When the work is finished he submits it to the art division of the library banks and it is recorded and cross-indexed under the name of the artist, the subject, the medium, the school, with sub-information on the painting's size, the artist's popularity, and so forth."

"Now wait right there. How do you mean his popularity? How is that decided?"

"By the number of reproductions of his past paintings. Also on file in the library banks are all the critical comments ever made on his work."

"By whom? I mean, who are these critics?"

"Anybody who wants to write about him, either pro or con. Of course, little-known critics are unlikely to have their papers read, but a person checking on any given artist would be inclined to read what the better-known authorities have to say about him."

"All right, to get back to it. Suppose you want one of his originals?"

"How do you mean?"

"Well, a reproduction is all very fine but a real collector wants originals."

"Oh," she said. "I thought the metallic-acrylic on presdwood-duplicator board system had already been developed in the late 1960s, but now that I think about it, it was only being utilized in France. The thing is, Jule, that not even the artist can tell the difference between his original and the reproductions. They're identical."

"What does one of these reproductions cost?"

"A very small amount. The exact cost, in man-hours, of reproducing and framing it. There are a wide selection of frames, of course."

"And what does *he*, the artist, get out of it?"

She twisted her mouth characteristically. "We always get back to that, don't we? The profit involved. This is what he gets out of it. If enough of his paintings are reproduced for persons who want them, he receives an artist's white ribbon. If still more are demanded, he goes up to a blue ribbon. If a fabulous number are taken, he even wins the coveted red ribbon, the highest award the nation can give. A handful of artists carry the golden international ribbon, the equivalent, in our day, of being a Picasso."

He said, "From what your father has already told me, writers must be handled approximately the same way. That is, anybody at all can write anything from a short story or essay to a book and it's filed in the library banks. I suppose that if it's read sufficiently he gets his white ribbon, or better."

"Of course. And musical compositions the same."

"Who records the music?"

"The composer makes arrangements with an orchestra, band, jazz combo, or whatever, to make the original recording. From then on whoever wants to record it, in possibly some new arrangement, does, and those recordings, too, go into the musical division of the library banks. The number of times the composition is listened to is recorded by the computers and the composer wins his award if he becomes sufficiently popular."

"Who pays the orchestra?"

She smiled again. "They too are artists. How can you evaluate the work of an artist?"

"But it takes the better part of a lifetime to become, say, a great violinist."

"What better way to spend the better part of a lifetime?"

"So it's all amateur."

"You might call it that."

He turned back to his cooking and took up the steamer he had selected. He said, "I'll need some cheesecloth or muslin. The holes in this steamer are too large, the couscous would fall through."

She ordered it for him.

He moistened the cheesecloth, put half of the couscous in it and bound a dampened piece of the cloth around where the pots met to prevent the steam from escaping. He put the steamer on the stove and in a few minutes added the balance of the cereal. He returned to the table at which she sat, watching him.

Julian said, "Look. Suppose a young fellow is a natural born violinist with all sorts of promise in the musical world. All right, then, when—what did your father call it—Muster Day comes along, he's eligible to be selected by the computers for some job, eh?"

"That's right. When he arrives at the age of twenty-five, he is eligible to be selected for any job for which he might be qualified. And he remains on the rolls until he is forty-five, the usual retirement age."

"All right. Suppose that the computers select him to be a plumber, or whatever. He'd have to take the job? Give up his music? Give up his chance of winning a gold ribbon as an internationally famed violinist?"

She was amused. "Theoretically, yes. In actuality, it would be all but impossible. Always keep in mind that only about two percent of our people are needed in production, distribution, communications and so forth. His musical abilities would be in the data banks, in his aptitude quotient, and his talent would undoubtedly be noted and taken into consideration. But there is another aspect. Most really outstanding artists show their embryonic talent early in life and begin training as youngsters. If their greatest interests while they are still in their school years are connected with the arts, it us unlikely that they will run up the aptitude quotient in some other field that would lead to their being selected to be a . . . plumber. If, in spite of all this, your potential world-famous musician was selected, please remember that his duties would tie him down for only six hours a day, four days a week. Many an artist, in all artistic fields, in your own times had to work at least that many hours. Besides, I suspect that even if he was selected the first year, on Muster Day, that he would soon be bumped."

"Bumped?"

"Remember, jobs are at a premium. There would be a good many mechanically inclined men and women, coming of work age each Muster Day, who would just love that job of his. When the computers select you for a job, you don't automatically retain it for the full twenty years until you reach forty-five. If somebody else—possibly with new techniques learned in school—comes along who has a higher aptitude quotient than you, you might well be bumped."

"If you want to be or not?"

"Yes. The computers select the best person available for the job. If you stop being the best, they bump you. In fact, precious few selected employees last the full twenty years. Technical changes are too rapid." She laughed abruptly.

"What's funny?"

"I was remembering father being bumped some years ago. He was indignant."

"What happened?"

"He had fallen behind in new developments in medicine. He had devoted too much of his time to his fascination with your case. As it was, he returned to his studies and was able to be selected again two years later."

"But he's still practicing now? He must be well over the forty-five-year retirement age."

"Oh, father retired from active practice years ago. He is now a student and also connected with research."

"Here we go again. You said that retirement age was forty-five. But now you tell me your father is connected with research and evidently is studying to keep up with the latest developments. When do you people actually stop working and retire?"

"Why, never."

The exasperation returned to him. He checked the couscous steamer and the mutton before turning back to her.

"You don't make sense. First you tell me only two per cent of the population is needed to do the work. Then you tell me the working age is between twenty-five and forty-five. Now you tell me nobody really retires. Doesn't anybody ever get tired?"

She laughed. "Jule, Jule. Did Einstein ever retire? Did Casals? Did Winston Churchill—until he reached the point where his physical and mental faculties were completely eroded away? Father will continue his interests in medicine and connected research until the end."

She switched a bit and said, "When your work is also your hobby and your play, then you never really retire. When the computers bump you from your job, or when you reach forty-five, you continue on what you might call an amateur basis. Just remember that your work is also your greatest pleasure, in this society."

"Well how in the devil are you going to continue farming, as an amateur, after you've been bumped or reach forty-five?"

She laughed at him still once again. "My basic interests in the field go far beyond supervising a bank of tractors, Jule. I've studied various facets of agronomy since I was a child, pleasuring away at my little gardens, my flowers, my plant mutations, my—"

"Your what?"

She was rueful. "I had ambitions, evidently beyond my talents. I was never selected by the computers to . . . well, let us just say that I was not able to be one of the two percent selected for the type of work I wanted to do most, but was lucky enough to be chosen for a less prestigious position, perhaps, in a related field."

"Good grief," Julian protested. "Two percent! Practically nobody gets to do what they want to."

"Don't misunderstand. You said something a day or

two ago that we got sidetracked from, before being able to answer you. You were indignant that such a small percentage of the people had to carry the load and do all the work, as you put it. In actuality, as you see now, they're the envied members of our society. But the rest don't sit around idle. We continue to work, if you wish to call it work—and then you've got to come to definitions about the difference between work and play—as amateurs, as students. There are precious few real idlers today, Jule. From earliest childhood the computers find what you *like* to do, and you are given every opportunity to do it."

"Suppose what you like to do is get drunk, make a glutton of yourself at table, chase women, loaf on the beach getting a suntan?"

She smiled her slow smile. "We've no objection to relaxation, in whatever way you like to relax. But given the educational system which we have today, there are few, few people who haven't found, and very early in life, an interest greater than loafing. I think that you'll find that the chronic loafers of your period were not happy people, they were frustrated people."

He shook his head, took the steamed couscous from the range, poured it into a bowl with a half-pint of water and a couple of teaspoons of salt and left it to dry a little. He checked the mutton, added the onions and put it back to boil.

He said, "Look, this new method of reproducing paintings so that even the artist can't tell the original from a copy. How about older paintings, old masters and that sort of thing?"

"They can't be copied so well, of course. You have to use the new mediums and the special board."

"What's happened to the great art of the past? Suppose someone had in his possession a, well, Rembrandt. How could he profit by it?"

"By donating it to a museum. The whole nation would be grateful."

"Ummm, but suppose he wanted to profit personally?"

She hesitated for a long moment before saying slowly, "Jule, we just seem to exist in different reference frames.

189

In the past, collecting art objects, owning them, was a status symbol. Only the very rich could afford such things as Rembrandts. Now we scorn status symbols. I would think very few people would want to have such a treasure hidden away from his fellow citizens so that none except he and his friends could see it."

"But you couldn't sell such an art object?"

"To whom? And how would you be paid for it? Possibly you could trade it to someone else for some other art object or objects that you preferred, but I'm afraid that everyone else would think that you were somewhat anti-social."

He thought about that, inwardly fuming. Then, "Look, is the whole world structured the way you are?"

"Why no. United America is the most advanced nation, if you could call it a nation, in the old sense of the word. But Common Europe has almost the same basic socio-economic system and—"

"But there are still some countries that use money?"

"Yes, the more backward areas in Africa and the Near and Far East, in particular, haven't as yet achieved a level where our advances are practical."

"Then if this hypothetical owner of a Rembrandt or two would take them to such countries he could sell them?"

"Why, I suppose so."

"And live on the proceeds, in comparative luxury, with servants and so forth? That is, assuming that he didn't like the setup in America."

"It seems a rather far-out trend of thought, but I can think of no reason why he couldn't."

Julian put the couscous back on to steam a bit more, then took it off, mixed it in the flat wooden dish, put the mutton in the middle, and poured over it the onions and a little liquid from the cooking pot.

"There we are," he said.

"I'll get the other dishes from the delivery," she told him.

He showed her how to eat Moslem style, using the right hand, the left only for breaking bread. She caught on quickly and they sat on opposite sides of the table, using the wooden dish community-style.

She congratulated him. "It's absolutely wonderful."

So were the Herrara soup, the pigeon pie and the braewats, he discovered to his chagrin. He suspected that they could have ordered just as good a couscous from the community kitchens.

She looked over at him in amused fashion. "You know," she said, "it's a strange experience for me to be sitting here with you."

He took a small piece of bread between the thumb and two first fingers of his right hand and dipped it into the dish. The bread soaked up some of the liquid, while his fingers took up some of the more solid stuff. He popped it into his mouth.

"How is that?"

She smiled. "I must have been all of ten years old when I first saw you. Father took me. You were stretched out in a glass compartment and looked exactly as you do now."

"I would think it a somewhat chilling sight for a ten-year-old youngster."

"To the contrary, I thought it very romantic, the whole story. I thought of you as a handsome, charming prince who would someday awaken and—"

"And?"

"And take me away with you. You see, I've had a terrible crush on you ever since I was that little girl. It even grew, when I reached my teens."

XVIII

The masters of the government of the United States are the combined capitalists and manufacturers of the United States. It is written over every intimate page of the record of Congress, it is written all through the history of conferences at the White House, that the suggestions of economic policy in this country have come from one source, not from many sources. . . . Suppose you go to Washington and try to to get at your government. You will always find that while you are politely listened to, the men really consulted are the men who have the biggest stake—the big bankers, the big manufacturers, the big masters of commerce, the heads of railroad corporations and of steamboat corporations. . . . The government of the United States at present is a foster child of the special interests.

> Woodrow Wilson
> *The New Freedom*

Then

The dream was a new one but came back with the usual clarity with which he revisited the past in sleep.

Julian West was the last of the group to arrive at the small dining room on the second floor of the Knickerbocker-Links Club. The others had finished eating and were sitting around informally over brandy or port. He had stopped off at the bar to pick up a snifter of Glenlivet. The club was the only place on Manhattan with which he was familiar where he could find the seldom-exported nectar of Scotland.

Jim Lynch, Andrew Scott and Hooker Armstrong were at the table and Julian walked over and stood there, glass in hand.

The broker, Lynch, looked up and nodded to him.

Hooker Armstrong, who was a distant relative of Julian West, said, "Hello, Jule."

Scott, a heavyset, harsh and florid man was saying, "Heard that Bernie Koch was proposed for this club the other day."

Jim Lynch grunted. "Jew, isn't he? One of these days somebody'll propose a Negro."

"And when that happens," Scott rasped, "I begin spending my time at the Metropolitan of The Brook."

Julian West took a sip of his drink and said, "As a matter of fact, with all this race stuff in the wind, it might be a good idea to have a, say, Thurgood Marshall in the membership. Very democratic."

Hooker Armstrong shot a glance of disgust at him. Julian subsided. He had a reputation, at least partly undeserved, for being a liberal and hence was seldom listened to in this type of discussion.

Armstrong said, "Bernie Koch isn't a bad chap to do business with."

Jim Lynch folded his hands over his belly. "Nobody ever said otherwise. But there's never been a Jew in the Knickerbocker-Links."

Armstrong said, "They've got a couple of the Warburgs in The Century." He savored the bouquet of his wine.

Jim Lynch grunted again. "Yes, and they had that bastard Franklin D. Roosevelt, too."

Davis Melville and Mark Ingersol came over from the side where they had been sitting and took chairs at the table.

Melville, next to Julian West the youngest man present, nodded at Julian and said, "Why so glum-looking, Jule?"

Julian shook his head. "I don't know. I'm having second thoughts about the Diversified thing, I suppose."

Hooker Armstrong shot a quick look at him. "What do you mean, second thoughts?"

Mark Ingersol snapped, "It's in the bag. It's too late for second thoughts now. We've got Percy by the balls."

Jim Lynch grinned. "And what's more, we're squeezing them."

Julian knocked back the rest of his drink unhappily. "That's what I mean. This overhead tender is going to push Bob Percy to the wall. I went to school with Bob. We were fairly good friends in those days. He's fighting this forced merger. He's sticking everything he's got into it, and everything Janice has as well."

Andrew Scott said, "To coin a phrase, business is business, or did somebody else say that before?" He beamed at his own wit.

"I still don't like it," Julian said. "We should give poor Bob some possible out. As it is, everything he's put into Diversified will go down the drain."

"You should have thought of that earlier," Hooker Armstrong growled. "This group of ours wasn't organized to be a schoolyears buddy sympathy league. There are six of us. Suppose each put up a howl every time a former friend stood in our way and might get hurt a little? However, if you want, you can drop out of this particular takeover. The rest of us can handle it alone. You want out?"

Julian West paused.

Melville said, "Well, Jule?"

Julian West shook his head. "I suppose not. It's the biggest deal we've undertaken. It's too good to let go by."

Andrew Scott looked at Jim Lynch and gruffed, "Now that's over, how about the reports on the public offer?"

The broker took up the briefcase which sat on the table before him, opened it and shuffled through some papers. He smiled. "Mark was right. We've got them by the balls."

Later, still unhappy, Julian West drifted into the bar again.

The white-jacketed Desmond said briskly, "Another of the same, Mr. West?"

"I suppose so," Julian said. He climbed up on one of the stools.

The bartender took up the bottle of Glenlivet and a brandy snifter glass and poured a double charge. He said, "A little ice, sir?"

"Desmond, you are a barbarian. Anyone who would put ice, water or anything else into prehistoric unblended

Scotch like this would vote communist. Where this precious stuff comes from, they make it with the intention of it being sniffed and sipped at room temperature, and they know what they're doing."

The other said, "Yes, sir. However, there's room temperature and room temperature. And the room temperature up there in Scotland, where when it gets cold they put on heavier underwear and sweaters instead of turning on central heating, isn't the same as here in the Knickerbocker-Links Club."

Julian West thought about that. "You know, Desmond, you might have a point there. It never occurred to me. However, even in Scotland the room temperature doesn't get to the point of ice. Though, come to think of it, it damn near does."

Bert Melville came up to the bar and stood next to Julian's stool. He said to the bartender, "A double Martell, and quickly."

"Yes, Mr. Melville," Desmond said.

Julian looked at the newcomer. "I didn't know you were in town, Bert. Davis is in the small dining room with Jim Lynch and some of the others."

Melville took up the glass of brandy Desmond served him and threw it back.

He said, "You were a friend of Bob and Janice Percy, weren't you?"

"How do you mean *were*? I still am—outside of business hours."

"He blew the top of his head off this morning."

XIX

This country, with its institutions, belongs to the
people who inhabit it. Whenever they shall grow
weary of the existing government, they can exer-
cise their constitutional right of amending it, or
their revolutionary right to dismember or over-
throw it.

Abraham Lincoln
First Inaugural Address

Now

Julian West awoke at first dawn. He tried to turn over
and get back to sleep but couldn't. He finally gave up,
arose and went through the routine of bath and shaving
and then ordered fresh clothing the way Edith Leete
had shown him.

He didn't expect any of his host family to be up at
this hour and went into the sanctum and beyond it to
the breakfast nook to order himself coffee on the auto-
table, or whatever they called it.

Back in the sanctum with the coffee, for a while he
stood at the window and stared out at the still strange
University City. It was becoming lighter.

His mind went back to the evening before and his discussion with Edie.

He had asked her what had happened to the old rich,
to people of his own class, when the big changes came
about, and it had been her opinion that they had become actually better off than before. To begin with, they
they had become some of the most valuable members of
the community since they averaged much better educa-
tions than most. To use an extreme example, did he think
for a moment that the queen of England did not have
the abilities to hold down a very serious job under any
socio-economic system? Or a scion of the Rockefeller,
Dupont, Mellon, or Ford families? They had started off
in the new society with an advantage, not a disadvantage.

They were, she repeated, better off than before. Under

the old society, pollution of air and water had affected them as well as everyone else. So had traffic congestion, the littering of highways and countryside. They too were the victims of the growing crime rate. They too wound up eating adulterated food. Their children too were exposed to LSD and marijuana and to the excess of the youth of the mid-twentieth century. A millionaire's son, indeed, was more apt to cop out and become a hippie or yippy than the son of an Appalachian poor white.

Besides, she had insisted, when you have a community where the Lodges speak only to Cabots and the Cabots speak only to God, you have a limited community—limited intellectually in particular—with which to have intercourse. In a world where all are equally well to do and all are as educated as their abilities permit, everyone's life is enriched.

She had thought of an example. Back during the Romantic period of British poetry, the three outstanding poets were Byron, Shelley and Keats. Bryon was a lord, Shelley a baron, Keats from a fairly well-to-do middle-class family. But how many of their contemporaries, born into the ranks of the poor and having to work, perhaps, in the textile mills of Manchester, were potential poets who would have added to the literature of the English-speaking world had they been able to possess the leisure time enjoyed by the big three?

And he had asked her what had happened to the cold war and to the Soviet Union and the competition between the two great super-powers.

War, she had told him, already no longer made sense in his own day, particularly between nuclear powers, and it was rapidly coming to the point where all could become nuclear powers. And the warning systems, the interception of missiles by anti-missile missiles, shelters, and preparations for retaliation were all obvious nonsense. No matter where the bombs were exploded, high in the sky, by anti-missile missiles, or on their targets, and no matter who launched them first and no matter how successfully, all the world would die from fallout.

Besides, the original reasons for war had faded away. The colonial empires, fought over so long by the Euro-

pean powers, proved unprofitable by the twentieth century and were given their freedom. Wars for sources of
raw materials such as petroleum and ores fell off when,
with modern technology and fusion power, the import of
raw materials became less necessary for the industrial
powers. And when trade lessened, finally, in the com-
puter-automated second industrial revolution where each
nation advanced to the point of producing its own, it was
no longer a cause for strife.

The Soviet Union? As production goals were finally
met first in the more advanced communist countries,
then the others, the Soviet bureaucracy became ever
more of a has-been. The old bolshevik type began to
disappear, inefficient in that they were politicians rather
than technicians, and the need in an industrial world is
for scientists, engineers, and technicians rather than party
hacks. A number equal to the western meritcrats arose
as the Soviets too began to utilize the computers and the
new educational methods to determine who was most
suited to hold down any given job. And, of course,
with the meeting of the production goals, the old needs
for limiting consumer consumption and devoting as much
as possible to industrial expansion dribbled away. The
Soviet Complex, a merging of most of the communist
countries, also became affluent.

"But there is still no world government?" he had asked
her.

She had shaken her head. There were still some differences between the East and West but they were rapidly reaching the point where the only thing that made
sense was an eventual world government. They had it
in embryo, based on the cosmocorps, especially in the
international communications and transportation net-
works, which were supranational. And such institutions
as the international data banks which had superseded
the national data banks. And such institutions as international higher education—

He had interrupted her there. "International education?"

"Higher education. Suppose that the greatest authority
on the anthropology of the area once called the Balkans

was a Bulgarian living in Sophia and you were interested in studying the subject. Wouldn't you wish to study under him?"

"I don't speak Bulgarian."

"Remember, the computer translators can translate any language into any other." She hesitated at that point, as though to say something further, but then didn't.

They had touched upon a few other items that had at least mildly surprised him. They were no longer bothered by such insects as flies and mosquitoes. Their clothes and the paint on vehicles and buildings were all impregnated with a chemical, odorless and colorless, which repelled insects. Bugs no longer had to be sprayed or otherwise killed, but lived out their lives and helped perpetuate the balance of nature—but they could no longer pester man.

Nor was there any longer obesity, nor unnatural thinness. Advances in balanced diet, and in psychotherapy and the nature of the glands, had eliminated both the abnormally and unhealthily fat and their opposite numbers. Julian had protested a bit at that on the grounds that everyone would soon look alike, but she laughed him to scorn. Some people were taller, some were shorter, some had stockier or more delicate bodies, and all, of course, had different facial characteristics, color of hair and eyes, and so forth and so on.

Yes, it had been quite an evening. She had mentioned no more about her crush on him, but the fact that she had said it at all increased his interest in her as a beautiful and desirable woman, beyond being one of his hostesses who was going far beyond the call of duty, as he saw it, to welcome him back to existence.

Now, as he stood at the window, something came to him. He put his empty coffee cup down on a table and went over to the screen at which Doctor Leete had sat the other day to demonstrate how news was spread. He scowled down at it, then took the chair that sat there. Sooner or later, he was going to have to get the hang of utilizing the national, no, now they were international, data banks.

199

He dialed information and immediately a voice responded, "Information."

He wondered why anyone should dial for what they wanted from the library data banks when this was so much easier. Perhaps it was because a certain amount of human effort was required to handle these screens on a verbal basis and they seemed to go overboard these days saving human effort when at all possible.

He said carefully, "I understand that you have complete records on . . . on everybody. I would like to have information on an Edith Bartlett: if she is still alive and, if so, where she is, if she is married, that sort of thing."

The voice said, "Edith Bartlett. What is her transceiver I.D. number?"

He said, "I don't know her transceiver number."

"When and where was she born? Does she have a middle name?"

He gave that information.

The voice said, "Do you wish a condensation of her complete dossier, or all information available to the public? Or, if you have the proper priority authorization, do you wish her complete dossier?"

He hesitated, not being quite sure where he stood. But obviously these data banks would not release all private information to just anybody at all. Doctors, police officials, government authorities and so forth would undoubtedly have priorities to dip further into these so-called dossiers than just any Tom, Dick or Harry. Or so he assumed—and hoped.

He said, "A condensation, please."

"In English?"

"Why . . . why, of course."

A printed page, looking much the same as the news reports of the other day, flashed onto the library screen.

It was all there. Just about everything he had known of Edith Bartlett and quite a bit more. He read the first page, then flicked the button he had seen Leete activate to turn pages on the screen. There were pictures of her at various ages. He spent long minutes at the one when she was at the age he had seen her last and hesitated before going on. But it was inevitable.

All right. She had married five years after his descent into stasis. He looked at the face of her husband. Clean-cut, aristocratic, undoubtedly a typical member of Julian's own class, and Edith's. She had had two children, one boy, one girl. There were pictures. Neither of them looked like Edith, to his thinking. There were other details.

Many, many of them and he could not help but wonder where the data banks had acquired it all. But then, Leete had said, all news went into the banks, all statistics, all medical information. He wondered how complete the full, restricted dossier must be.

And then, of course, finally he came to the end.

She had died approximately seven years before. He didn't recognize the name of the disease, if it were a disease. Evidently some new medical term.

He flicked the set off, momentarily, and leaned back in the chair, his eyes closed. And once again the story of the doctor's last fistfight came to him.

She had married five years after Pillsbury had put him under. What could he have expected? She had been normal, beautiful, alive. Undoubtedly she had come to know that his awakening had to be postponed far beyond the time originally estimated—if it were possible to revive him at all. He wondered whether she had even remembered his name, by the time her last years were upon her. A husband, two children, a new way of life. Had she even remembered his name? She had died some twenty-five years after his going into stasis. A quarter of a century.

He shook his head and stared at the screen, then reached out for the information dial again. In turn, he dialed his own name, that of his parents, and finally that of one of his friends, taken at random: Roy London, of whom he had dreamed the other night in the Chicago riots matter.

Yes, it was all there. As complete as the dossier of Edith. Things about his own life that he had forgotten; things he had never known about his parents, the Wild Wests. He wondered vaguely at an international data bank that would contain such information. His mother and father had died half a century ago. Who cared about such information as the fact that his father had once been a champion skindiver, or had won this automobile rally, or that? Of what possible interest was it today that his mother had been expelled from three different girls' schools? But then, come to think of it, the Wild Wests had been prominent members of the jet set. If a present-day writer desired accurate information on the period, he would not have to stir out of his home to research it.

The section of his own dossier which dealt with his being put into stasis by Pillsbury and finally being revived a third of a century later was so technical that he gave it up. Otherwise, he had little difficulty with the stories of Edith Bartlett, his parents and Roy London. There were a few words, a few allusions to technical matters he didn't understand, but largely he was on home ground. London was the worst. Evidently he continued to write into the 1980s and some of his papers were on subjects that left Julian West blank. He couldn't more than skim them.

Roy London, he found, was still alive and currently living, retired, in Costa Rica. He would be about seventy, Julian decided. Seventy! But one day he would have to look up the one-time journalist. It came to him that in many respects Roy London would be in a better position to brief the newly awakened Julian West on the new world than were the Leetes. Edith, for instance, had not even been born when he went into stasis, and the older Leetes must have been in their early twenties or even younger.

The library screen fascinated him.

He thought for a moment, dialed information again, and said, "I would like a résumé of the space program. That is, what has transpired in the exploration of space."

"How complete a résumé, please?"

"Why . . . why, say, about a few thousand words."

A paper faded onto the screen before him. However, within moments he was at sea. The terminology baffled him. It was all he could do to recognize two words out of three. He leaned back in disgust and thought about it. He could get a dictionary, of course, but it would take forever.

Finally, he dialed information again and said, "I would like a résumé of the space program for young people. A juvenile report."

"For what age group, please?"

He began to say fifteen, but then remembered how precocious teenagers were even in his own time, and said, "For a child of twelve."

He had trouble enough as it was.

He hurried through the early origins, through the launching of the Sputniks and Explorers, and through the material on Yuri Gagarin and John Glenn and the other firsts into space. He had lived through that.

When he got to the section on the Apollo lunar-landing program he took a deep breath and muttered, "So they made it."

He read about the early set-downs with their EASEP—Early Apollo Scientific Experiments Payload—scientific equipment, including a solar-powered seismometer to check on moonquakes and a mirror to bounce back to Earth a laser beam to measure the distance from home. And of the later expeditions with their more sophisticated payload called ALSEP. Toward the end of the Apollo landings they were staying as long as seventy-two hours and were at work on a shelter for more permanent occupancy.

Meanwhile, the Russians were still evidently in the game. If he understood the report correctly, they hadn't been particularly interested in the so-called race to the moon. That had been largely in American minds. The Russians had decided to leave landing on the moon for a time when they had more sophisticated equipment, and the equivalent of a lifeboat, in case of tragedy. They had concentrated, instead, on an orbiting laboratory, a space platform. And began its earliest stages at the same time the Americans were embarked on the Apollo projects.

They had evidently flung specially designed spaceships, not all of them manned, into orbit and then assembled them in such manner that the interiors, once largely devoted to fuel, became the living quarters of the sizeable crews. They had evidently been the first to send up scientists and to get orbital telescopes into action. The figures on that set Julian West back. A two-hundred inch telescope in space turned out to be one thousand times as effective as one based on Earth. Knowledge of the other planets and deep space was expanded many fold overnight, since foreign bodies appeared ten times closer and at least a hundred times sharper.

But already he was beginning to run into trouble with terminology. "This is for twelve-year-olds?" he muttered.

A Russian maneuver had made the first breakthrough in cooperation, although once the prestige of being first on Luna had been gained by the Americans they seemed to be far from loath. The Soviets had invited the scientists of other countries, including the United States, to take advantage of the facilities offered by Satellite City.

"Satellite City!" Julian ejaculated.

The Americans could do nothing less than make equal offers to share the experiments taking place in their rapidly expanding moonbase. It seemed to develop that men living in a tiny moon shelter, or in the cramped quarters of a space platform, are not inclined toward nationalism. The spirit of comradeship that sprang up between American astronauts and Russian cosmonauts went far toward influencing populations at home toward the same trend and, in time, reluctant governments toward a détente.

However, there seemed to have been a fall-off in the speed of the race into space following the Apollo program and the launching of the Russian space program. The same reaction against the military machines, in the Soviet Complex as well as in the West, had evidently applied to the space programs as well. Appropriations fell off abruptly.

But even while the moonbase and Satellite City were being developed, the other planets were not ignored. Both Russians and Americans sent probes to Venus and Mars, achieving soft landings on both. And the Americans were first to send their Venus-Mercury "minitaur" to Mercury by using the Venusian gravitational force to whip a satellite on toward the small planet. In 1976 several so-called grand tour flights to the outer planets were achieved, since Jupiter, Saturn, Uranus and Neptune were aligned in such a way from 1976 to 1978 that a single craft would fly by all of them.

By now, Julian West was running into such technical terms that he could barely follow. He muttered in disgust, once more, "This is for twelve-year-olds?"

Edith Leete entered the room and said, "Good morning, Jule. You're up early. What are you after?" She walked over toward him.

He looked up, scowling. "I was trying to check up on what has happened in space in the past third of a century."

She frowned and hesitated. "Don't you find it a bit . . . technical?"

He laughed self-deprecation. "I'm reading an account for juveniles and refuse to admit the age group. I'm already out of my depth."

She said, "We could have answered any questions you had."

He flicked off the set. "I thought I might get it quicker this way. Every time we start talking about the developments since my time we get off on side roads and sometimes never get back to the subject we started with. But, all right, what are the latest developments in space?"

"It's not really my field, but briefly, with the coming of nuclear fusion engines—"

"Nuclear fusion engines? You mean you fire off nuclear fusion engines into the atmosphere to lift off from Earth now?"

"No, certainly not. The ships are assembled in space, in orbit either around Earth or the moon. Using fusion power, we can reach even the outer planets in comparatively short periods. In fact, a base on Titan is currently being planned."

"Titan?"

"The largest of the Saturn satellites, it's almost as big as Mars."

"How about Mars? Has there been a landing?"

"The first one, quite a time ago. There's a preliminary base there now. With the speed the nuclear engines give us, we can shuttle back and forth to Mars in no time at all."

"Was there life?"

"Intelligent life? No. And nobody really expected it. But there are some very primitive life forms, lichens and so on."

"Well, look. How is the base on the moon? What turned up there, finally?"

"There are several settlements on the moon now. Various experiments going on in regard to whether a permanent Luna City should be largely underground or—"

"Luna *City!* How many people are up there now?"

"Why hundreds. Possibly thousands. I really don't know. We could check with the data banks."

He was staring. "Thousands! You mean you can send air, water, food, fuel and all the rest for thousands of people on the moon?"

"Of course not. No need to. Remember, we have unlimited power now, with nuclear fusion. Water is present in various minerals on the moon. They extract it and break some of it down into oxygen and hydrogen, for air and for fuel. Our chemists are able to synthesize most foods we need from such basics as lime, phosphates, carbon dioxide, water and ammonia. Also, on the moon we have hydroponic farming. There is no real problem. The colonies are largely self-sufficient. But look, Jule, mother and father are in the breakfast room. Would you like to eat with us?"

He got up to follow her, saying, "I got the impression from the juvenile report I was reading that the dash into space had more or less slowed to a walk after the early successes."

"It sped up later again. It was a bit ridiculous to spend so much money on space research when people were still hungry on earth. But when we had solved all our production problems, research into all the sciences really began to get under way. You'd be surprised."

"No I wouldn't," he said dryly. "I've long since got

over the ability to be surprised at anything anymore."

She turned to lead the way, but he hesitated. "Edie," he said.

"Yes?" She turned back again.

"Before you came in, before I looked up space travel, I checked out the dossiers of some of the people close to me."

"Oh?"

"Among others, that of Edith Bartlett—my fiancée."

Compassion came into her face, as it so often did when something more than usually upsetting to him developed.

He took a breath and said, "She died about seven years ago."

She laid a hand on his arm. "Yes, I know."

He looked at her. "How do you mean?"

"She was my maternal aunt. I was named after her."

"Your aunt! You mean your mother—"

"Yes, Edith's sister. You met her two or three times when she was only a girl."

"Of course! How stupid of me. I remember when I first saw her that she reminded me of someone. I didn't really know her. She was usually away at school."

"It was through you, actually, that she met father. She had gone out to the laboratory where you were kept, with Edith. Father, as a young medical technician, was already working on the project."

It all came back, all over again, in an agonizing awareness and he closed his eyes in pain.

She stepped closer and took him in her arms, as though he were a child. "Jule, Jule," she said in extreme sympathy.

XX

Our enormously productive economy . . . demands that we make consumption our way of life, that we convert the buying and use of goods into rituals, that we seek our spiritual satisfactions, our ego satisfactions, in consumption. . . . We need things consumed, burned up, worn out, replaced, and discarded at an ever increasing rate.

Victor Lebow, Marketing Consultant
in *Journal of Retailing*

(Basic utility) . . . cannot be the foundation of a prosperous apparel industry. . . . We must accelerate obsolescence. . . . It is our job to make women unhappy with what they have. . . . We must make them so unhappy that their husbands can find no happiness or peace in their excessive savings.

B. Earl Puckette, Chairman
Allied Stores Corporation

United States industrial firms are grinding up more than half of the natural resources processed each year on this planet for the benefit of six percent of the planet's people. In the lifetime of many, if not most, of us, Americans will be trying to 'mine' old forgotten garbage dumps for their rusted tin cans. . . . Historians, I suspect, may allude to this as the Throwaway Age.

Vance Packward
The Waste Makers

Now

Doctor Leete and Martha were already at the small breakfast table when Edie and Julian entered.

The doctor looked up quizzically and said, "How are you feeling, Julian?"

"As usual, confused."

"I mean physically."

Martha said, "Good morning, Julian."

"Good morning . . . Martha." He looked at the doctor. "I feel fine physically. Getting increasingly tired of the inactivity and actually beginning to react against spending so much time in the confines of the apartment, if you don't mind my saying so."

The doctor said, "I'll check you out some more after breakfast. If the truth be known, my first inclination was to keep you in bed for these first few days."

"Well, thank goodness you didn't. I would have gone around the bend."

Julian began to make the gesture of holding Edie's chair for her while she seated herself and she made a moue at him.

"I don't hold your chair for you, why should you hold mine for me?"

"Sorry. A custom of my time."

"Would you have helped seat an older man?"

"Why, no, unless he was really so old as to be practically fragile. I suppose he would have resented it."

"Fine. So do I," she said. "When I am old and fragile, then you can hold my chair for me, Jule."

He grinned at her wryly and said, "All right, I'll try to remember."

Martha said, "We heard you coming and I ordered. A breakfast dish I though you might like to try. I originated it myself."

Julian sat down himself and said, "Great." He looked over at his hostess. "Edie tells me you're Martha Bartlett. I should have recognized you."

She cocked her head slightly at her daughter, but then turned back to Julian. "Yes, of course. But I'm afraid that a third of a century has changed the teenager you met glancingly. Did you know that I had a terrible crush on you at the time?"

"No. I'm afraid not." His grin was rueful. "I was rather deeply involved with your . . ." his voice caught and he couldn't keep it light ". . . your sister."

Martha frowned at Edith. "I thought we were going

209

to wait awhile, to keep poor Julian from having too much heaped on him at once."

Edie said, "I found him in the sanctum at the library screen. He had discovered that Aunt Edith passed away seven years ago. I . . . I tried to add a little comfort. I'd already told him that your crush went into the second generation."

"Let's forget about it," Julian said. "It's hard for me to conceive. You see, in my memory Edith Bartlett was a bright, lovely girl, only last week."

"Of course," Edie said. She looked at her father. "Julian was also checking out the progress of the space program."

The doctor looked at his patient, a somewhat strange expression on his face, an element Julian couldn't put his finger upon. He said, "How did you find it?"

"Too technical, even though I was reading a juvenile summation."

The doctor nodded. "That's the difficulty with the information explosion. In the old days a man of Benjamin Franklin's time and intellectual stature could keep abreast of all scientific development. There were various universal minds. But even by your time it had become all but impossible. As I recall from my youth, we used to have quite a few popularizers of science who did an amazingly good job of keeping up themselves and simplifying for their readers. Men like Isaac Asimov and Willy Ley, and Arthur C. Clarke and Gordon Rattray Taylor, over in England. But by today it is practically impossible to keep abreast of scientific developments except in your own narrow specialization, save on the very broadest of popularized scales. There are hundreds of new sciences I know nothing about, save possibly their names."

The food had arrived and Martha Leete served it. Her own breakfast dish turned out to be an herb omelet which Julian West found superlative and said so.

He said, to get conversation going, "For nearly a week now you've been setting me back with the new developments in the world. I've been surprised, over and over again. But tell me, looking backward, what do you find most surprising about my world—now that you've evolved into a new one?"

They thought about it, obviously intrigued by the question.

Martha Leete said, "I've never been able to understand how you put up for so long with adulterated foods, shoddy clothing, inferior products ranging from, well, candy bars to yachts. Why didn't consumers revolt and demand the best capable of being produced?"

Julian said, "Well, there were outfits such as Consumer's Union and Consumer's Research that tried to buck the tide."

"But without success?"

"Largely without too much success, I suppose. You mentioned candy bars. When I was a little tike I used to be able to buy for a nickle a candy bar composed largely of good chocolate, sugar and nuts. By the time I was in my twenties, the supposedly same bar was selling for a dime, was half the size, and the big brains in the candy company's laboratories had figured out various ways of cutting costs by using less and less chocolate, few nuts, substitutes for sugar and various fillings based on, I think, soy beans." He shook his head as though hating to admit the validity of her charge.

Edie said, "It's impossible for me to understand how your people continued to participate in wars, and the threat of war, for so long after they had become a left-over from man's infancy." Her tone was intense.

Julian scowled and sent his mind back. "I was in one myself, of course. We discussed it a bit the other night. I hated it, so did almost every non-pro I knew. The professionals were another thing. They spent their lives in the atmosphere. Only in times of actual war, or at least high-pitched cold war and preparation for war, did they find their fulfillment. It was then that glory was to be found—and rapid promotion."

That didn't seem to quite cover it. He added, still scowling, "It was part of the system. Part of the way things worked. The purpose of the State was to defend the nation from outside pressures, and also from internal ones. The military handled the first part of that, the police, courts, prisons and so forth, the second."

"Thank goodness we're doing away with the State," she said grimly. "But I was more interested in the average person's reaction against war and preparations for war."

"Theoretically, everybody was against it. But somehow or other the first toys our kids played with were guns. Their comic books, which they stared at even before they could read, were full of war and other fighting. I imagine that three out of four movies, TV shows and radio programs had considerable violence in them—war movies, crime movies, westerns in which the frontiersmen killed either each other or multitudes of Indians. Even Disney's kid films *Pinocchio, Bambi, 101 Dalmations* and *Snow White and the Seven Dwarfs* wound up in big scary chase scenes."

"Something like the Romans taking the youngsters to the arena to see the games, the gladiators and so forth," Edie muttered.

Julian looked at her. "Possibly something like that. It didn't occur to me at the time. As I say, it was part of the system—and so was I."

He turned his eyes to the doctor who had been pursing his lips in continued thought.

Leete said, "No, actually I think the thing that surprises me most was the utter waste that we put up with back in the early and middle half of the twentieth century. Martha touched on it from a slightly different angle than I had in mind."

Julian returned to the lighter approach, after taking a sip of his coffee. "Waste! We considered private enterprise the most efficient system that had ever come down the pike. The very theory was that competition drove the inefficient out of the market. New methods, better methods, new inventions, new techniques were continually driving the old into oblivion. Progress was the theme."

"Oh?" There was an unwonted sarcastic element in the doctor's voice.

Julian said, "Well, we were the most prosperous nation in the world, with a gross per capita income of close
to four thousand dollars."

"Producing four thousand dollars per capita has nothing to do with the amount of waste in the economy. It
would be quite possible to produce that and then throw
three thousand of it away. For instance, did you know
that five hundred dollars a year was spent for every man,
woman and child in the country on packaging? Often
the package in which the product came was more expensive than the contents.

"I think a good example was the aspirin you mentioned the other day. In a drug store usually a customer
would buy a neatly packaged tin for, say, twenty-five
cents. Available, possibly, was a cheaper brand for fifteen cents, but the consumer was so conditioned by advertising that he'd buy the more expensive brand,
although, of course, aspirin is a chemical compound
called acetylsalicylic acid and by law one brand could
not differ from another. Very well. Had the customer
bought his aspirin in hundred pound lots in polyethylene
film bags, he would have gotten it for fourteen cents a
pound, or in carload lots for eleven cents a pound. I
leave to your imagination the amount of profit made by
the aspirin-selling companies.

"But still sticking to the field of medicine, I might
mention U.S.P. grade milk of magnesia—the chemical
name is magnesium hydroxide—which sold for about six
dollars a ton, and you'd have one thousand quarts in that
ton. Buying it beautifully packaged and fully advertised,
you'd pay up to a dollar and twenty-five cents a pint
for it in the druggist section of a supermarket.

"Your drug companies used to pour four times as much
money into selling as they did into research. Everything
was sell, sell, sell but what the consumer received for his
money wasn't especially important. Advertise, advertise,
advertise. Get people to buy things they don't want or
need with money they don't have."

The doctor was in full voice now. "And to speed it up,
this continual milking of the consumer, the producers
would turn out electric light bulbs that were deliberately

designed to burn out after a few hundred hours, although it was possible at the time to manufacture light bulbs that would last almost the life of the house. They produced automobile batteries timed to last one year, or eighteen months, before needing replacement. In Europe, the batteries would last as much as ten years. And European tires would give twice the mileage American ones did. They turned out razorblades that became dull after two or three shaves and—"

He skidded to an abrupt halt and took off on another tack. "I could go on indefinitely but that's only part of it. Let me give you another example of waste under your system. Suppose an inventor hit upon a new type of tubular electrical discharge lamp. I think you usually called them neon signs. This one, say, flashes off and on with a mother-of-pearl-like color. He patents it, then interests an entrepeneur who puts up the money after investigation by his highly trained staff and his bankers. Engineers are found to design the new type sign and then a factory is tooled up to construct it. A great deal is now spent in exploiting the new device by advertising and other methods. Finally it goes on the market and, possibly, falls flat on its face. But even if it is a success, it's beside the point. Not only is this new device absolutely injurious to the eyes with its rapidly flashing on and off, but destructive to the attention of the motorist, who should be watching the road.

"In short, inventor, patent attorney, patent office employees, entrepeneur and his staff and bankers, engineers, factory workers, advertising and other exploitation workers, sales staff, installers of the signs and those who maintain them are all doing nothing-work. Worse, they are actually doing the nation a disservice."

By this time Julian was laughing at Leete's emphatic presentation of his case.

The doctor glared at him, caught up in the heat of his argument. "Waste, waste, waste. Wasted production, wasted labor. Why, consider the institution of feather-bedding. Hundreds of thousands of highly trained mechanics and craftsmen, deliberately lying down on the job even during the years when there were labor shortages.

"And here's another example. Back in 1959 there were 551 different brands of coffee on the market, 249 brands of powdered soap and 177 brands of salad dressing. If that isn't rediculous waste and duplication of effort, I don't know what is. Efficiency indeed!"

"Just a minute there," Julian protested, finishing the last sip of his beverage. "Do you mean to tell me you have only one brand of coffee?"

"No, of course not. We have every different type of coffee our people might want to drink. Light roast, dark roast, chicory-flavored, Italian expresso, powdered coffee, Turkish coffee and all the rest. But we have no such thing as inferior types of coffee. Each type is the best we can produce. The same applies to everything else."

"All right, now. Suppose somebody came along with a desire for some type of coffee you don't have available in your ultramarkets? Possibly he comes up with a new type, a blending of say coffee and vanilla beans, heaven forbid. How does he go about getting it?"

"The same way he would any other consumer item he might wish. He requests it from Consumer Products and his request is put onto the New Consumer Products reports, available to all in the data banks. If enough others vote for producing the product, it is produced and made available."

"Suppose he is the only one that wants this offbeat type of coffee?"

The doctor shrugged. "Then it is unlikely that the trouble would be gone to to produce the product.

Martha said in her usual placid way, "In which case he could always make his own in the privacy of his home. Or get together with a local handicrafts group and turn it out. Do-it-yourself clubs are all over the place."

Edith said, "It eliminates far-fetched products in which only a very small minority might be interested."

"That seems like discrimination to me. In my time, if anybody wanted something badly enough, and had the money for it, he could have it made."

"The same thing applies now," Leete said. "There is nothing to prevent you from using your credits to produce, say, a nuclear powered pogo stick, even though not another single soul in the whole nation is interested in such an item. But it would not go into mass production unless others signified that they too would like one."

The doctor pursued it. "In your day, production was simply chaotic. It was up to the individual, or the individual company, to try and determine what it was the public might want. Sometimes they would come up with the most outlandish things and through fantastic advertising budgets manage to put them across. I remember from my boyhood days such items as electric martini stirrers, gold-headed golf putters, hula hoops. A new product would come out which everybody wanted, immediately, and prices would soar so that businessmen would dash into that field and try to get on the gravy train. Shortly there would be more of the product, or copies of it, than could possibly be sold and prices would drop. Thousands or tens of thousands of the product would then be dumped, destroyed, burnt, or thrown away. The hula hoops I mentioned are an example."

Julian grunted remembrance. "How do you get around that now?"

"The computers do a remarkable job of continually evaluating supply and demand. Everything requested of Consumer Products, from an ice cream cone in Florida to the occupancy of a house in Point Barrow, Alaska, is recorded and the supply of ice cream cones is increased or decreased according to need as is the number of houses in Point Barrow. As a result, supply equals demand. Seldom is there a temporary shortage or overabundance of anything. This eliminates the overproduction of the past and the underproduction which used to temporarily send prices soaring. You see, yours was a system of production for sale and profit; ours is a system of production for use."

Julian said, "I'm not quite sure I got that last."

"We produce things for use, you produced them for a profit."

"All right, but in the long run the things we produced had to be useful or they wouldn't sell. So it all comes to the same thing."

"Not necessarily. If there was a sales opening for a

commodity somebody would produce it, even though it was deadly. Take LSD. As dangerous a drug as it was, particularly in the hands of the layman, your system of private enterprise found ample numbers to manufacture it, wholesale it, distribute it and finally retail it—at tremendous profit, of course. Or look at your automobiles. Time and again it was pointed out how overpowered they were, how devoid of safety devices, how thin the sheet metal considering the speed they traveled. How their exhausts were polluting the air to the point where life on the whole planet was threatened. But did that speed the private enterprisers in Detroit to their drawing boards to design vehicles that were less destructive, more sensible? Certainly not. Internal combustion vehicles were too profitable, and that was all that counted."

"So today you've eliminated the production of such items as, say, LSD and marijuana, I suppose, not to speak of racing cars."

Edie said hurriedly, "Oh, not at all. It's just that such things are not in the hands of persons, or businesses, that are motivated by personal gain. When racing cars are produced, they are made as safe as they possibly can be. Marijuana is produced to the extent it is requested but most of it goes to research organizations; there is an education program on narcotics that weans almost all would-be experimenters away from such items. LSD is also available, but we've gone far beyond in our research into the hallucinogens and it's seldom resorted to, even by those silly enough to want to take a trip to unreality."

Julian tried to stifle an irritation which these discussions continually brought out in him, a feeling he realized as being invalid to the point of childishness. He said, "This matter of supply and demand always equaling each other, because the computers keep such a close check—that can't be quite accurate. There must be occasions when something brand new is devised and before your factories, no matter how efficient, can begin turning out sufficient quantities for everybody, there's a shortage. Take that hula hoop example you used. Suppose some new fad hit for kids, something like the hula hoop. Everybody becomes anxious to get it soonest. All right. If I

217

understood you correctly, you have a per capita income now of the equivalent of something like twenty thousand dollars a year. If some people are silly enough to want to shell out a thousand dollars for a hula hoop—or its present day equivalent—in order to get one first, you mean your society doesn't offer any manner in which they can do it? This comes under the head of Big Brotherism. People should be allowed to do what they want with their income—including waste it."

Leete was waggling a finger negatively in despair. "Julian, I am afraid that in some respects we aren't getting through to you."

Edith was speaking simultaneously. "As far as fads are concerned—"

"As you say, as you say. You don't have them any more," he said in disgust.

"Not as you knew them."

The doctor said, "The thing that seems most incomprehensible to you in our discussions is that we have achieved the point where we can produce plenty, absolutely plenty, for everyone. You always run aground on that conception. You mention that we now have a per capita income of the equivalent of twenty thousand dollars. In actuality, I rather doubt it, though it would be difficult to figure out in our present terms of evaluating objects by the amount of time involved in producing them. You see, we have slowed up the race for greater production which was such a fetish in your time. We no longer need greater production. Production is such that, if need be, we could double it or triple it almost overnight. We simply are not concerned any more. That bee has flown out of our bonnet. When it went, many of the motivations of your time went with it. We no longer burn to keep up with the Joneses, to acquire status symbols, to climb higher on the totem pole, at least in so far as the owning of *things* is concerned. We strive now in being of greater use to the community and the nation, not to get a larger car than the neighbors have. It just doesn't make any difference.

"But to get back to your example. Suppose that some new item which a fabulous number of people wanted was suddenly developed. Something considerably more difficult to manufacture than your hula hoop. An item such as a hula hoop we could produce in quantity between sunset of one day and the following dawn and get it to the supply distribution centers a few hours later. But, say, some new type of sport equipment which would take a bit longer. Not much longer—a bit. Do you think our present day, highly educated people would be so ridiculous as to fret over the fact that they couldn't get one the first week? We simply aren't motivated by the same burning impatience that you were.

"So far as the twenty thousand a year income of each person is concerned, why, Julian, if there was occasion, we could double that amount of production in six months or quadruple it within the year. There is simply no *need*. We don't *need* a national product of eighty thousand dollars per capita a year and don't want it. We are simply not pushed by the desire for things that you were in your day."

Breakfast was over. He stared at them in frustration.

XXI

*If they prove nothing else the widespread Amer-
ican riots, increasing and spreading from the
1940s and 1950s into the 1960s, prove that the
American ruling class, given the political instru-
mentalities of its rule through low-grade stooges,
is unable to rule at home. The general cry goes
out for law and order, yet there is steadily less
and less law and order, more and more crime
and insurrection as Lyndon B. Johnstn calls for
national days of prayer. For prayer rather than
science or reason is the tool of the political medicine men. What is happening as the average
citizen looks on in disbelief is that an outworn,
patched politico-economic system is cracking,
while no serious steps are taken to ascertain the
causes and remedies.*

> Ferdinand Lundberg
> *The Rich and the Super-Rich*

Now

When Julian West awoke in the morning it was with
the realization that, for the first time since his return to
living, he had spent a night without dreaming. Was it
because at long last he was beginning to accept the reality of this new world?

He stared up at the ceiling and recapitulated. In actuality, the changes were not as world-shaking as he had
first thought. The events that had taken place could all
have been foreseen in his own time; indeed, most if not
all of them had been.

The real basics of human existence were still the same.
A baby was born to man and woman and went through
childhood and adolescence in a family group, prepara-
tory to taking his place in society as an adult. He lived
in a community, received his education, found his niche
in life, formed new family relationships and had children, and then eventually faced death.

All right, those were still basic. It was up to him, Julian

West, to adapt to the changes that had taken place in the politico-economic setup and go about the business of living his life.

Following breakfast, the day before, he had finished out the balance of the day in much the same manner as he had been doing ever since his awakening. The doctor had once again thoroughly checked him out and evidently could find nothing whatsoever physically wrong with his patient. In fact, Julian West could not remember a greater feeling of well-being in his life. So much so that he was increasingly rebellious of his being cooped up in this manner for such a long period.

He had awakened, once again, at earliest dawn, which had not been his custom in the old days. He decided that one reason was the fact he got so little physical exercise that he customarily went to bed without being tired and hence needed less sleep.

Lying there, he reviewed the various discussions, arguments and revelations of the day before.

For a while he had had it hot and heavy with Martha and Edith Leete on a return to the subject of so few persons having to work in production, distribution and communications. His original claim was that it was undoubtedly making the nation into a race of loafers.

That had amused them.

Edie had said, "Did you get the impression that in our educational system we concentrated on only one aptitude a child might have? Something that would direct him to one or another position in production when he reached Muster Day?"

"That was the impression you gave me," he said, puzzled.

"Then we put it badly. The growing child is observed not only for scientific and mechanical aptitude but for artistic and scholarly ones as well. There are few people who don't have more than one special interest. Even Einstein had his violin for moments of leisure. For instance, my own greatest interest has been in various branches of agriculture, but I am also an amateur anthropologist, play the flute with considerable élan and love ceramics. Mother went into medicine and for a time was a nurse before she was bumped. But she also plays piano and is a national authority on Crewel embroidery for which she won her blue ribbon."

"All right, that's fine, but everybody can't be an artist or a handicraft expert."

"Why not?" Martha had said mildly. "In your day there were whole villages in countries such as Mexico where nearly every family was producing fine handicrafts: pottery, silverware, glass, jewelry, serapes, furniture, copperwares—or perhaps fake pre-Columbian artifacts. Wouldn't this indicate that every normal person is a potential craftsman, if not an artist? The same thing applied at an earlier day on the American frontier. For all practical purposes, every woman was a handicraft worker and so were many of the men. They had to be if they were to have even the necessities of life, not to speak of their little luxuries."

Edie had said, "You might say that there are two economies in United America. One, the industrial economy, the other an art world. Many more of us participate in the second than in the first. It includes music, painting, writing, ceramics, hand printing, book binding, even making paper, quilting, embroidery, tapestry, wood carving, weaving, silver, gold, copper and other metalwork, lapidary, sculpture and a dozen others."

"But what do you do with the finished product? You already produce, with your highly automated industry, everything you need."

Edie shook her head at him. "A factory never produced a work of art and I rather doubt that one ever will. Obviously, with so many of us in the arts and handicrafts there is no need for large production of the things we turn out. We strive rather for quality, each of us trying to produce masterpieces."

"But if you can't sell them, in this moneyless economy, what do you do with these masterpieces?"

Martha said, "We exchange them with each other. How much more pleasant to have personal gifts than something purchased. Today we do a great deal of exchanging of presents—and it's considered good taste to give as much as one receives."

The doctor had put in a word then. "I suppose, in a way, it is a return to primitive barter, but on a high level. Suppose, for instance, somebody interested in painting presented Edith with a sample of his work which she had admired. Edith is a ceramist of first caliber. There is no hurry, but sooner or later she would present her benefactor with a lovely bowl."

"Suppose he didn't want a bowl? Suppose his house was chock full of bowls?"

Martha said, "The same as Christmas presents in your day. He would probably pass it on as a gift to the first person who admired it."

"Suppose the ceramist wasn't as competent as Edith? Suppose the bowl was a horror?"

Edith twisted her mouth in amusement. "Then I suspect it would soon be accidently broken, or, at best, stored away in some closet or other storage area."

Julian had finished it off by saying dryly, "We used to have a joke about people making a living by taking in each other's washing. In fact, they said that the Arabs made their living by stealing each other's washing. But now you seem to make a full-time occupation of taking in each other's handicrafts."

But it had been the discussion on civil government that had brought on the big debate the previous day.

There were quite a few odds and ends that he wasn't at all clear about, but if he had the basics right it looked as though the State was at long last withering away, as once predicted by Marx and Engels.

It turned out that United America now consisted of not only what was once the United States, but all of North America right down through Panama and the Caribbean Islands, including the Bahamas and Bermuda as well. There was some discussion of taking into the union the South American countries, but evidently thus far it was considered too geographically remote. The uniting of the northern hemisphere hadn't been a matter of conquest. All had voluntarily joined. It was simply a matter of practicality in the modern age of communication, transportation and production. Residents of what was the United States had no more privileges in the union than did those of Canada, Mexico, or even Panama or Haiti.

Government as he had known it was on the wane. You might say there were two governments, productive and civil, with the productive by far the more important. There was still a president, complete with cabinet, but he was largely a figurehead, a chief of state, something like the queen of England had once been. His duties were largely involved with diplomatic affairs with Common Europe, the Soviet Complex and other foreign groups or nations.

In United America, the states of the United States, the provinces of Canada and the various other political divisions of the nations which had amalgamated had been shifted about into more realistic lines. There was very little civil government on a wide-area level, and no need for there to be. Almost all civil government was local.

That had set Julian West back as much as anything he had heard for the last several days. But even worse had been when Leete had calmly announced that there weren't laws any longer. At least not in the former sense. Evidently they were currently of the opinion that any law can be wrong, under certain circumstances.

Leete had explained. For instance, suppose you had a speed law of a hundred kilometers an hour. Did it apply when a physician was hurrying to a patient? Would the law be valid? Thou shalt not kill. But suppose you are a police officer up against a berserk madman who is slaughtering citizens right and left, and the only way to stop him is to kill him? In the present world, each case that came up was dealt with on its own merit.

Evidently there were considerably fewer cases come to the present day equivalent of court than in the past. According to Leete, nine-tenths of court matters in Julian's day dealt with property questions, with money. Such matters were negligible now, since there was so little private property and no money at all.

Leete had used as an example of local government the officers of the high-rise apartment building in which they lived. The mayor, as he was sometimes called, had a staff of three assistants, elected, as was he, by all the adults in

the building. At any time he, or any or all of his assistants, could be replaced when and if a majority of his
constituents voted against him. At any given time, the
data banks contained a record of how many of a man's
constituents still wanted him in office and how many
didn't. If and when he were removed, an election immediately took place, every voter who wished nominat-
ing his candidate directly into his transceiver and into
the computer data banks which then revealed to all who
the candidates were.

Julian had said, "But who decides upon the candidates
to be voted for?"

The doctor said, "That's an important point. In the past
those who controlled the political parties were the real
ones who nominated the candidates and often the same
elements controlled both political parties and both candidates stood for the same thing. For instance, what was
the difference between Goldwater and Johnson, or
Humphrey and Nixon?"

"I know. I was in on it to a certain extent. But the
question still stands, who nominates the candidates
today?"

"Each citizen is a candidate, that is, if the computers
agree that he had the qualifications to fill the office. In
your day it made no difference if he had the qualifications
or not."

"But suppose he doesn't want to run, doesn't want to
hold office?"

"Then he refuses. But if a man's background is such
that a majority wish him to hold the office, he most likely
has the desire. Of course, as soon as he is elected he is
released from duties in production, if he held down such
a job."

"I can see that with so many running, few persons
would get much of a vote and a man could be elected
with but a handful of constituents."

"Oh, that's the first run-off. Although usually constituents are acquainted with the most suited for the office and
vote for him. However, after the first run-off we take the
ten candidates who polled the largest vote and a new
vote is taken on them. If no one receives an absolute

majority then the top three candidates are voted upon in a new run-off. If there is still no absolute majority, the two top candidates are voted upon."

"And, once elected, how long does he stay in office?"

"Until he either reaches retirement age or his constituents remove him. Usually, we feel that the longer a man holds such an office the more experienced he becomes in it and consequently the more valuable. There are many fewer elections than you might think."

"What is his motivation for taking a job like that, with all its responsibilities, if he doesn't get paid any more than anyone else?"

"It's an honor to serve the community. The best administrators have always been so motivated. Using the example of the early American presidents once again, do you think they were motivated by the pay they received? Not a one of them but lost financially in taking the burdens of office. It wasn't until the twentieth century that the office of President paid enough to make it worthwhile to take the job, financially speaking. By that time, we Americans were scornful of our politicians, knowing them for the opportunists they had become. Today, with the profit factor completely gone, we honor them since they serve the community without personal gain."

Evidently the mayor's three assistants acted as judges in any cases that came up in conflict between two residents of the building, or any other matters requiring a decision—judges and jury. However, if a citizen did not accept their decision he could appeal it to a general vote of all his fellow inhabitants.

The next largest unit of government was the whole university city and it largely duplicated the smaller unit. If a dispute came up between two citizens of differing buildings, all six of the mayors' assistants acted as judges. If their decision was unacceptable to either of the disputants, the matter was put to the vote of all residents of both buildings. If the subject to be decided upon involved all citizens of the Julian West University City and could not be resolved by the city officials, then all voted.

Leete insisted that it was a present day democracy, if

you wished the term, based on the same theories as those of ancient Athens, or, perhaps better, the Town Hall government of early New England.

The next highest level of government pertained to an area somewhat similar to the states of the former United States and involved matters common to all the pseduo-cities and the smaller towns and rural areas which were organized into groupings somewhat similar to the counties of old.

The federal government, if it could be called that, co-ordinated all these to the extent necessary. Leete contended that there was much less government than before and that a great deal of what there was was in the hands of the Congress of Guilds, which had evolved from the super-corporations and the cosmocorps, rather than the civil government.

Well, Julian decided now, undoubtedly he could go into it further later on.

He flung aside the bedclothes and swung his legs out to the floor. He took a deep breath and repeated to himself that strange though the new world might be, the job was now to adapt to the changes and go about the business of living.

After shower and shave, he dressed and as he did so his eye caught the shell briar pipe sitting on the stand next to his bed. For the first time, the sight of it failed to bring on at least a slight wince. He had never gotten around to ordering tobacco from Central Warehouses, or wherever, and felt no desire for the once-important nicotine.

He took the pipe up and stared at it. Present from Edith . . . the old Edith. The never-again-to-be Edith Bartlett. Part of the past. The never-again-to-be past. The job now was to adapt to the changes and get about the business of living.

He snapped the stem, took the pipe and tobacco pouch into the bath and tossed them into the disposal chute. That was that—the last contact with the past.

He hadn't expected any of the Leetes to be up yet. He went through the sanctum, into the living room and out the front door into the hall. He went over to the elevator Edie had told him was especially reserved for the Leete's apartment and, as before, its door opened for him.

He entered and said, "Car pool, please."

"Thank you, Mr. West."

The compartment began to sink and he bent his knees to accomodate the acceleration. He was beginning to get used to the working of this ultra-ultra-high-rise building. Given time, he told himself grimly, he might even get to like it, five-thousand-apartment anthill or no.

The elevator came to a halt and he stepped out and retraced the route he had taken with Edie the other day. At this time of morning he ran into no other occupants of the building.

In the enormous room that had reminded Julian of a large underground parking area of his own time, he duplicated the process to which Edie had introduced him. He stepped before one screen and said, "Information, please."

"Yes, Mr. West."

"I want to take a vehicle to a town called Woodstock, in the Catskill Mountains of the area once known as New York. I would like to make the trip as quickly as possible, uh, on the underground highway, not by air."

"Thank you, Mr. West."

He was pleased with himself. That had gone very well, he thought. He could see no reason for his being so highly screened by the affable Leetes. There were no handicaps to his getting around. Right this minute, it was a relief to be out of the apartment.

A four-wheeled vehicle, only slightly different from the one he and Edie had ridden in the other day, hurried up to the curb and its plastic canopy slid back. Julian West stepped into it behind the manual controls. He stared at them, scowling. He should have had Edie check him out the other day. However, the hell with it, he had watched her. There was no reason to believe he couldn't handle them, if the occasion came up.

He didn't know if it would be necessary for him to repeat his destination into the car's screen or not, but found it not needed. The little vehicle smoothed away from the curb and shortly was into the mainstream of traffic.

His trip differed little from the one with Edie, save that he was evidently shunted into a traffic lane involving top speed whereas the other morning—their destination being only the countryside—that hadn't been required.

In what seemed to him a fantastically short time, the car shuttled off on a side road and he caught the name Kingston on the wall. He was already only ten miles from his destination.

And that was achieved shortly indeed. The car turned off onto a side road and the dashboard red light began to flicker. Julian West took the wheel and a quick breath and put his foot on the accelerator. He didn't really know what any of the other controls were, save the brake. Accelerator and brake were located as on cars of his own period, but he would have had to experiment to find how to turn the engine off or start it. Well, he could always ask the data banks, if he couldn't figure it out himself. He could begin to realize the value of those data banks.

He emerged on the outskirts of the little artist colony he had once known. Surprisingly enough, it had altered little in the third of a century since he had been there last. He was to find later that a deliberate effort had been made to keep the typical town as it had been: something like the French Quarter of New Orleans, the colonial town of Williamsburg, Virginia. Stores were no longer present but he recognized several little bars and restaurants.

It was still quite early, with few persons on the streets. He headed up the Rock City Road and suddenly stepped on the brake pedal.

Before him, on the slopes of Overlook Mountain, rose the shapes of a dozen high-rise apartment houses of the type he had become familiar with in the Julian West University City. His eyes bugged. He could hardly recognize the mountain he had climbed so often in his youth.

He reactivated the car, but now progressed at a lower speed.

The clearing he had known as Mead's Meadow was

only barely recognizable. And from it, an excellent road let upward to the summit.

He stopped there. There was no purpose in going on. Overlook Mountain had become a garden; no longer was it all but virgin forest. Every tree was an art object, every blade of grass, every bush, all individually trimmed.

There was a buzzing in his pocket which he at first ignored, as he stared in dismay. Finally, he could ignore it no longer and brought the transceiver out.

He had never utilized it as a phone before, but there was no question. He flicked the cover back and looked into the screen. Edith Leete was there, her face worried.

"Jule!" she said. "Where are you? What are you doing?"

He said, very slowly, ruefully, "I thought I was out picking up a wedding present. But evidently I'm mistaken, darling. I don't have even that."

XXII

. . . it is provided in the nature of things that from every consummation will spring conditions that make it necessary to pass beyond it.
                                                    Walt Whitman

Now

He drove back to the underground ultrahighway slowly, more in disgust than despair. It had seemed such a wonderful gesture to be able to make. She could have kept the paintings for their own home, had she wished. More likely, from what they had told him, the masterpieces would have wound up as a presentation to some museum or museums, and without doubt such a gift would have been acclaimed by United American and possibly even eventuated in a decoration for the donor, although he wasn't quite sure if you could be awarded even a white ribbon for such a notable contribution to the nation's art.

He had no trouble whatsoever in returning to the building which housed the Leetes. He left his vehicle at the car pool and looked after it for a moment as it took off and headed for, he supposed, some parking area where it would remain until summoned by someone else. He shook his head. Julian West still wasn't used to seeing the present-day automobiles zipping around without benefit of drivers.

He turned and headed for the elevators.

Just as he was about to step in, a couple passed. They were dressed, as usual, almost identically, and were possibly in their mid-twenties.

The girl was saying, *"Li estis kisonta sin."*

And the man, evidently slightly surprised at that, replied, *"Tio mirigis min. La doma estas—"* And then they had passed beyond earshot.

Julian West scowled puzzlement. But then it came back to him. The little girl in the park. And then something else came to him. Save for the Leetes, he had spoken to no one, no one at all, since coming out of stasis.

He entered the elevator, still scowling, trying to fight down the unease coming over him. He licked his lower lip, and, for an unknown reason, held out his right hand to see if it were shaking.

The door opened before him at the Leete apartment and he went in to find Edie, still obviously worried, in the sanctum.

She looked up from the chair she sat in. "Jule! Where have you been?"

He sank down into a chair opposite her, frowning. He said, "Evidently on a wild goose chase. I'll tell you about it, but first tell me something. I just passed a young couple, on the way up. They were speaking some language I couldn't place. But it occured to me that it was the same as that alien child was using in the park. Is there quite a foreign colony in this building?"

She looked at him unhappily for a moment, then evidently came to a decision. She said, "Jule, the child wasn't an alien. It was a perfectly normal American child, speaking Interlingua."

"Speaking what?"

"Interlingua, the international language. You see, with the revolution in communications and transportation, it only made sense to adopt a universal language. You had the roots in your time, with Esperanto. I think some eight million people were already speaking it when you began your experiment."

"This Interlingua is similar to Esperanto?"

"It has many similarities. But it also has elements of the original Interlingua and Ido. An international congress was held, not too long after you went into stasis, to compose such a scientific language and Interlingua was the name decided upon."

"What was wrong with English? I thought it was well on the way to becoming an international language."

"The same as what was wrong with French, Spanish, German, Russian, or Chinese, for that matter. None were scientific languages. All have evolved from primitive times. Look at English. It was originally Celtic, then the

Romans conquered England and Latin was imposed. When the Romans left, the Angles and Saxons moved in with their Germanic language and later the Danes and other Northmen came. The French took over under William the Conqueror and added their bit. It was a bastard language, Jule, and utterly impossible not only as an international language but as one that could be utilized in a burgeoning scientific age. It simply is not suited for really higher education, and neither were any of the other old languages."

"All right. And now everybody speaks this Interlingua?"

"Everybody in the advanced countries, and everybody in the less-developed ones with any education at all. We had a crash program, first in the West and then in the Soviet Complex too, and then it spread geometrically. It became a required subject in all schools; and all the mass media, TV, radio, and so forth were pressed into service to spread its use. At first classes in school were handled in both languages, but as the students became practiced classes were held in Interlingua alone."

"At first? You mean that now children don't bother to learn English at all?"

She hesitated. "Not unless they are particularly interested in linguistics, or in studying some subjects in the original. For instance, Chaucer, or even Shakespeare, don't translate in the original meter, rhythm and rhyme very well."

"You mean that child I met out in the park has never learned English?"

"Probably not."

"And that young couple down below?"

"They possibly spoke it as children, but a language slips away from you if you don't practice it daily."

"And people don't practice it daily any more, eh? Not even people of my own generation?"

"Well, no. As a spoken language English isn't practical in the modern world. Interlingua is just about universal. Even people in their sixties and seventies and older find it easier to utilize the new language."

"I see." He looked at her, his face empty. "How is it

233

you and your father and mother have such a good command of a language that evidently has been out of common usage for a generation?"

She twisted her mouth in her characteristic moue. "Jule, father has been specializing on your experiment for the greater part of his life. We have been making special preparations for your revival for some time—years. We both, and mother as well, have kept boned-up on English, on the customs of your times, on the food you ate, the things you drank, all of it. All in preparation for the time when you came out of stasis. It was thought that when you discovered how long you had been out of this world, that you would have a considerable . . . well, shock. And we were prepared to . . . well, cushion it for you."

He said, at long last, "You three. You . . . you talk baby talk to me, by your standards I mean—don't you?"

There was misery in her eyes. "I'm sorry, Jule. I suppose I sound cruel. Besides, that's not the way I'd put it."

"How would you put it? This morning I decided to ask you to marry me, or whatever you call the relationship now."

"Jule."

"I went up to the Catskills to retrieve some old masters I had hidden there. I was going to give them to you as a wedding present. They were the only thing I thought I had in the world. I know . . . I know, don't tell me. You don't have weddings any more. However, I'm still a bit old-fashioned, I suppose. I thought perhaps we could go through the old ceremonies and all. I was raised an Episcopalian."

The misery was still in her eyes, and compassion. "Oh, Jule. Don't you see it's impossible? Can't you see?

He shook his head, not expecting exactly that reaction. "Why?"

"Jule, Jule. We've been telling you for almost a week now. Human knowledge, even in your day, was doubling every eight years. The pace has accelerated. Jule, I don't want to hurt you. None of us want to hurt you. But can't you see? It is as difficult for us to communicate with you as it would have been for you to communicate with an

Australian Bushman. We live in different worlds. We don't even have our language in common."

"You said you had a crush on me. I thought you were in love with me."

"I know I'm not doing this right." She seemed exhausted. "Love, as you use the word, we don't have any more, Jule. The relationship between man and woman has . . . evolved. I said I had a crush on you, as mother did when she was a child. It was all so romantic. You were so handsome—the touch of gray at your temples, the . . . But I seem to have given a wrong impression. Don't you see how impractical any relationship between us would be?"

He came to his feet in a start of anger and slammed his right fist into his left palm.

"No, dammit, I don't! There's no reason in the world why I can't learn Interlingua. I learned French. I even have some Spanish and German. Why the hell can't I learn Interlingua? I'll go back to school. I'll pick up the big changes, the big advances you keep talking about. You won't have to be ashamed of me! I'm not a dolt."

He sank back into the chair he had just deserted and stared at her, defiantly.

She closed her eyes in pain. Finally, she said, lowly, flatly, "Jule. How long did it take you to learn to drive?"

"Drive? What the hell's that got to do with anything?"

"How long?"

He tried to think about it. "Why, I don't know. I never remember learning to drive. We had cars in the family long before I was born. As far back as I can remember, I used to know how to drive. I suppose my father used to set me on his lap and let me steer, when I was a few years old."

"So, seemingly, you were practically born knowing the world of the automobile, a thing that would have astonished your grandfather. Now, Jule, think. A boy of ten, in the world today, is *born* knowing things about physics that a . . . well, a top nuclear physicist of your time would not comprehend. He's *born* into it. It's in the atmosphere. It's in his earliest schooling, in the Tri-Di shows he sees daily on the screens in his home. It's in the conversation of the adults around him. In his toys. It's everywhere."

"All right. I'll go back to school. I'll pick up where I left off. I'll catch up."

"Jule, I understand you have a bachelor's degree. What did you specialize in?"

He scowled at her. "Schooling never made a great deal of difference to me. I didn't have to specialize. I more or less drifted through. I was . . . don't laugh, a gentleman with more means than I'd ever need."

"Very well. You probably never learned to study. Probably most people didn't, in your time. You studied just enough to get through. Now, you're in your mid-thirties. I don't mean you don't have an averagely good I.Q., but at your time of life it's difficult to pick up the art of really studying. You've passed through that period of life when the training is most easily acquired.

"Fine. Suppose you make the effort and do return to school. It will take you a concentrated year or two to learn Interlingua to the point where you can study in it well. The vocabulary is extensive, as it must be."

"All right," he snapped. "But it can be learned, even by a stupid jerk like me."

"Please. This isn't easy for me. I am not pulling punches, it would be no kindness to you in the long run. By the time you have learned Interlingua sufficiently well and can start into . . . the first grade of grammar school, that ten-year-old boy we mentioned will be twelve, and human knowledge will still be geometrically progressing. You'll have to go back and learn, bit by bit, the information he was *born* with, that he assimilated as though by osmosis, in home and kindergarten. By the time you have got through elementary education, as we know it now, he'll be seventeen or eighteen and, Jule, by that time, human knowledge will have again doubled and we will possess somewhere between thirty-two and sixty-four times the amount you had in your day. By this time you will be in your forties, and ready to go into what you used to call high school."

He sank back into his chair, in despair.

"What happens? With whom do I associate, if I'm such

a moron? The people of my own generation? People like Roy London, an old friend now in his seventies, now retired down in Costa Rica"

She was agonizing for him, but she shook her head. "Even your friend London lived through all these intervening years. I assume he was at least an averagely intelligent man. He kept up as best he could. He learned as matters progressed, although even he would find difficulty in communicating with the present generation."

"You mean even Roy would have his work cut out carrying on a conversation with me—that is, of course, after the initial hail-fellow-well-met greeting?"

She looked at him, in compassionate misery for him.

He said, "You'd made all sorts of arrangements with the computers, and the elevators, and the data banks and all the rest of it, to take care of my needs, didn't you? Everything was set to baby . . . the mental baby."

She could say nothing.

He said bitterly. "Thirty-three years, only thirty-three years. I've been continually labeling this new world of yours utopia. It isn't utopia for me, is it? It's dystopia, the exact opposite. I'm a freak. Why did you ever awaken me?"

She shook her head sadly. "It wasn't my decision to make, Jule. I was against it."